The Leather Burners

Center Point
Large Print

**This Large Print Book carries the
Seal of Approval of N.A.V.H.**

The Leather Burners

Bliss Lomax

CENTER POINT LARGE PRINT
THORNDIKE, MAINE

This Center Point Large Print edition
is published in the year 2014 by arrangement with
Golden West Literary Agency.

The text of this Large Print edition is unabridged.
In other aspects, this book may vary
from the original edition.
Printed in the United States of America
on permanent paper.
Set in 16-point Times New Roman type.

ISBN: 978-1-62899-347-9 (hardcover)
ISBN: 978-1-62899-354-7 (paperback)

Library of Congress Cataloging-in-Publication Data

Lomax, Bliss, 1888–1979.
 The leather burners / Bliss Lomax. — Center Point Large Print edition.
 pages ; cm
 Summary: "When range detectives Rainbow Ripley and Grumpy Gibbs
embroil themselves in the problems of some rustled cattle and some
mysterious activity in the Lost Angel mine near Crazy Horse, Nevada,
there is no rest for anybody"—Provided by publisher.
 ISBN 978-1-62899-347-9 (hardcover : alk. paper)
 ISBN 978-1-62899-354-7 (pbk. : alk. paper)
 1. Large type books. I. Title.
 PS3507.R1745L43 2014
 813′.52—dc23
                                                      2014028583

The Leather Burners

1

Tossing his cigarette aside, Rainbow Ripley pushed through the swing doors of the old National Saloon in Cheyenne. Instead of moving to the bar, he ran his quiet glance over the men in the place. After a moment he spotted the leathery little man he was looking for, seated at a card table in the rear.

Grumpy Gibbs, crusty, dour faced, would never see forty again. Hard and irascible, he bore little resemblance to the experienced and capable range detective he really was. Casting a look of irritation over his shoulder as Rainbow paused behind his chair, he growled, "Don't stand behind me." Then his tone changed. "Oh, you, Rainbow? What yuh want?"

There was still a trace of irritability in his voice, for he was deep in the card game. A slow smile appeared on Rainbow's lean, bronzed features as he answered, "Break it off, Grumpy. There's a job waitin' for us."

Instead of throwing down his cards, Grumpy frowned. "It kin wait till I finish my game, can't it?"

"It can, but I don't see why it should—seein' what you're holdin'."

Grumpy started to argue with him when one of

7

the other players thrust in brusquely, "Okay, Gibbs. Ante up."

Grumpy made his bet. He fingered his cards as if he wished Rainbow would go away and leave him alone; but the latter stuck. Presently the hand was played out. While one of his opponents raked in the pot, Grumpy whirled on his partner. "There yuh go," he rasped, his indignation severe. "Yuh made me lose again, takin' my mind off what I'm doin'!"

Rainbow laughed shortly. "Cash in and we'll be shovin' off," he insisted.

There was nothing else Grumpy could do. When he got up with a long face, Rainbow waved him to the bar. They made an ill-assorted pair as they stood there; the one tall and quiet and still young; the other short, iron faced, almost ugly. Drinks were set before them. Grumpy downed his at a gulp and grunted, "What is this job that's so dang pressin'?"

For answer, Rainbow handed him a telegram which he had just received. Taking it suspiciously, the other read the words:

RUSTLED FOR SIX STRAIGHT MONTHS CAN'T STOP IT RUIN STARING IN FACE YOU AND PARTNER RECOMMENDED BY U. S. MARSHAL GRAHAM GOOD PAY ASSURED IF YOU LL UNDERTAKE CLEAN UP THIS RANGE

It was signed, "J. Goodnight, for Tuscarora Cattlemen's Association."

Grumpy stared at the paper. "Crazy Horse, Nevada!" he snorted, naming the address from which the telegram had been sent. "We can't go shovin' off into that Godforsaken country!"

"Why can't we?"

There was no good reason, but the fact did not faze Grumpy. He went on in his querulous, crusty manner until Rainbow finally cut him off crisply. "Nonsense. You've had a week to play cards and take things easy. Accordin' to this wire, we're needed and needed bad. We're goin' to the hotel right now for our things. Then we'll have supper, and we can get away by the evenin' train."

They did as he said. They were just comfortably in time to catch the U. P. Flyer for Salt Lake and the West. Once he had given in to the idea, Grumpy's grouch slipped from him; but as they settled themselves in the smoker a new idea struck him. He turned to Rainbow.

"Seems to me yo're answerin' this call in a gosh-awful sweat. Yuh know this Goodnight?"

"I never heard of him before," was the prompt reply.

"Then why . . ."

"It's there in the wire," Rainbow told him. "Goodnight may be a stranger to me; but I know these Nevada buckaroos. If the telegram says

9

conditions are bad, it's a safe bet they're even worse than it sounds. That's enough to assure me that there's no time to be lost."

It was a shrewd surmise. Goodnight's wire was an understatement in every respect save its reference to the imminence of ruin. Almost at that very hour, while Rainbow and Grumpy were riding west in the train, old Tas Johnson, who owned a little spread a few miles away, was riding into the ranch yard of Goodnight's huge Wishbone outfit in northern Nevada. There was a man with him. It was Bart Galey, of the Circle G on Misery Creek: a burly, hard-looking individual with a red face.

Goodnight's foreman met them. Johnson's nod was brief. "Jim around?"

"Yeh. He's grabbin' himself a bait—"

Goodnight appeared in the kitchen door at that moment, picking his teeth. He called out, "Here I am, Tas. What's up now?"

Rawboned and lanky, Johnson turned toward him. Salty as Tas was, it was plain that he deferred in many things to the younger man as the head of the local cattlemen's association.

"Bart here wants some extry help," he explained. "He thinks he spotted some hombres snoopin' round the edges of his range today—figgers there's probably a raid planned. Wants us to give him a hand guardin' his stuff."

Tall and lean hipped, with level gray eyes which attracted one to him at first sight, Goodnight was yet on the happy side of thirty. Capability showed in the set of his broad shoulders, nor was the appearance misleading; Jim had made a name for himself on this range since taking over the management of his father's big spread on the latter's death a year ago. It was a tribute to his fairness that even the owners of small outfits, ordinarily suspicious of any large ranch, held him in high esteem.

But if Goodnight was generous, he could be severely just on occasion as well. His regard switched to Galey. There was a touch of curtness in his manner.

"That's hardly a reasonable request, Galey. We can lend you a few of the boys, maybe. But yours is the smallest outfit on the range, and up to now it's suffered the least. It 'll be pitch dark tonight, with no chance of a moon. If there's a raid—and I'm satisfied there will be—it's scarcely likely it will be directed at you."

His tone said how serious the matter was, but Galey chose to take umbrage at his reluctance to comply with his demands. The red of his face deepened to plum color.

"Hell, Goodnight!" he burst out. "I don't think that's square. I'm a member of the association in good standin'. I've always held up my end of things—there ain't no call for yuh to throw me

11

down now! I've got reason to believe the rustlers aim to git into my stuff tonight; this may be jest the chance we been lookin' for to snag 'em! I'll do what I can by myself, o' course; but if I was to lose out for lack of a little help . . ." He broke off significantly.

It was a telling argument. The forays of the cattle thieves who were demoralizing this range had been so bold and persistent of late that only the most rigid co-operation served to keep some of the weaker spreads from folding up. Even the powerful Wishbone had suffered heavily. As yet the rustlers had succeeded in keeping the secret of their identity. No cowman would be justified in passing by a chance to bring them to book. Still Goodnight hesitated.

"You've brought us tips before," he told Galey, "that got us nowhere in the end. If I could be sure this one was any better . . ."

"Dammit, I ain't got nothin' but my brains to go by!" Bart exclaimed wrathfully. "No man kin read the minds of those rustlers, Goodnight! If I was dead shore of anythin', I'd go straight to Lint Granger with it, 'stead of gittin' down on my knees to you!"

Goodnight didn't turn a hair at this evocation of the sheriff's name. He knew Galey for what he was; a crabbed, small-minded man perpetually afraid that someone was attempting to take advantage of him. It weighed against him none at all in Jim's mind. It was plain Galey had never had any advantages; perhaps his two-bit spread meant even more to him in toil and effort than the vast Wishbone holdings meant to Goodnight himself. It was that which decided the latter.

"Since you put it that way," he said slowly, "we'll do as you want this time, Galey." He turned to Johnson. "You'll see that the boys get word, Tas? Tell them to be at Galey's Circle G before midnight."

Old Tas cleared his throat with a rumble and nodded. "I'll do that." There was nothing in his mien to tell whether he approved or disapproved; the glance he bent on Bart Galey as he turned his bronc was inscrutable.

Meeting that look, Bart said, "I'll carry word along the South Fork, Johnson; yuh can take the North Fork. That way it 'll save time." A moment later he was jogging away on his errand, brisk and matter of fact. Goodnight remained where he was for a long time, looking after Galey. At last he shook his head.

"I wish I could satisfy myself about that gent," he murmured. "It ain't right to hold his looks and his manner against him."

It was the measure of his squareness that his dislike of Galey's personality troubled him. Mean or small as the man might be, he was a member of the local organization; that fact alone entitled him to full consideration. Goodnight

13

warned himself against taking the other's concerns too lightly.

The cattlemen's association members, nearly a dozen grim-faced, silent men, gathered at Galey's little spread on Misery before midnight. "Bart says he saw prowlers on his range today," Goodnight told them. "We'll let him give us the rest of it."

Galey complied with what he had seen and what he suspected. "As Goodnight says, the rustlers 've left me pretty much to myself up to the present. They may be figurin' to polish off my whole herd at one clip," he summed up. He went on with his suggestions for its defense.

None of these men were the arguing kind: a plan of action was soon hit on. They swung away from the Circle G ten minutes later. The high, dim stars seemed only to accentuate the darkness. Not a word was said until, half a mile from Galey's bunched cattle, Goodnight gave his orders for the disposition of the men in a low tone. They split up, threading the brush with the silence of shadows, drawing an unbroken cordon about the steers.

Time dragged by. The failure of anything to happen did nothing to lessen the tension of these men. They had been forced to do so much of this kind of riding that their nerves were rasped raw with disappointed expectation. All would have welcomed a sharp clash with the rustlers who were slowly but surely bringing them face to face

14

with ruin. So far none had occurred. Would it be the same tonight?

It appeared likely. Hours later the first streaks of the false dawn appeared in the sky and still the dreamy peace enfolding the Circle G herd remained unbroken. Tas Johnson snorted his disgruntlement. He *was* on the point of voicing a gloomy remark to Goodnight when the silence was split abruptly by gunfire from over west. Both men jerked taut in a flash. They headed that way and struck in the spurs, Goodnight in the lead. Old Tas was not far behind.

"By grab, mebby this time there 'll be somethin' doin'!" the latter burst out harshly.

Goodnight was equally hopeful but he said nothing. Nor did he show disappointment when the firing broke off and sharp cries rang out.

Several men were gathered on a ridge when Goodnight and Johnson rode up. They were staring their hostility at a rider a little apart, menacing him with their guns.

"Who is that?" Goodnight jerked out.

"It's me, Jim! Tell those fools to lay off! I fired a signal shot to find yuh and they tried to jump me!"

Goodnight recognized his foreman. He pushed forward, old Tas at his side. "What are you doin' here, Steve?"

"Yuh figured yuh was layin' out in the right spot tonight," Steve exclaimed; "but there was a

15

mistake somewheres! Them wolves got into yore own stuff—there's been eighteen or twenty head of Wishbone stock drove off! Curly spotted the rustlers; there was some lead thrown. But they made a clean getaway!"

"Damn!" Goodnight packed all his exasperated wrath in the word. Then, "How long ago did this happen?" he rapped swiftly.

"Two hours."

"Which way did the steers go?"

"North, as near as we kin figure," came the answer. Quickly Steve told his story.

"They're headin' for the Idaho border!" Bart Galey struck in. He cursed the rustlers loudly. "By God, Goodnight, if they git away with it this time—!"

"If they do, it 'll be because you insisted on havin' your way!" Goodnight cut him off flatly. The others had come up. To them he said, "We're strikin' north, boys! There ain't nothin' to keep us here any longer. Let's go!"

They swung away at a round pace. An hour later Galey pulled up beside Goodnight. Light was gathering strength now, and still they had seen no trace of either cattle or rustlers. But the ground was so flinty, the going so rough, that it was impossible to be certain they had not come this way.

"Yo're makin' a mistake, Goodnight," Galey declared. "I told yuh them rustlers was makin' for the Idaho border. I'm shore of it now! This headin' north was nothin' but a ruse to throw us off."

Goodnight met his stare stonily.

"You may be right, Galey; but this time I'll prove myself wrong before I believe it!" he retorted.

Bart was quick to make capital of his stubborn attitude. "Yuh won't let a man tell yuh a thing!" he stormed. "Shore, I made a mistake tonight; I'll admit it—but who else is doin' any better? Small wonder we ain't gettin' anywheres!" he added significantly.

Goodnight looked at him sharply. It struck him that Galey's vehemence was designed chiefly for the benefit of the others; but he might be wrong about that. Bart had always been unnecessarily noisy. Either he was something of a fool as well, or he was one of those unfortunates whose blunders only succeeded in directing unjust suspicions against themselves.

They were still pressing forward at noon. Their luck had not improved; they had no more inkling of where the rustlers had faded to than before. It was no new experience for them: this thing had gone on in much the same manner from the time the rustling had started. Who the rustlers were, where they hid out, by what mysterious and unvaryingly successful means they succeeded in getting the stolen steers out of the country—these problems seemed destined to remain unsolved.

For this reason no one suggested giving up until at last Goodnight reined in on the edge of a vast stretch of badlands.

"We've come far enough," he declared. "If they got into these breaks, we'll never clap eyes on them. Personally, I'm satisfied they never came this way at all," he added.

"Where do yuh think the steers went, Jim?" a man asked.

"I don't know." Goodnight was frankly at a loss. "But if it was this way, we'd have been sure to spot some sign of it before now."

"Dang it all, I told yuh—" Bart Galey began argumentatively. Goodnight rounded on him.

"You tell us more than any sensible man can afford to listen to, Galey!" he threw out before the other could go on. "But this time I'm goin' to forestall you before you have time to yell stubborn! There's nothin' else we can do—so on the way back we'll loop over northeast and have a look at the Idaho trails. That ought to satisfy you."

If it did, Bart failed to signify as much. But he said no more as they headed back by the course Goodnight indicated. There were half-a-dozen Idaho trails to be crossed, leading up to the passes in the hills; but as one after another dropped behind, it became increasingly clear that no steers had been driven this way for a long time.

"It don't prove a thing," Galey insisted when

this was called to his attention. "No reason why the rustlers should stick to the trails. We're all fagged out, anyway. We may 've passed plumb over their sign without even bein' aware of it!"

It was logic of a kind, but Goodnight rejected it on short consideration. "If guesses are what we're workin' on, hereafter my own will suit me as well as another's—and maybe a bit better," was his grim comment. "Far as that goes, we'll soon have somethin' a whole lot better to depend on."

His tone was arresting. Old Tas said, gruffly curious, "What's that, Jim?"

"I received an answer last night from those range detectives I was to wire. They're on the way now. We're to be in Crazy Horse tomorrow to meet them."

"Yeh?" Johnson was attentive. "They're acceptin' our offer, then; is that it?"

"Looks like it."

None was more interested in the news than Bart Galey. At the first word he pricked up his ears; nothing that was said on the subject escaped him. But he said nothing as the men prepared to split up and head for their own spreads.

Goodnight arrived back at his ranch late at night. He felt burned out; but all the men were worn down, for that matter. Consequently he was the more surprised when his foreman routed him out at dawn with the news that Bart Galey and one

19

of his own men were here to see him. Hastily pulling on his boots, Jim went outside.

In the yard Galey and his puncher were holding three steers. They were Wishbone stuff, their hides matted with dried sweat; most of the beef had been run off them, and they were bellowing for water.

"Where 'd they come from?" Goodnight barked.

"Picked 'em up on the edge of my range," said Bart easily. "Looks like they was some of the stuff the rustlers run off."

Goodnight stared. "You mean you haven't had any rest yet—you took the time to haze these steers back here for me?"

Galey appeared embarrassed. "That's right. I reckon they got away from the bunch. Figured I'd do somethin' about it before the rustlers come back to gather 'em in."

It was Goodnight's turn to evince diffidence. "I'm sure obliged, Galey," he said. "It's mighty white of yuh."

"Not at all," Bart told him. "I'd expect yuh to do as much for me." He appeared to be satisfied if the matter was forgotten.

Jim didn't know what to say. Galey's unexpected favor made him ashamed for some of the things he had said yesterday. The whole incident convinced him the man meant well. He promptly dismissed any vague suspicions he had harbored against Bart for things which had happened in the past.

"You'll be in town tomorrow for the meetin', I expect?" he queried.

Galey nodded. "I'll be there."

Galey was in Crazy Horse early the following morning, attending every move as the Tuscarora Association prepared for the arrival of the heralded range detectives. And yet he was the last to head for the Humboldt House, where Goodnight had said they would wait, as train time drew near. There was something on Bart's mind while he stood at the bar in his favorite saloon and kept a wary watch on the street through the door.

At last came the signal he awaited: a blanket thrown over the high fence of the wagon yard opposite. Galey finished his drink, wiped his lips and walked out. Crossing over to the public yard, he paused in the gate with elaborate casualness; then, after a sharp glance up and down the street, he turned inside.

He was gone for a good five minutes, to reappear just as casually. After a scrutiny of his surroundings to make sure his movements had not been observed, Galey crossed back to the other side of the street and set out at a brisk pace for the Humboldt House.

A few minutes after he disappeared, a second man walked out of the gate. With a similar darting glance over the street, he turned on his heel and started off in the other direction.

2

Swinging along the plank sidewalk of Crazy Horse's main street, his spurs jingling, Slicer Cully paused before the doorway leading to the floor above the Northern Nevada Mercantile Company's store. A hard-looking individual, with a sliding glance and a traplike slash of a mouth, he slipped in and mounted the wooden steps, to knock softly at a door in the dusky hall. A flat, grating voice bade him enter.

The man seated at a table near the window was big, middle aged, dour faced. A cigar smoked in his fingers. Closing the door softly, Cully moved toward him.

There were no greetings. "Bart Galey just got word to me," Cully's words were a grumbling murmur, "that those two stock detectives the cattlemen's association sent for are on the way. They'll be here in a few minutes on Number Five." He paused, his beady eyes glittering with speculation. "How's that goin' to make things for our game, Slack?"

Dan Slack's steel-gray glance cut into him unwaveringly. If Cully was a man to awaken instinctive distrust by his gnarled, ferretlike appearance, Slack was his direct opposite. Broad faced and bluff, he looked solid, prosperous. Just now he was thinking hard. His lips parted in a grim smile.

"Rainbow Ripley and Grumpy Gibbs," he laughed contemptuously.

"You can laugh," Slicer snarled at him. "*I'm doin' the rustlin'*! Things are hard enough as it is; and now that pair is showin' up—the best range detectives this country's ever seen! They're the ones who put the Hole-In-The-Wall gang away; how do yuh know they won't do the same thing for us?"

Slack rolled it over. He knew all about Ripley and Gibbs and was secretly worried. "What else did Galey have to say?"

Slicer submitted further information about the stockmen's meeting even then in progress in another part of town. Slack listened attentively. He put a dozen crisp questions. Slicer told him what he knew.

At last Slack nodded heavily. "Leave these gents to me," he grunted. "I'll take care of 'em."

"Okay." As if this was his dismissal, Slicer turned toward the door, leaving him alone with his reflections.

Number Five rumbled into Crazy Horse on the Western Pacific main line twenty minutes later. Two men looking like cowpunchers descended from the smoker, carrying saddle and war bag. One of them, tall and lithe, with a magnificent pair of shoulders, was ten years younger than his hard-bitten companion. Yet it was plain he was their leader. The other, of a remarkably lugubrious cast of countenance, was just as obviously no fool.

From a safe distance, Dan Slack watched them, his gaze calculating, as they deposited their belongings with the station agent and headed down the street for the Golden Palace Saloon.

"So this is Crazy Horse," was Grumpy's disparaging comment as he looked the town over. "Why don't they call it Dead Horse an' be done with it?"

Rainbow smiled tolerantly. "Maybe the name 'll fit better with us around."

Range detectives for half-a-dozen years, and inseparable pals despite the difference in them, they had worked for stockmen up and down the West, acquiring a varied and violent past. Few indeed were the men who had defied their investigations successfully. They were in no hurry to get to the work which had called them here after a hard chase and a bitter showdown with stock thieves in Wyoming. Both knew what it would be. In good time they would take hold with competence and thoroughness. In the meantime a little relaxation would do no harm.

Crazy Horse they found to be much the same as a hundred cow towns they had known. There was a single dusty, wide business street, lined with false fronts and sun-baked adobes. A row of aged cottonwoods shaded the frame hotel, its upper-story windows shot out in some long-forgotten spree by the cowboys who rode exuberantly into town on payday. Just now, however, there was little to hold the interest of newcomers. A fat and lazy Mexican shambled along the plank sidewalk; a dog dozed or snapped at flies in the inch-thick sun-pounded dust. There was a bank, but it didn't look overly prosperous.

"Dang queer they got two railroads runnin' into this town," Grumpy observed. "Yuh'd think one was too much."

Rainbow had noted the second station. "Probably it belongs to some jerk line runnin' into the hills," he gave his opinion. "Raisin' beef is not the only business around here; they still take quite a bit of ore out, if the mines haven't all closed down."

They were bellying up to the bar in the Golden Palace when they were accosted by a big man who had just come in. "Howdy, boys," he said affably. "Have one on me?"

Turning in surprise, they took him in from head to toe. His whole manner and appearance were amiable enough; yet Grumpy was inclined to immediate suspicion. "Who 're you?" he queried bluntly.

"The name's Slack, Dan Slack." The man stared at Rainbow. "You're Rainbow Ripley."

"That's right. I don't remember you—"

"I didn't figure yuh would," Slack broke in

smoothly. "I never forget a face. Wasn't it in Salt Lake we met? It don't matter. I know why yo're here. Reckon there's a cryin' need for yuh on this range." He seemed determined to make himself agreeable, his words flowing on easily. "Signed up with the Tuscarora Association yet?" he broke off.

Grumpy only stared at him with growing distrust, but Rainbow answered promptly, "No, not yet."

"Don't be in a hurry, then," was Slack's cool proposal. He added in explanation that with the recent rise in the price of gold, he had decided to ship out mine tailings from the old Buckskin Mine at Lost Angel Camp on Superstition Mountain, some eighteen miles north of Indian Wells. There was an old tumble-down railroad line running out there from Crazy Horse, still in operation as far as Indian Wells. As soon as repairs were completed in the track from that point on to the deserted ghost camp, he would begin. "I've got a prop-osition of my own that may interest yuh," he concluded. "Far as the money goes, I'll pay yuh twice what they offer yuh."

On the verge of telling Slack irascibly what he could do with his money, Grumpy subsided when Rainbow jabbed an elbow into his ribs.

"We'll keep you in mind," Rainbow promised in an interested tone, "but right now we'd better be huntin' up these stockmen. I understand they're waitin' for us."

"At the Humboldt House," Slack nodded. "Well"—he lifted his glass as they turned away— "see you later, gents."

Grumpy's expression as they left the saloon was one of puzzlement. "What's the idear of swallerin' his oily talk?" he groused irritably. "He lissens like a dang smooth hombre to me. 'Wasn't it in Salt Lake we met?' he says. Like hell yuh did!"

"I never saw him before in my life," Rainbow admitted, "and that's what interests me. He's goin' out of his way to make us a proposition when he knows why we're here. Looks mighty queer. What's he got in his mind?"

"I reckon yo're slated to find out, the way yo're goin' at it," his partner returned.

Nearly a dozen men were crowded into the little parlor of the Humboldt House when Rainbow and Grumpy entered. The talk died down. A cowman still young in years who was acting as chairman of the meeting ran his eye over them appraisingly.

"Ripley and Gibbs?" he queried. And at their nods, "We've been waitin' for you. Boys, these are the men we sent for. Now we'll get some action!"

There was a chorus of gruff greetings. Bart Galey, of the Circle G, old Tas Johnson, who ran the Lazy Lightning, and others pushed forward to shake hands.

To their spokesman Rainbow said, "You're Jim Goodnight, I expect." It was the name signed to the wire which had called him and Grumpy to Nevada. Goodnight assented.

For some reason, Rainbow took to the latter at once. There was a forthrightness about Goodnight which said that he was to be trusted; his earnest blue eyes in themselves were a guarantee of his character. Rainbow had seen men such as this go far; with luck, in time Goodnight might make almost anything of himself that he wanted to. He was young yet; his very sincerity might give him trouble until experience had knocked the rough edges off. But the stuff was there.

Tucking these reflections in the back of his mind, Rainbow asked for an explanation of the situation.

Goodnight complied at length. The men gathered here were cowmen from the Indian Wells range, twenty miles to the north. For months their herds had been raided by some mysterious agency. Steers were disappearing steadily. For some reason the thieving appeared impossible to stop. Not once had the rustlers been seen. Although the trails leading west toward the desert and north through the mountains into Oregon were being watched closely, it had not yet even been discovered in what direction the steers were going.

"We're relyin' on you to get results, Ripley," Goodnight declared. The fact that he was the owner of the Wishbone, the biggest spread in the Indian Wells country, plus the hard drive of his iron will, had made him the spearhead of the Tuscarora Cattlemen's Association.

Rainbow shook his head with apparent reluctance when Goodnight mentioned the amount the association was prepared to pay them.

"That's a pretty good figure, Goodnight," he acknowledged. "But I'm afraid we can't see the work at that price. If that's the best you can do, you'll have to get someone else."

Surprise silenced the assembled ranchers for a moment. Then Bart Galey burst out, "Hell, Ripley, yuh can't walk out on us like that! If this is a shakedown, it won't work!" Plainly a hot-head, he would have run on angrily, but Goodnight stopped him.

"Ripley," he said, "you knew from my wire what to expect. What's changed your mind so suddenly?"

"A better proposition," was the prompt answer.

"You mean since you stepped off the train?"

"Yes. A man named Slack offered us a job, lookin' after his operations at Lost Angel."

"Slack!"

It was old Tas Johnson. He spat the name out like a curse. "Damn his gall, how'd he even find out we sent fer yuh?" He shifted his intent suddenly. "Leave his job alone, Ripley. That's a warnin'!"

Rainbow was immediately curious. From the dark looks and the muttering, it was trebly clear that Dan Slack was cordially hated by these men. Bart Galey was louder than any in his condemnation of Dan. Rainbow inquired, "Just what have you got against Slack, if you don't mind my askin'?"

Goodnight enlightened him tersely. The previous summer Slack had organized a water district around Indian Wells, planning to tap the headwaters of the Owyhee. All present had invested heavily, but upon a survey being completed, the project had proved unfeasible. No one ever saw the color of his money again, but Slack had done well for himself. The inference was plain.

There was even further reservation in Jim's mind where Slack was concerned. Shortly after the failure of the water district, Goodnight's father had been picked up on the range, murdered. He had told his foreman on leaving the Wishbone that he intended facing Slack and demanding an accounting. Inevitably the latter had been believed guilty of the crime. Although a jury had acquitted him, Jim had never been satisfied with the verdict. He still believed Slack responsible for his father's death. But he said nothing of all this to Ripley.

He waited for some sign of a natural indignation as he finished his story. It did not come. Rainbow said calmly, "Reckon I don't blame you gents any, but—"

"But, hell! You'll never take Slack's job, Ripley!" Bart Galey jerked out fiercely, shrewdly

measuring his man. Others seconded the sentiment.

"That so?" Rainbow sounded unimpressed. If
the gathering menace of this moment got to
him, he gave no sign. "I reckon we'll have
another talk with him, anyway."

"Don't yuh come back here, if yuh do!" Tas
Johnson grated. Jim Goodnight added slowly, "I
don't think yo're bein' on the square with us,
Ripley. I'll promise you we won't forget it!"

Rainbow was not disposed to argue the matter.
Sliding a glance at Grumpy, they started for the
door. "Stop 'em!" a man exclaimed harshly. "By
God, if they throw us down an' sign up with
Slack . . . !" But something in the self-reliant look
of the pair prevented anyone from hindering their
departure. Grumpy was impelled to fire a parting
shot from the door, but Rainbow pushed him
through and followed.

Once in the street, Rainbow headed back to the
Golden Palace. "Seems to me yo're in a danged
almighty sweat to grab yoreself a handful uh
trouble," Grumpy growled. He did not hold back,
however.

Slack was waiting for them when they reached
the saloon. Easy as his greeting was, his glance
held a sharp question. Without preamble Rainbow
said, "We'll listen to that offer now."

"Interested, eh? Fine!" Slack lost no time in
acquainting them with his proposal. With gold

31

hovering around twenty-five dollars an ounce for several years, the mines at Lost Angel on Superstition Mountain had been forced to close down. Now that gold had skyrocketed to thirty-three dollars, even the tailings of the mines had once more grown sufficiently valuable to work. As an experiment, Slack had leased the old Buckskin and intended to start shipping as soon as he could get the ore cars up there.

"I've been lookin' for a couple good men to guard the railroad right of way through the canyons," he lied smoothly. "It's wild, lonely country up there an' needs watchin'. You and yore partner just suit me." He made them his offer.

"Don't look for no bed of roses," he warned frankly as they nodded their acceptance. "You may run into plenty of grief."

"That 'll be okay with us," Rainbow told him.

Slack said he wanted them on the job without delay. He told Grumpy where to go to get horses. And to Rainbow, "Come down to the Nevada Midland Station with me and meet Miss Longstreet. Since her father died she's the owner, president, general manager, ticket agent and about everything else on her road," he explained.

The Nevada Midland offices were in a dilapidated station standing beside rusty tracks on the edge of town. Clearly the little road was tottering on the verge of dissolution. Rainbow saw half-a-dozen worn-out and disused coaches on a spur.

An old engine that would never run again stood across from the station.

In the cluttered office, Slack introduced him to a slim, clear-eyed girl whose astonishing good looks had nothing to do with her self-possession or her shrewd common sense.

Sharon Longstreet took in Rainbow's capable shoulders, his level gray eyes and dead-black hair with plain approval while she listened to Slack's smooth explanation of who and what Rainbow and his partner were, and for what they had been engaged. It did not influence her judgment in the slightest, however. She shook her head decisively when Slack finished.

"It may be an excellent idea, but I simply can't afford guards," she said in a tone vibrating with reserves of strength. "That will have to be my final answer."

"You're not listenin'," Slack returned suavely, with his heavy smile. "I said *I'd* hired these men, Miss Longstreet. Don't you understand? They'll be workin' for you, but I'll foot the bill. Ain't that fair enough?"

She wasted no time on false attitudes. "It's not fair at all; but since the advantage is all with me, I won't pretend to protest. If it weren't for you, I wouldn't have this extra freight to haul."

It satisfied Slack. After talking a few minutes longer he departed, leaving Rainbow and Sharon together. So interested was Rainbow in this capable, auburn-haired girl that he seemed scarcely to notice. And yet, Slack was barely beyond ear-shot before Rainbow spoke of something else that interested him.

"It appears to be generally agreed that a guard over the railroad between Indian Wells and Lost Angel is advisable," he said. "Why?"

"Because of the Indian Wells cattlemen," she answered without hesitation. "Two years ago, we had a cloudburst in the mountains. It weakened the track. I refused to bring ten cars of cattle down until the road was reballasted. Rocky Goodnight, who owned the steers, insisted on shipping. He gave me a waiver and the cars came down. There was a wreck. Two cars went into the canyon at a washout and Tim Bucktoe, one of the Wishbone punchers, was nearly killed. The accident left him crippled and unable to get range work. It embittered him and, I think, made a madman of him. He's ripped up track several times and tried to wreck our only locomotive. Of course the stockmen sympathize with him."

"Which don't make matters any easier for you," Rainbow commented.

"We manage to get along," Sharon answered without self-pity. At his inquiry, she explained that her father had built the Nevada Pacific at a time when Lost Angel was a roaring gold camp. In those days the receipts had been heavy, and there was even a little freight from north of the

34

camp. When the mines petered out, business gradually slacked off, until now, although the road continued to serve Indian Wells and the Pine Valley Indian Reservation hauling freight and ties and making occasional cattle shipments, it was getting harder and harder to make both ends meet. The refusal of the Indian Wells ranchers to give her their business didn't help matters any.

"They don't care much for Slack, either," Rainbow nodded.

"No, they don't." She flashed him a look. "He attempted to organize a water district which failed. Soon afterward, Rocky Goodnight, one of the heaviest losers, was murdered—"

"That's Jim Goodnight's father, I take it?"

She nodded. "Mr Slack was accused of the crime. Tim Bucktoe testified in his behalf, and he was acquitted. But the cattlemen have their own idea of what happened."

Rainbow understood young Goodnight's bitterness against Slack better now. "Is Bucktoe still around?" he asked.

"No, he disappeared a few weeks ago. I understand he has left the country for good."

Rainbow asked other questions. They were still talking when a man barged into the office roughly. "Sharon . . ." he began half angrily.

Rainbow whirled. He found himself gazing into the stony features of Jim Goodnight. Goodnight broke off whatever he had been about to say to stare sharply. His tone held a rasp of antagonism.

"What are you doin' here, Ripley?"

Though he watched Goodnight closely, Rainbow did not miss the swift color which flamed in Sharon Longstreet's face at the tone the rancher used. Plainly she was accustomed to different treatment from him. Rainbow had gathered from her manner of speaking about Goodnight that her interest in him was strong. She seemed saddened by the happenings which had thrust a barrier between them.

"I happen to be workin' for the Nevada Midland," was the dangerously quiet reply, "if it really matters."

"What!" Goodnight was genuinely surprised. "But I thought Slack . . ."

"Mr Slack has hired Rainbow and his partner to guard the railroad above Indian Wells," Sharon put in calmly.

"Against my kind, eh?" Goodnight gave her a freezing look. "I just heard about the deal you've made with Slack to carry his tailings down from the Buckskin. I could hardly believe it. Is it true?"

"Yes, it's true."

"But you can't do that!" Goodnight stormed. "Slack is the man who murdered my father— everybody knows it! Good God, Sharon, what can you be thinkin' of?"

"I'm thinking of the railroad," she told him

steadily. "Since you and your friends have ceased to look to me, I've had to turn elsewhere. My business is to haul freight, and Mr Slack has offered an opportunity to increase that business. I have no other interest in him, if that is what you mean."

Goodnight's face went scarlet with anger, indignation and injured pride. "It's plain you've got none in me, to have anything to do with that wolf!" he threw at her bitterly. Sharon went white to the lips but her gaze did not waver, nor was her proudly held head any less erect.

"You will have to reach your own decision about that, Jim," she returned quietly.

It had not escaped Rainbow that more than a casual interest lay between these two. Just as plainly it promised now to come to an abrupt end. He could not altogether persuade himself that he was sorry. And yet, he put in in a conciliating tone,

"Now you're talkin' hasty, Goodnight. Why not look at her side of things?" If there was censure in the words, there was approval in his manner, for he could not honestly condemn Goodnight's attitude. However it appeared, he was still working in the man's interests.

Goodnight turned on him. "I've said my say to you, Ripley—you can mind your own business!" he whipped out. Rainbow shrugged.

"Maybe there's a slight difference of opinion as to what's mine and what's yours," he drawled.

Goodnight flushed with fury at the coolness of it. "By God, if that's the way you feel, we can settle this right here and now!"

In the crackling tension left in the wake of this challenge Sharon stiffened with dread. She need not have worried, however. Rainbow gave Goodnight the benefit of his twisted smile.

"Maybe it 'll dawn on you finally that I didn't come here for love of you, Goodnight, any more than to fight over nothin'," he dropped. "Until you hunt up a better excuse than the present one, we won't!"

With the words, he turned on his heel and walked out.

3

Procuring broncs for himself and Rainbow, Grumpy saddled up and led them back to the Golden Palace. Rainbow had said they would meet here. Racking the horses, Grumpy entered the saloon for another drink.

The first person his glance fell on was Bart Galey, the hot-tempered Indian Wells rancher. The meeting at the Humboldt House had broken up; Galey and the other ranch owners stood lined up at the bar. A cold warning ran along Grumpy's nerves at the hostile battery of eyes turned on him. But it was not in his book to turn his back on trouble. Making for the other end of the bar, he poured himself a drink and stood before it.

Galey, Tas Johnson and the others glared at him with mounting ire.

"Them two hombres 've got a gall, paradin' themselves after turnin' us down fer Slack! Oughta be run out of town, they had!" old Tas averred harshly.

"What's the matter with doin' jest that?" Galey caught him up in an ugly tone. "There 'll never be a better chance! They had their warnin'. We'll get this sour mug first," he ran on, "then handle the other . . ."

The proposal caught like a spark in dry tinder. Wicked tempered as a result of their grievances, ready for anything, the cattlemen edged toward Grumpy, pretending meanwhile to carry on a loud conversation among themselves. Keenly aware of what was afoot, Grumpy chose to stand his ground. Saner men would have taken warning from his forbidding cast of visage. But not these. Slowly but surely, urged on by Galey, they crowded him to the end of the bar.

A potential violence stirred in Grumpy as he considered his situation. He mastered it with iron control, playing for time; for he read to a hair-breadth the danger packed in this setup. Where was Rainbow?

Grumpy finished his drink and started to pour another, his hand steady as rock, when without any warning the bottle was batted out of his grasp roughly. A growl rose in his throat and he found himself staring into the bleak eyes of Bart Galey. "Wal, what about it?" the latter snarled, plainly trying to force an issue.

Instead of satisfying him, Grumpy backed away warily, eyes darting, his itching fingers hovering close to his six gun. He didn't open his lips. A glance in the back bar mirror, moments ago, had shown him a pool table directly behind him; it was toward the heavy table that he maneuvered now.

"Hell, don't fool around with the skunk!" the flat words exploded in this tense silence. "Pull him down!"

Naked murder was in the air. Grumpy read it in the reckless drive of this bunch, inflamed by Galey's fierce hatred, so sure of themselves that they had tossed reason aside. Another moment and they would swing into concerted action.

Grumpy didn't wait for it. Wheeling sharply, he sprang to the pool table. A heave sufficed to tip it over on edge. Its slate bed and hardwood frame would provide excellent cover when the lead began to fly. Before he had time to duck behind it, however, things were sailing through the air. A bottle crashed against the table. A hurtling pool cue glanced off Grumpy's head, knocking his hat aside and bringing him to his knees.

The blow left him groggy. The room rocked while he strove desperately for control; a sharp cry sliced through the rising storm of guttural talk.

"Now we've got him!"

It stung Grumpy to a final effort. With what seemed the last remnant of his strength, he wrenched out his gun and shoved it in front of him. Its muzzle wavered across the moving front of these men, holding them at bay momentarily.

"Finish it—finish it!" Bart Galey bellowed in a wild, infectious rage. "He can't pull trigger if he tries!"

Why they didn't come at him with a rush, he couldn't understand; for despite his display of clear grit, it would have been easy. Still they closed in with the deadly slowness of a wolf pack. He was beyond doing anything for himself; he saw that with fatal clarity. To attempt to reach his feet would be to crash headlong. It was a deadlock without an end; and when the end did come, it was completely unexpected.

"Just a minute, gents," said a calm voice from the door. The cowmen spun toward it. Rainbow stood there, taking them in with cold contempt in his lean cheeks, his blazing eyes.

"There's the other one!" Galey ripped out truculently. "Let's make a clean sweep of this!"

Rainbow's lips were pressed into a thin line. He opened them to ask, "Are you okay, Grump?" His partner's answer was to fold forward on the floor. He was out cold.

Concern flashed across Rainbow's features. He never paused to ask what the odds against him might be. Whipping his gun out of the leather, he started to slide crabwise down the side of the saloon toward Grumpy.

"Take it easy, boys," came from him in a gentle murmur. "Don't make any mistakes."

There was a sibilant rustle amongst these men, watching with hawklike care for the first break in his attention. His cold defiance was like raw alcohol flung on the flames of their anger. "You'll never get in the clear, Ripley!" Galey swore furiously. "You ain't got a chance!"

Rainbow bit back a stinging retort, his face set and stony. What he had set himself to do spoke louder than any words a man could find. Carefully he pressed on. Grumpy was at his feet now. Leaning down, he got a grip on the other and with a heave swung him up. His bulk was a dead weight across Rainbow's shoulder. Rainbow grunted as he settled that burden, his narrowed eyes flicking here and there.

"One side."

Thin and low, crackling in the electric tension of this room, the words were both challenge and declaration. The ranchers had begun to shift toward the door, cutting Rainbow off, an ugly determination stamped on their faces. Slowly Rainbow crowded them, cold steel in his look. No more had been said or would be said; there was

42

this fine-drawn combat of wills, like menacing thunder behind the curtain of silence, and the soft scuffle of boots, no more.

Rainbow gained a yard, two yards. There was still a long ways to go. He didn't spare a look for the door, keeping his iron regard glued on the faces in front of him, alert for the first quick move. Another six feet and he was hard up against a solid wall of men: men who itched to lay hands on him, yet held off.

But they didn't break away before him. Considering that bleakly, he knew he was cornered unless he broke it up somehow. The means wasn't clear, and Rainbow was asking himself if this was the end of his trail when a fresh voice said:

"Drop this, boys."

Rainbow recognized Jim Goodnight's rasping tone. Without removing his gaze from the smoky eyes directly before him, he answered, "It's a funeral, Goodnight. It ain't yet decided whose— but you're invited!"

The silence which met his retort at length impelled him to glance around. Beside Goodnight stood a lanky, gimlet-eyed man with a stringy mustache and a lawman's star on his floppy vest. Sheriff Lint Granger took in this arrested situation shrewdly and grunted,

"Yo're Ripley, ain't yuh? Jim was jest tellin' me about yuh. Go on an' pull yore stakes—if that's what yuh was aimin' to do. There ain't nothin' goin' to happen here."

The air in this place cleared at once. It brought the saner ones to their senses, a little sheepish. "All the same—" a man began hotly, argumentatively, only to break off. Except for Galey, they started to turn away. A lane opened up before Rainbow. Wasting no time, yet coolly deliberate, he pushed through.

At the door he came close to Goodnight. Their eyes clashed. "Much obliged, Goodnight," said Rainbow. Anger flashed across the rancher's flat features.

"Save your breath. This don't change anything between us!"

Rainbow nodded curtly without words and pushed on outside, conscious all at once of Grumpy's whalebone and rawhide weight over his shoulder. Letting him slip down, Rainbow looked him over anxiously. There was no blood on him. "Knocked out," Rainbow grunted in a relieved tone.

Dragging Grumpy toward the near-by horse trough, he ducked his head in the water. Grumpy remained passive for a moment and then began to struggle and sputter. He came up red faced, fire in his eye.

"Tryin' to drown me?" he rasped irritably.

"Why no," was the serene reply. "Jest tryin' to wash your neck."

From the tone of Grumpy's disgusted cursing, he read that the other was rapidly returning to normal. "Finish your drink, and we'll head out for Lost Angel," he said as he examined the broncs which his partner had procured. "I understand it's quite a jog away from here."

"Go to hell," Grumpy told him amiably.

A few minutes later, with the latter fully recovered, they swung up and headed out of Crazy Horse. To the north as they came out upon open range, the hills rolled up in the sere brown fold on fold of the mountain desert. Magpies skimmed the sage. There was every prospect of a peacefully dull afternoon following the rapid events of the morning.

They would not have felt so sure of this, however, could they have heard the talk between Dan Slack and Slicer Cully which occurred while they were still almost within hail. Slicer moved to a position near Slack and flat words issued from the side of his mouth.

"We've got nigh onto two hundred head of steers in the Buckskin Mine right now, Dan; what's the idear of invitin' them birds to nose around up there?"

Slack cast a wary glance about before replying. Isolated in the street, they were in no danger of being overheard.

"Well, they're on their way now. Knowin'

exactly where they are and what they're doin' is better than wonderin', ain't it." It was not a question. He went on, "Of course, if you can suggest anything better—" and broke off thinly on that note.

Testing its satire, Slicer grunted. "Mebby a little lead throwin' would persuade 'em this country ain't so healthy fer range detectives. If yuh wasn't so thin skinned, you'd o' thought of that yoreself!"

"Yuh mean rub 'em out?"

"It 'd be all right with me," Slicer began callously. Slack vetoed the proposal decisively: "No, but maybe there's something there at that. Ripley's the one for us to worry about," he declared shrewdly. "If he was to be winged, say, and hustled off to the hospital in Salt Lake . . . ?" Then, after a pause, "You can see where the blame would fall, after what happened in the Palace."

Cully straightened up from the hitch rack against which he had been leaning, purpose in his manner. "Which way are they goin'?"

"I told 'em to take the road," said Slack. "I'm goin' to cut across the hills myself."

Slicer's thin brows lifted. "You goin' up?"

"Yeh." It was said blandly. "I want to see how things are gettin' along."

They started down the street together only to part a block below. Shortly afterward both rode out of Crazy Horse, each taking a different direction.

Slicer's course paralleled the Indian Wells road. He rode at a brisk pace, yet it was half an hour before he got a flash of Rainbow and Grumpy jogging far beyond. Another twenty minutes passed, and they were in the hills before he drew up on them; and when he did it was to circle on ahead. He worked toward a rocky defile in the brush-covered slopes overlooking the road. There he drew his rifle from the boot and got down.

Settling to wait, his face was lean and wolfish. His lip curled as he recalled Slack's instructions. He had no intention of winging either of these men whom he had set himself to bushwhack; he'd do considerably more than that, but he anticipated no real trouble to come of it. It would be easy to explain how his aim had been better than he intended.

A glimpse of Rainbow and his companion, advancing along the trail, interrupted his thoughts.

It had become habitual with these two not to ride too close together. They were tossing remarks across a space of a dozen feet and interestedly scanning the hills as they rode. Grumpy's thoughts had been running on cattle for some minutes.

"A hot note this is," he grumbled. "Couple old cow pokes like us, hirin' out to ride herd on a tin-pot railroad!"

"You may get your bellyful of steer chasin' before we get through," his partner returned cryptically.

47

Grumpy said "Huh?" blankly, but Rainbow offered no explanation of his remark. He had just thrown back his head to glance at a soaring yellowhammer when the unwarning crack of a rifle rang out on the iron slope above them and a slug whined past his face.

Rainbow's ducking slide and the answering crash of Grumpy's six gun, seasoned with an angry curse, were simultaneous. Mastering his spooky bronc, Rainbow jerked his rifle out and darted a look up the rocks.

"He's up there in that gulch—the danged skunk!" Grumpy gritted, pointing. "I got a flash of his smoke!"

Rainbow's face was white and taut. There was no need for instructions. Whipping a shot up there, he jammed his mount that way in a curving course that would bring him out above the ravine. Grumpy took the other side. It was tough going; before they had covered half the distance, the rasp of shod hoofs on rock reached their ears. The assassin's rifle cracked again; slugs droned about them, screaming off the granite; but they saw no more than a flitting shadow, vague against the dun background and gone in an instant.

"Right after him!" Rainbow jerked out.

By the time they reached the point where the cut sliced through the ridge crest, empty silence alone awaited them. It was not unexpected. They shoved on, alert for the first crashing announcement of a fresh ambush. The riven, tumbled rocks and boulder patches here were cover enough for an army. But the danger of being cut down without a chance for their skins could not deter them now.

"Take that side of the gulch," Rainbow snapped, jerking his chin up, "and comb it out!"

"Mebby it 'd be better sense to jest locate this Galey's spread an' ride over there. He seems to be the number-one bad boy of this bunch—"

"Do as I say!" the answer whipped back. "If we can square accounts on the spot, we'll do that. I don't like unfinished business!"

For ten minutes they were busily employed. The gravel and hardpan underfoot showed no trace of tracks; each knew it to be a case of smoking out their quarry or letting the matter drop.

At last Grumpy reined in to flick a rueful glance at his friend. "Looks like he's give us the slip."

Rainbow nodded. Busy as his thoughts were, he had nothing to say. It was Grumpy who went on, "Jest like old times, danged if it ain't! Here we are again, plumb in the middle of poppin' hell!"

"What of it?" his partner grinned at him unfeelingly. "You wouldn't want it any other way."

4

Riding hard, Dan Slack came across the tumbled hills to Lost Angel in the late afternoon. It lay in an irregular valley, hemmed in by barren, rocky slopes; to the north the vast bulk of Superstition Mountain cut the sky. It was on the flank of this mountain that gold had been discovered. The Buckskin Mine, at the end of a Nevada Midland spur, lay at its foot, a gaping tunnel mouth.

It was toward this that Slack headed. To the left, around a jutting granite shoulder, was the all-but-deserted ghost town. On the flat before the mine entrance, amidst ancient rusted machinery and great heaps of old tailings, half-a-dozen hard-looking men were collected. They were idle, unless keeping a sharp lookout could be said to constitute their work. Slack knew them. They were his men, waiting to start the task for which the mine had ostensibly been leased, as soon as the railroad had been repaired to this point.

They came forward as he rode up. One took his bronc when he swung to the ground. If they expected orders from him now, however, he soon disposed of the notion, waving a hand in careless denial. "Just lookin' around, boys," he said. "I'll take a walk down to the camp. No, I don't want anyone with me." He started down the trail toward Lost Angel and a moment later disappeared from sight, humming to himself. His men exchanged looks of inquiry, shrugged and returned to their own concerns.

Once beyond view around the shoulder of the mountain, Slack dropped his pose of casualness and hastened forward with every appearance of purpose. The deserted camp opened out before him. Chinatown, where hundreds of coolies had lived during the heyday of the mines, lay at this end of Lost Angel's long and crooked street. On either side ran a line of single-storied tumble-down buildings—old shops, chophouses and fantan joints, their doors and windows gaping. Everywhere, on pillars and blank walls, fluttered the tattered remnants of Chinese posters covered with hieroglyphics.

It was deathly silent here, the walls sun baked and crumbling. Alleys ran between most of these adobe warrens in which rats scurried as Slack moved past. At the mouth of a certain devious alley he turned in after a sharp glance along the street. He moved down it for some distance before he slowed.

The echoes of these sleeping walls awakened suddenly to the startlingly realistic hoot of an owl. The sound came from Slack's lips. He repeated it. But not until he had done so half-a-dozen times was there an answer. Even then it was only a rattle of dirt at a blank doorway behind him. Slack turned that way. His manner seemed to have undergone a change during the last few minutes. His habitual assertion was gone. "That you, Tim?" he muttered.

"Stow the racket and get in here in a hurry," said a heavy, grating voice in a tone of impatience.

Slack entered a dusky low-ceiled shell of a room. A large deformed figure detached from the shadows, monstrously distorted by the half-light. This man had once been huge; he was still big. Some accident had twisted him all out of shape. His massive shoulders were bent and warped and beamlike arms hung almost to his knees, one longer than the other. His face was scarred and ugly; a steady glow of potential power lay in his deep-set, shaggy-browed eyes. The incredible roughness of his appearance only enhanced the suggestion of immense strength and animal-like shrewdness that lent him a peculiar fascination.

He was Tim Bucktoe, the man who had been in the Nevada Midland wreck two years before. Slack gave him a direct, probing glance and at once felt impelled to avert his eyes from that hideous face.

"Well?" came the short, imperative growl.

"Somethin' came up today that I had to fix in a hurry," Slack told him. Rapidly, as though the words were dragged out of him, and yet with some hesitancy in the telling as if uncertain of its reception, he related the arrival of the range detectives called in by the Tuscarora Cattlemen's Association, and how by quick thinking he had managed to hire the pair. "I figured—" he began in explanation.

Bucktoe silenced him with a gesture of his apelike arm.

"That was a fool play," he rasped disgustedly, his eyes crying scorn. "A danged waste of money! There's cheaper ways of gettin' rid of their kind than that. I don't want no damned stock detectives either for or against me!"

Slack's brows shot up. Cowed by this domineering cripple and yet secretly hating him, he was stung to argument by the other's tone. "What do yuh mean, cheaper?" he demanded. "Yuh told me there's a fortune in this mine, and all we had to do was get the money to work it. It's why we went into rustlin' together." His voice gathered assurance as he ran on. "I'm no doughhead; I can do some thinkin' for myself!" he wound up defiantly.

Bucktoe stared at him in silence for so long that he grew fidgety despite his bluster. That maimed face did things to him.

"Gettin' big, are yuh?" the menacing rumble came at last. "Don't fool yoreself a minute about throwin' in with me! Yuh didn't—I saved yuh at that trial for a purpose; just remember that that's one thing it ain't healthy to overlook!" Slack would have protested vehemently, but Bucktoe beat him down with a look. "What was you, before I took yuh in hand?" The biting words dropped from the corner of his misshapen mouth. "Not a damned thing! *I* made yuh rich in that water scheme; *I* saved yore hide by lyin', when yuh had to knock off old Rocky Goodnight on account of it! *I'm* offerin' to lay the money in yore hand that 'll make yuh anything from governor to U. S. senator. But meantime, you're doin' exactly as I say. Paste that in yore hat, Slack!"

Bucktoe was speaking the literal truth in referring to the water district as he did. The plan had originated in his shrewd brain. He had given his instructions to Slack, and the latter had carried them out. The plan was, briefly, to cut through the hills to the headwaters of the Owyhee, bringing that extra irrigation into the Indian Wells range. Many men had invested, some heavily. And when the scheme had gone glimmering, like so many desert dreams of water, Slack had appropriated the funds, taking refuge in subterfuge and technicalities.

Slack was on the verge now of blurting out the story of his instructions to Slicer Cully, but Bucktoe's cantankerous assumption of dominance dried him up. He clamped his teeth on his rage in bitter silence. At last he got out, grudgingly, "Those detectives can be fired quick enough, if it comes to that."

Bucktoe grated, "Forget it! They're comin' up here—I'll take care of 'em!" His flattened, grinning face became utterly forbidding.

"And meanwhile they've got to be paid; them and the others," Slack came back at him significantly. Bucktoe glowered at him for a moment, his jaw thrust out; then without words he turned back to a crumbling door. He was gone for several minutes, and when he reappeared it was to lay a heavy buckskin bag in Slack's palm. The latter gauged its value by hefting it and thrust it into a pocket.

"Just see that yuh make that go further 'n the last," Bucktoe told him in a miserly tone. "An' don't be showin' up here so often, either. Stay away till I signal yuh. An', Slack, I don't need to repeat what'll happen to you if yuh ever breathe a word 'bout me bein' here or where the gold comes from! Like it or not, nobody 'll ever get me; but *I'll get you!*"

There was a lethal whine in the threat from which Slack took refuge in injured dignity. The next moment he said, "This new vein yuh discovered in the Buckskin, Tim—I want to see it. Take me down in there, can't yuh?" There was a mixture of urgency and greed in the request.

Bucktoe told him thinly, "You'll lay eyes on the vein when I get ready to have yuh, and not before." The words said his decision was immovable, and Slack shrugged his disappointment. He knew how far he could go with this strangely twisted man, and at what point he must haul up short. After talking a few minutes longer they parted, Slack making his way back toward Lost Angel's street, a look of deep discontent brooding in his eyes. But dark as were his own designs, a shiver shook him at the thought of Bucktoe; that deformed, hate-ridden vulture bent him to his will with an iron grip that he despaired of breaking.

North of Indian Wells the road paralleled the railroad right of way through the canyons on the extension running up toward Lost Angel. Rainbow and Grumpy at length deserted the trail to cling to the rails, for this was the stretch which they had been hired to guard. It was lonely country, rough and wild.

The sun swung low in the west when Grumpy squinted ahead and said, "There's some men workin'. Must be the track gang Slack was tellin' yuh about."

Rainbow nodded. Presently they drew near enough to watch an antiquated, bell-stacked Baldwin locomotive pushing a flatcar loaded with rails and ties back and forth with a busy chuffing, while a dozen or more men worked on the track under the supervision of a tall, blocky and granite-visaged individual whose reddish stubble, keen blue eyes and biting sarcasms proclaimed him to be an Irishman. Rainbow accosted this man.

"Con Murphy?" he said.

"That's the name." There was sharp appraisal in the regard that was turned on Rainbow. "Jest who might you be?"

Rainbow introduced himself and Grumpy and handed over a note which Sharon Longstreet had given him, explaining why they were there. Murphy read it, his lips thrust out. He snorted half contemptuously, "Who in hell ever heard of guardin' a railroad? Has the colleen gone crazy?"

Grumpy stared at him as if about to erupt, but Rainbow struck in with a smile, "Dan Slack has somethin' to do with it, Murphy. It's him wants the guardin' done. He made us the offer, and I understand he's footin' the bill."

"Oh, Slack," Con grunted, only partially mollified. He was a salty old railroad veteran of many years' standing, almost as grizzled as Clem Rucker, the white-haired engineer, and the fireman who peered interestedly from the locomotive cab.

"Wal," he continued, "there ain't nothin' much to guard now. We ain't done our work yet. Reckon you'll have to wait."

Rainbow cheerfully assented. "Where's your camp?"

"We're puttin' up in Lost Angel. Yuh can go on up there. It's only a mile or so." He told them where to go.

Among the men who watched the partners pull away was Slicer Cully, pretending to busy himself with the work. He had pushed on here in a hurry after his unsuccessful attempt on their lives, intent on establishing an alibi in the event of need. Rainbow's glance fell on him without particular interest, for he had never seen the other before. His sole thought was that Sharon had some tough customers in her crew, if Cully was any criterion.

Lost Angel was reached shortly. The slanting rays of the sun outlined Superstition Mountain in bold relief and filled the valley with a golden dust in which the sway-backed roofs of dismantled stamp mills with their rusty smokestacks only emphasized the lonely desolation of this once-populous camp.

"That's probably the Buckskin over there," Rainbow pointed to the mine entrance at the base of the mountain. "And those 'll be Slack's men."

"Jest waitin' to dig into them tailin's, the minute the cars arrive," Grumpy agreed acidly.

At one side of the mine apron stood a recently erected, rambling board shack. Rainbow's glance rested on it momentarily. It was probably where Slack's men bunked. "Slack must be figurin' to use considerable of a crew, judgin' from the size of that bunkhouse," he commented to Grumpy.

They did not go that way, but struck the end of Lost Angel's street at the jut of the mountain's shoulder. The place was well named. Chinatown, with its spooky antiquity, laid a hush on them. Beyond were the abandoned stores and saloons, boardinghouses and even a bank, its doors standing open. Battered tin signs everywhere proclaimed past glories. Bottles and rusted cans lay about. Grumpy looked the place over and shook his head. "She's seen some ripsnortin' times in her day," he hazarded.

Near the foot of the street they passed an abandoned hotel with blankets hung from various upstairs windows to air. Farther on was a store which showed some signs of occupancy. There were heaps of ore samples, a few cans of tobacco and the like in the window. An old man stepped to the door as they swung down.

Climbing the steps, Grumpy and Rainbow nodded to him. There was a second old-timer inside; both wore faded woolen shirts and battered hats and bore every sign of being old inhabitants.

"Glad to meet yuh," the first responded, when Rainbow introduced himself and Grumpy. "I'm Sukey Withers. I run this place; been hyar nigh onto thirty years. Meet the mayor—Cyclone Bradley." He waved toward his grizzled companion. "We jest about run Lost Angel, I reckon." There was a note of pride in his voice, and a tinge of curiosity as well. "Have a little nip o' somethin'?"

Sipping his drink, Rainbow ran his eye over the scanty stock of supplies on the shelves as he explained why he and Grumpy were here. Triumph rose in Sukey Withers' eyes at the end.

"Didn't I tell yuh?" he exclaimed, turning to Bradley. "This camp's comin' back, like I allus said she would! With Slack openin' the Buckskin an' hirin' guards an' all, others 'll be driftin' in. The railroad 'll fetch 'em. Before the month is out, things 'll be hummin'!"

Cyclone Bradley, who looked about as swift as a sunning lizard, brightened at that. "Reckon yuh hit 'er plumb center, Suke," he declared. "It shore looks like old times was comin' back!"

There was kindly amusement in the glances Rainbow and Grumpy exchanged. But they liked these old junipers and the talk flowed easily. The old hotel, they learned, was where everyone staying at the camp slept. Withers was cooking for Con Murphy's boys and for Dan Slack's crowd at the Buckskin. He thought Rainbow and Grumpy could be accommodated for their meals.

"We'll have a real cook in here 'fore long, if things keep on pickin' up," he added.

Discussion swung back to the revival of Lost Angel. It was an obsession with these weathered desert rats; they had lived their lives in anticipation of it. Before long, however, Withers was forced to break off to make preparations for the evening meal.

With waning light, Slack's men drifted down from the mine. Glancing them over, Rainbow thought he had counted more on the way here, but he couldn't be sure. Con Murphy's gang put in an appearance soon afterward. Dan Slack was with them. He had come up to make sure the work was being pushed along, he told Rainbow.

"My job 'll be done in another day," Murphy assured him. "The cars 'll soon be rollin'."

For dining room an empty store building had been commandeered and improvised tables set up under the smoky light of old oil lamps. The laughter and talk of rough men filled the place as supper progressed. Withers and Cyclone Bradley ate with the others and soon had them on the subject of the camp's threatened return to life. It was coming none too soon, old Sukey averred, declaring Lost Angel to be a real ghost town. He related a shivery tale of spirits at night that only a lively fancy could have fathered.

The rest took him up with interest. "Reckon that's the answer to them noises in the Buckskin," said one of Slack's men. Slack turned on him with surprising sharpness.

"What kind of noises?" he demanded.

"Why, rumblin's and the like," was the answer. "Once we heard what must 've been a whole drift crashin' in. Timbers rotten, like as not."

Slack seemed relieved. He withdrew into silence while Cyclone Bradley narrated the story of a gruesome murder which had taken place during the camp's heyday and told how the victim's ghost haunted Lost Angel on stormy nights in the dark

61

of the moon. Rainbow chuckled as he saw Grumpy taking it all in soberly.

After supper they pulled away to ride back along the railroad right of way, looking the ground over. Star-shot darkness at the end of a long twilight found them far from the camp. Grumpy hauled up and started to turn his pony.

"We've come far 'nough," he declared. "It'll be late when we git back."

To his surprise, Rainbow did not turn with him. "We'll go on a little farther," he said.

"What fur?" Grumpy was inclined to argue. "We can't see a dang thing now, anyways!"

"You don't care," was the easy reply. "You'd rather ride than sleep."

Grumpy stared at him. Disgruntled as he was, he realized there must be something behind his partner's course. "Can't yuh tell a feller what yuh got in yore mind?" he growled.

Rainbow grinned, "If I did, you'd swear I was lyin', it's so near empty. Where's your romance?" he pursued banteringly. "This is a swell opportunity to take advantage of the peace and quiet. Just look at them shinin' stars, Grumpy—feel that cool breeze blowin' on your face. Great, eh?"

"Huh!" Grumpy's tone eloquently expressed his reaction to these suggestions, but he no longer held back. A few minutes later he began thoughtfully, "Wal, here we are, a million miles from nowheres—jest like I warned yuh in Cheyenne.

Bad luck doggin' us, its teeth sunk so deep in our leg it can't even take time out to bark. Not much chance of nailin' a bunch of rustlers if we take this job of Slack's very serious, Rainbow."

Rainbow took time over his answer. "It looks as though we'd run our heads against a blank wall," he confessed then. "But when I think of the lead that was thrown at us on the way up here, I feel better. Somebody's either awful interested in us, or plenty disgusted with Slack."

"Jest who is Slack?" Grumpy put in, an edge to his voice. "Knowin' somethin' about him would help a lot."

As they talked it over, Grumpy came to the realization that this was precisely the question which had occupied his partner ever since they had signed on with Slack.

"I don't know who I can ask on this range," Rainbow said musingly. "I may think of someone. In the meantime, there's one bet I came near overlooking."

"What's that?"

"Goodnight's wire to us in Cheyenne said we had been recommended to him by Matt Graham. That means to me that Matt must know something about the setup here. Maybe he knows Slack's story as well."

Grumpy nodded his comprehension. "You'll git in touch with Graham, eh?"

Rainbow waved toward the distant patch of

lights, shining across the range. "We ought to be able to send a wire off from Indian Wells. It may mean a delay if Matt is out on a job himself. But an answer from him should tell us where we stand."

Arriving at Indian Wells, they soon got a wire off to their old friend, the U. S. marshal, asking for such information as he possessed concerning Dan Slack's past.

"Where do you want the answer sent?" the station agent asked, before turning to open his key.

"I'll ride in and pick it up," Rainbow told him. "It may be a day or two before it comes. Let's go, Grumpy."

Leaving the little cowtown behind, they headed back up the hills in the direction of the old mining camp. It was nearly midnight by the time they arrived. Turning their horses into a makeshift corral of roofless adobe walls, they found their way to the tumble-down hotel.

A number of upstairs rooms were occupied, but they located an empty one at last, its windows long innocent of glass. Spreading out their bedrolls on the floor, they quickly made ready for sleep. For Grumpy at least, it proved no easy task to drop off. Half-a-dozen times Rainbow jerked up out of a doze to hear his partner moving about, muttering to himself. He knew what was bothering the other—those wild yarns they had heard at supper.

"What's eatin' you, anyway?" Rainbow was impelled to snap at last.

"I been hearin' a thumpin' down below," Grumpy muttered. "Sounds like hammerin' or somethin'."

"Nonsense! This place has been still as the grave for the last hour—except for the danged racket you're makin'!"

"Go on an' sleep then, if yuh can," Grumpy retorted with asperity. "I can't!"

But he quieted down at last and Rainbow thought no more of the matter until he was awakened by the early flash of sunlight on the wall above his head. Grumpy was yawning in his blankets. There was a murmur of voices from other parts of the hotel.

Quickly they got up and pulled on their boots. Grumpy was the first to push through the door and head for the stairs. To his astonishment, Rainbow suddenly grasped him by the arm and yanked him back violently. He turned a face twisted with indignation. "What's the big idear?" he demanded.

"The floor," Rainbow grated. "Can't you feel it saggin'? Get back, for God's sake!"

Even as he spoke he whirled Grumpy toward the window; and none too soon! With a kind of accelerating deliberation the floor bellied in, lower and lower, until suddenly a large section tore away to cave in. There was a ripping crash, in the midst of which the yells of startled men could be heard; a column of adobe dust burst upward, choking in its density. Minor crashes followed as beams and portions of the near walls tumbled into the pit.

Climbing out through the window frame and dropping with a jar to the ground outside, Rainbow and Grumpy found that every man who had spent the night in the hotel had followed their example. None were injured beyond scratches and bruises; and yet, it had been a near thing. Dan Slack came hurrying up as they stood there. He alone had refused to spend the night in the place.

"Now maybe you'll find some other place to roll in besides that dang deathtrap!" he burst out. "I told yuh what yuh could expect someday, with them walls saggin' in that way!"

He made it sound as if the eventual collapse of the hotel due to its own weight had been inevitable, but for his part, Rainbow was not so readily satisfied. Into his mind flashed remembrance of the mysterious sounds which Grumpy had declared he heard during the night. They had a new meaning now.

When the dust cleared away, he and Grumpy started to look for a way down into the wrecked building.

"Don't go in there!" Slack warned sharply on seeing this. "The hotel's built over a mine drift;

the whole shebang may come smashin' down any minute, now she's started."

Rainbow merely nodded. "We'll take our chances of that. We want to fish out our blankets and war bags if we can." Slack wanted to dissuade them but was afraid he would tip his hand.

Cautiously they clambered down into the pit which the falling beams and heavy walls had torn. It was risky to say the least, but they were not concerned about that. Nor did the discovery of their half-buried belongings particularly elate them. Rainbow climbed here and there, peering and prying in the dim light. Suddenly he gave vent to a low exclamation.

"Huh! Will you look at this, Grump."

Near the edge of the hole into the mine gallery underneath lay a rusted steel sledge but lately used. Near by the butt of a sagging beam support showed the marks of heavy blows. Grumpy nodded slowly, taking it in.

"So that's what it was!" he muttered, an edge to his tone. "Reckon I was wrong about the ghosts. Rainbow, somebody with two good hands was down here last night, knockin' the props out from under this hotel: somebody who wanted to finish us"—anger made his tone rise—"and damn near did it!"

5

Tim Bucktoe lurched down the stygian mine tunnel under Lost Angel like a specter, his apelike arms swinging. He was in a black mood. He knew that Rainbow Ripley and Grumpy Gibbs had escaped from the hotel crash, for he had waited to see; had overheard too their murmured words in the pit and was satisfied that they must be put out of the way with the least possible amount of delay. Dan Slack himself came in for no small portion of his anger, for it was Slack's doing that the pair were here at all. Had there been any way to dispense with Slack in carrying out his extensive plans, Bucktoe would have moved toward that end without compunction.

Misanthrope was a word which might have been invented to fit Tim Bucktoe. He hated all men for what had happened to him. He meant to bring suffering and disaster to all who came within his reach.

Grave as had been his injuries in the train wreck which had made him a monstrosity instead of a man, the greater damage had been done to his spirit. It had not always been so. At first there had been hope. He had soon learned, however, once his bent and twisted body healed, that the honest work of the world was no longer for him. The

Nevada Midland had been unable to give him compensation. Rocky Goodnight had not even held his old job open for him, because he said Tim could no longer do the work. Other outfits had turned him away on the same excuse; but actually, as he soon came to understand, because he was so ugly they didn't care to put up with the sight of him.

Once the truth came home to him, Bucktoe had undergone a profound mental change. His blood seemed to have turned to venom in his veins. The water district, suggested to Dan Slack in such a manner as to appeal to his greed and ambition, had been the first step in a slowly forming scheme of revenge. Rocky Goodnight's murder trial, in which by perjured evidence he had been able to bind Slack to him with bonds of steel, had shown him his opportunity.

It was true that once Jim Goodnight had taken over his father's great Wishbone ranch he had sought out Bucktoe with the offer of work. But by that time the acid of hate had worked too deep into Bucktoe's bones. He didn't have to tell himself that Goodnight's offer had sprung from neither desire or need of him; it had been a gesture of belated pity which only inflamed Bucktoe's sense of grievance. He had brushed the offer aside and gone on in the course which it was plain a pitiless fate had designed for him. Carefully planting the rumor that he had left the country,

Bucktoe had retired to the Buckskin Mine, from which he directed his far-reaching plans with a sure hand.

Although he seldom came out into the light of day and for months had been seen by no man but Slack, he lived fairly comfortably. For food, he beefed a steer occasionally and had a little garden high on the flank of Superstition Mountain. As for his strange home, he knew all the miles of the Buckskin Mine like his pocket. Little went on in the mountain, or in Lost Angel for that matter, that he did not know about. The vein with which he lured Dan Slack on was his one hope; he lived with the dream of developing that, and thus making himself so rich and powerful that no one could touch him. He had no intention of allowing Slack to lay hands on any part of it.

Meanwhile, however, there was much to be done. Just now Bucktoe was headed toward the main tunnel of the mine. He had no means of lighting his way, but he needed none. In places where the footing failed he swung himself along through the mine timbers by his long prehensile arms.

Soon he was in the lower tunnel. Many of the drifts were boarded up, a circumstance wholly to his advantage, since it enabled him to hear words spoken within a few yards from behind the boarding without running the risk of discovery. There were always men in the mine, watching the rustled steers being held here. He had long kept his fingers on the pulse of affairs by listening in on their unguarded talk.

At present he hoped to overhear some discussion of the stock detectives. He was therefore the more surprised, on stealing close to the boarding as usual, to catch the tones of Rainbow and Grumpy themselves, out in the main tunnel. A few moments served to explain their presence to Bucktoe. Coming down from the camp, they had stepped in the mine for a look around. They had not been stopped, since there was nothing at this point to arouse suspicion. Pretending they had no inkling their every move was being watched, they did not appear interested.

But Bucktoe was not fooled. Knowing what they knew, he asked himself how much more they guessed, and his veins hammered with hatred. Putting his eye to a crack, he peered through. In the smoky light of a flare, Rainbow and Grumpy were standing squarely on the dump-car track, where it ran through under the boarding, talking to several of Slack's men. A blaze leapt up in Bucktoe at the sight. His eyes gleamed with the plan taking a sudden form in his brain.

Turning away, he stole swiftly up the drift. The grade was fairly steep. At its head he sought an old dump car lying on its side, and with deft hands oiled the wheels by means of an oilcan tossed aside years before. He stood the car on the track then. It was child's play for his strength.

The wheels blocked, he set about filling the car with chunks of quartz, his great shoulders making short work of the task. He lost no time when it was done. Knocking out the chocks, he started the car down the incline, running it to a good send-off, his dragging leg no impediment.

Carrying well over a ton's weight for momentum, the car swiftly gathered speed. Soon it was rocketing madly down the tunnel. It was impossible to avoid hearing its rumbling progress altogether; but Bucktoe counted on its unexpectedness to accomplish his object. He ran forward and bent down to watch the result of his work.

The dump car struck the boarded-up mouth of the drift with a splitting crash. Wood splintered and flew in a dozen directions. Yells rang out hollowly, drowned in the clang and clash of metal as the car struck the switch into the main tunnel, jumped the track and slammed into the opposite wall, its freight of rock bursting outward and showering the spot with flying missiles.

Nothing but sheer luck had impelled the group of talkers in the main tunnel to move aside only a moment before. Had they not done so, a good share of their number would certainly have been killed. Rainbow and Grumpy had remained standing on the track as it was; but at the first whining rumble of the advancing car, Rainbow thrust his partner back instinctively, and himself leaped aside. He was only just in time. The crash sent them staggering back; then they were ducking the flying pieces of quartz.

Rainbow was the first to recover from his surprise. He had seen one man knocked flying. There might be others. "Get that flare lit!" he jerked out, springing to the injured man's side.

In its flickering light he saw his fears confirmed. Struck by a ragged piece of rock, the man lay unconscious, his head bloody; Rainbow thought his leg was broken. Possibly he was injured internally as well. Others were banged up; Grumpy bore a gash on his leathery cheek.

"This man must be got to a doctor!" Rainbow declared. "Get hold of his shoulders, Grumpy; we'll carry him out of the mine!"

"It come dang near bein' the undertaker fer all of us," one of Slack's men spoke up angrily. "What in hell made that happen, anyway?"

The rest were no less puzzled. "Mebby the mountain moved an' started that car off," hazarded one. "I've seen loaded dump cars standin' on the track in these drifts. A jar might knock out the blockin' . . ."

Rainbow paid no heed to this at the moment. He and Grumpy got the unconscious man out in the open. "We'll rush him down to the end of track," Rainbow decided.

Their saddled broncs were near at hand. They started off without delay, Grumpy carrying the accident victim across his saddlebow. Rainbow rode at his side in silence for some minutes before he said finally, "So they think maybe the shakin' of the mountain was what started that car rollin' . . ."

What they had learned only a short time before in the pit under the hotel was present in Grumpy's mind as he nodded. Yet he grunted, "Any good reason fer usin' that tone?"

"Yes. I noticed fresh oil on the wheels of that dump car, Grumpy."

Grumpy's jaw dropped, then closed with a snap. A dangerous look came into his eyes. "So it's like that, huh?" he said softly. "Reckon we got hell starin' us in the face from a dozen directions!"

The Nevada Midland locomotive was shunting a flatcar along a mile down the right of way. Ties were being tossed off when they arrived. Dan Slack was there, watching the work. He and Slicer Cully turned to stare at the burden across Grumpy's saddle. It was Slack who spoke up. "What happened?"

Rainbow acquainted him with the accident in the mine, adding that the injured man was in immediate need of a doctor's care. Slack's face set in stubborn lines at the end, for he knew what was coming. "Then it means a ride to Indian Wells for you," he said brusquely.

Rainbow stared at him. "Nonsense! It 'll take three or four hours to ride there, Slack! The engine can do it in a quarter of the time! It may mean the difference between life and death for this man."

"I don't give a damn!" Slack told him, brutally frank. "The engine can't be spared. This job's goin' to be finished today and that's that!"

Rainbow's lip curled with his blazing contempt. He had suspected Slack's ruthlessness from the beginning. Now it was coming out with a vengeance. Before he could give voice to the sharp words hovering on his tongue, however, a new sound advancing along the completed track turned them all that way. It was the staccato bark of a gasoline scooter which drew near with Sharon Longstreet in the driver's seat. She had come up alone this morning from Crazy Horse.

Slack advanced in an ingratiating manner as the girl stepped to the ground. "What brings you way up here, Miss Longstreet?" he inquired smoothly, dissembling his concern.

"I'm afraid you may not like what I have to say," she told him, "but it means a lot to me. The Raven brothers are cutting ties on contract at the head of Singer Canyon. They've got several thousand piled along my spur track. I've been asked to shove half-a-dozen flatcars up there for loading. They want the cars today. Later they'll have to be hauled down to the main line. It will mean a slight delay for you, I'm afraid."

Slack frowned and shook his head. "They'll have to wait," he declared. "My work comes first. If it wasn't for me, there wouldn't be any engine up here; and my tailin's are contracted for, the same as Alf and Ed Raven's ties."

That he should tell her what to do so plainly came as a surprise to the girl. Watching her, Rainbow told himself that whatever else she was, she was levelheaded. She reasoned with Slack quietly, trying to make him see how much depended on this extra business for the road; the ties would be regular freight from now on, the Ravens had assured her. She got nowhere until Rainbow spoke up,

"His anxiety's runnin' away with him, Miss Longstreet. Murphy's sure to get done today; what matter if it's an hour or two later? Slack 'll have to load his tailin's anyway. And here's this man, badly hurt. He can be got out to Indian Wells and the flatcars taken care of at the same time."

Slack whirled on him. But the furious words boiling up in him did not come. Meeting Rainbow's steady eyes, a change occurred in him. He calmed down.

At Sharon's swift inquiry, Rainbow explained about the accident in the mine. "That settles it," the girl decided crisply. "The engine will take him to Indian Wells at once. The flatcars are on a siding there. They can be run up Singer Canyon on the way back. It'll not take more than a couple of hours at the outside."

Slack said, "Well"—thinking hard and fast—"this is what we'll do. We'll start the engine off for Indian Wells right away. Meanwhile you and yore partner pull across the hills for Singer Canyon. Tell Alf Raven you've come to see to the loadin' of those ties, Ripley, you may have to help out yoreself, but make sure the cars are ready to roll first thing in the mornin'. Stay with them and come back here with the engine from Crazy Horse; I'll send a man over after yore broncs. If it's got to be worked this way, I don't want so much as a minute lost."

He spoke with an authority to which Sharon acquiesced, and matters were thus arranged. The injured man was put aboard the engine, and it started down the hills. A few minutes later Sharon followed on the scooter; Rainbow and Grumpy saw her flying down the rails as they headed across the range.

Slack and Slicer Cully were left standing near the track, and it was Rainbow on whom the former's gaze lingered longest. "Damn him, he seems to 've been born with a slick tongue, and a rabbit's foot in his hand," he grated. Suddenly he whirled on Slicer. "That was a hell of a job yuh made of puttin' that pair out of the way!" His tone was savage with accusation.

Slicer's snaky eyes met his briefly and slid away. "Couldn't be helped," was his muttered answer. "It come near bein' the other way around when they come foggin' after me. Yuh told me not to finish 'em," he was quick to fasten on an out.

His face darkened with his own grievance against the pair. "But I kin do that if yuh pass the word."

"No, I don't want any more of yore damned bunglin'!" Slack was brusque. "I've got Ripley and his partner taken care of for the time bein'. Meanwhile I may hit on some plan myself."

Tim Bucktoe was in his mind as he spoke. Slack was under no illusions concerning the cause of the accident in the mine. He read Bucktoe's hand in it. It warned him that his next attempt to dispose of Rainbow and Grumpy had better be successful.

Daily, when the crest of Superstition threw its shadow over the eastern slope, Tim Bucktoe tended the little garden that lay hidden in a tiny cup high on the mountain shoulder. A prospect tunnel in the Buckskin Extension gave him easy access to the spot. A trickling spring supplied what water the plants needed.

Bucktoe was in his garden today. Here— surrounded by the flowers and growing things he loved, and believing himself safe from the prying eyes of the world—his mask of cruel, implacable hatred was lowered. Some strange inner alchemy seemed to soften his bitter, gruesome face. These green things that he tended so faithfully did not mock nor turn away in disgust. They were the chink in his armor of hate.

Bracing his deformed foot, he bent down to lift

a blossom trampled into the earth by the passage of some marauding coyote. A woman's hands could not have touched that flower with greater tenderness. A long-drawn ghost of a sound drifting across the hills brought him up abruptly. Eyes blazing suspiciously from under bushy brows, he scanned the tumbled horizon.

Miles away over the pines in the direction of Singer Canyon he descried minute puffs of white smoke which could only be those of a railroad locomotive. The fact was instantly significant to him.

"Train over there!" he growled savagely. "Goin' up to haul ties, eh? Well, I'll put a stop to that! Slack 'll answer to me for this!"

Plunged in brooding thought, he forgot the garden. Whatever the conclusions he reached, they were decisive. Swaying toward the mine entrance in his ungainly way, he penetrated the mountain and swung down through the long drifts.

It took him half an hour to reach the lower level. He made for the gallery which ran in the direction of Lost Angel, and presently hauling himself up through a hole, was in the midst of Chinatown's crowded buildings. A rat could not have threaded the wilderness of alleys with more expertness. Finding himself in one giving upon the street, Bucktoe stole to its mouth like a shadow.

Long he prospected the sunning street in either direction. There was no sign of life. Near at hand was a pillar bearing the tattered scraps of Chinese posters with their strange markings. To this Bucktoe darted. Producing a fragment of charcoal from his pocket, on the blank corner of a poster he fashioned a bold flying U. It looked remarkably like all the other incomprehensible markings. Then he scuttled back into the protection of the alley.

It was noontime before Dan Slack came by on his way to dinner and saw the sign meant for his eyes alone; nearly an hour later before he could answer the summons. When he did, Bucktoe was waiting. In a few words Slack confirmed his surmise that the Ravens were getting ready to ship ties. As usual, mention of the railroad inflamed him.

Bucktoe rumbled fiercely, "I don't like it! I'm boss of this railroad, remember that; it 'll carry what I say it will and nothin' else!"

Slack told him hurriedly about the injured man who had been taken to Indian Wells, and what he had done about Rainbow and Grumpy. Bucktoe's eyes glinted craftily in their sockets at that. "They're over there now, you say? And ridin' the cars down the hills in the mornin'? Good! For once yuh done better 'n yuh thought!" Something he saw which Slack did not moved him to dark amusement. With his next words he terminated the meeting abruptly, in cryptic fashion. "Okay, leave things to me. I'll see to them hombres, and no slipup this time!" Turning his back, he lurched down the alley in which they had been murmuring together and disappeared through a crumbling doorway, a human gorilla, grim, implacable and cunning.

Slack turned away, the weight of the world resting on his shoulders, as always when the repulsive sight of that man reminded him afresh of his bondage. He wanted to get away, to forget for a few hours. Getting up his bronc, he turned his face down the hills toward Crazy Horse. Even so, Bucktoe succeeded in riding with him, at least in spirit.

"I'll have to shove lead through him!" Slack gritted, a red haze before his eyes. "With Bucktoe in the discard, things would sure be comin' my way! God! If I only dared!"

He forgot, as he had done before, that Bucktoe's diabolic cunning had placed him where he was. All he remembered was that with the other out of the way, he would be firm in the saddle, a master in his own right, with no one daring to oppose him.

Yet with this prize dangled temptingly before his eyes, the fear of Tim Bucktoe remained stronger. Were that twisted man ever to learn he had entertained these thoughts, he would be ruthless! Slack shivered at the prospect. Once more he put temptation away from him, without realizing that each time he toyed with it a little longer; and that someday hatred, ambition and revolt might prove stronger even than his fear.

Arriving at Crazy Horse, Slack went heavily to his office above the Northern Nevada Mercantile Company's store. Here he put in a couple of hours' work, always with the malign visage of Bucktoe hovering just behind his shoulder. It was enough to drive a man crazy. Abruptly Slack got up and strode out.

Intending to stop in at the Golden Palace, where a drink or two and the feel of life about him would presently dispel his dark mood, Slack first headed for the Nevada Midland station. There were some arrangements about his shipments of tailings to be made.

Although the office was open, Sharon was not there. Pausing in the door, Slack met the sardonic glance of a lanky, dark-featured man wearing a green eye-shade and a pencil stuck behind his ear. They exchanged short nods of perfect familiarity.

"Where's the girl, Lafe?" Slack queried.

"You oughta know," was the answer. "Been up in the hills for the last day or so, ain't yuh?"

Slack said, "I knew she was at Lost Angel, of course. Then I lost track. She hasn't come back, eh?"

"Don't expect her till tomorrow sometime," said Lafe.

A sour-visaged individual of unprepossessing appearance, he was Slack's ace in this office. Whenever unavoidable business took Sharon Longstreet away for a day, she was forced to leave a substitute in charge. Slack had recommended Lafe Bailey. The small salary Lafe asked had decided the girl.

"What's new?" Slack inquired easily. Bailey gave him such a peculiar look that he found himself waiting for the answer with real concern.

"Maybe it'll surprise yuh," Lafe returned, "and maybe not. But there ain't much question it's somethin' to think about, Dan. Take a look at this," he broke off, handing over a telegraph blank on which a message had been scrawled.

For a minute Slack stared at it, expressionless. "A wire for United States Marshal Graham, askin' for all available information about me, eh?" he said softly at last. "And signed by Rainbow Ripley."

"I reckon," Bailey nodded, "yuh know what that means . . ."

Slack was curt. "It may mean plenty, or nothin' at all. Ripley's got no reason to be suspicious of me. He may just be checkin' up to make sure I'm good for a fat salary." But he didn't sound very assured. "Where 'd this come from, Lafe?"

"Came over the wire from Indian Wells, to be relayed via the Western Pacific."

"But you didn't send it on?" Slack rasped sharply.

"Hell! Do I look as dumb as that?" Bailey barked a short laugh. "I've been waitin' for you to show up and decide what yuh wanted done about it."

"Hmm." A furrow of concentration appeared in Slack's brow. "It's awkward, Ripley's knowin' Matt Graham. But maybe we can get around that."

"Just send Ripley an answer," Lafe suggested shrewdly. "He won't have any reason to think Graham didn't send it."

Slack nodded. "That's my idea," he admitted. "But what would Graham be likely to say in a telegram that nobody else would—somethin' that'll convince Ripley and throw him off the track?" He was speaking half to himself. Taking a block of telegram blanks, he tried two or three times to compose a message which wholly satisfied him. At last he shook his head.

"No sense in tryin' to get between Graham and Ripley," he decided. "I don't know either of 'em well enough. It 'll have to be short and simple."

With that object in mind, he scribbled a few words out and handed the blank to Bailey. The latter read it.

KNOW DAN SLACK WELL CAN VOUCH FOR HIM HE'S AN ARIZONA MAN CLEAN RECORD PAST LIKE OPEN BOOK ANY-THING ELSE WANT KNOW?

"Send that to Ripley sometime tomorrow," Slack directed. "And sign it, 'Graham, U. S. marshal.'"

Lafe hesitated, pursing his mouth up. "This last

84

here, Dan . . ." he began. "If Ripley *did* want more information, and his request came through while I wasn't here, it 'd spill the beans!"

Slack scoffed, "That's just the point that'll convince Ripley he's barkin' up the wrong tree. He'll figure he's closed out in this direction and let it go at that."

Bailey shrugged. "Maybe you're right."

"You send the wire as it's written," Slack directed flatly. "Ripley 'll be taken care of before he has the chance to follow many more such leads." He felt safe in saying that, for he had not forgotten the veiled threat in Tim Bucktoe's talk.

After a few more words which straightened out his business here, Slack took his leave. But walking back to the Golden Palace he found plenty to think about.

His explanation of just why Rainbow had seen fit to investigate him had not sounded satisfactory even to himself. Walking into the saloon and bellying up to the bar, a chill ran down his back as he poured himself a drink and downed it.

"What can Ripley have found out about me?" he wondered. "Somethin' got him figurin' along that line. What was it?"

He was not deceived in the slightest about Rainbow's abilities. The man was sharp as a steel trap, wary as a wolf. Once he fastened onto a course of action, he was likely to follow it up with unshaken tenacity unless convinced that he would get nowhere in that direction. Would the telegram Slack had sent him succeed in accomplishing that result?

There was no way of being sure. Without realizing the irony of it, Slack took refuge in the hope that whatever move Bucktoe contemplated would solve his own problem. Bucktoe would get rid of Ripley and Gibbs if anybody could.

Downing another drink, Slack tossed a coin on the bar, wiped his lips with the back of his hand and turned out of the place. It was evening, but he didn't even think about supper. Getting up his bronc, he headed back into the hills. The necessity to know what was going on up there was so strong that he forgot even his need to get away from the proximity of Bucktoe for a time.

It was a quiet hour in the hills. Always at twilight a hush descended. No vagrant breeze stirred the brush to rustling life. The hoofs of Slack's pony sounded loud on the trail; more than once he pulled up to stare about, wondering what it was that pressed so insistently on his consciousness. It was exactly as if he was being trailed; there was the same creepy warning along his nerves, the same vague intimation of portending trouble.

Once, at a likely spot, he circled and watched his back trail from cover for ten minutes, only to find the range apparently as empty in that quarter as in every other.

"Hell, I'm all spooked up over nothin'!" he growled.

He had almost succeeded in persuading himself that his snarled nerves were responsible for his uneasiness, when the ringing crack of a rifleshot jerked him taut. There could be no doubt that the slug had been meant for him. It struck the trail a little to one side, kicking up the dust and snarling away. That was enough to tell Slack the direction from which it had come.

He took no chances. Jamming his bronc into a run, he headed the opposite way. Two minutes served to put him beyond range. He drilled on till the night had thickened to full darkness, then slowed his horse to a rack and turned once more toward Lost Angel. His face was long. Who wanted to dry gulch him?

One after another he cast up the possibilities, only to reject them all till he came to the last. "Was it Ripley and Gibbs?" A real fear knifed through him. "Have they got wise to me? Are they followin' every move I make?"

One thing was certain. Slack put it into words while the sweat burst out on his brow in a fine dew, "Responsible or not, their comin' here has been the cause of more hell in a week than we've had to deal with in the past six months! One way or another, that pair's got to be shuffled out of the deck for keeps, and damn soon!"

6

Leaving his little ranch on the edge of the Calico Hills at noon, Bart Galey jogged across to the protection of upward-running folds which concealed him from the view of a possible watcher. The very rocks had eyes, the way things were going on this range; and Galey had occasion to be cagey. Putting his bronc to a brisker pace, he struck a course which brought him out a couple of hours later on the shoulder of Superstition Mountain.

Lost Angel huddled below in the blinding sunshine. Beyond in the valley, Con Murphy's crew was putting the finishing touches on the spur track reaching up to the Buckskin Mine. Shading his eyes, Galey stared down there.

He was looking for Slack but did not find him. Galey had missed the other by half an hour; Slack was now well on his way to Crazy Horse. Bart did see Slicer Cully, however. He was just as good. The problem was how to get in touch with him.

Working down the slope, Galey fell to watching Cully's movements. Obviously Slicer had no interest in the track repairing. Soon he turned to his horse and rode toward the Buckskin. On the flat before the mine he stood talking to Slack's men for ten minutes. When they turned away he remained where he was, his pony's reins hooked over one arm, rolling himself a smoke.

Galey didn't relish the idea of riding down there. How to attract Slicer's attention was a puzzle, until he thought of the pocket mirror he carried in his pocket. Pulling it out, he flashed a reflection across the brush. The bright patch hovered on Cully, but it wasn't strong enough in this incandescent sunlight to catch his notice.

Galey centered his beam on the side of the tool shed beyond Slicer and twitched it from side to side. Cully saw that, for he looked intently at the shed, then spun around. Immediately Galey flashed his reflection in the man's face. Pocketing the mirror then, he cautiously waved an arm. Slicer made no direct response, but a moment later he swung up on his bronc and headed out.

They met behind a rocky butte a mile from the mine. That Cully knew whom to expect was plain from his first words. "What's the meanin' of this horseplay?" he snapped. "Yuh wanta git spotted, hangin' around here?"

Galey said, "Don't be worryin' about me. Where's Slack?"

"He ain't around." Slicer was not disposed to pass the time of day. "What yuh want?"

"I'm after some money, Cully," Bart told him thinly. "I was promised some a week ago; I ain't got it yet."

"Dan's got some for yuh. You'll have to wait till

he gits back—he jest went to Crazy Horse. What's doin'—anything new?"

"Never mind the run-around," Galey threw back bluntly. "Sure, I got some information; but you don't git it till I lay hands on a little of what it's good for, savvy?"

Slicer gave him an ugly look. "So yuh know somethin', eh? Yuh know too damned much fer yore own good, Galey," he said softly. "Let Dan know yo're holdin' out, an' it 'll shore be bad news."

"Holdin' out! Me?" Bart snorted sarcastically. "That's a good 'un. I s'pose Slack ain't doin' the same thing; I s'pose he didn't start it first! But what burns me is here he's hirin' birds like Ripley an' Gibbs—payin' 'em good money at that; an' his own boys, who're in this as deep as he is, can go to hell!"

"I said you'd git yore money, didn't I?"

"And I said I want it now!"

Slicer's grin was twisted. "So what?" he retorted.

A warning ran along Galey's nerves at that. He had not forgotten that this man was Slack's gun slinger and right bower. Cully must have read his thought, for he continued smoothly, "Jest spill what yuh know, Galey, an' we'll forget the little unpleasantness." Only his tone suggested what might happen if Bart refused.

Reluctantly, a sullen light in his eyes, the latter

muttered his information concerning the proposed activities of the Tuscarora Association. Slicer listened stolidly and nodded at the end. "Okay, I'll speak to Slack about yore money." He turned his horse and started away. "Don't come here again, Galey!" he tossed back. "We'll stick to the regular meetin'-place. If it means a little delay, all right."

Watching him ride away nonchalantly, Galey was a prey to gathering wrath.

"Blast his hide, he got my information outa me an' I didn't get a thing!" he grated. He didn't understand precisely how it had been done, but the fact was enough to gravel him.

There was an element of mystery in the whole business. The sums he had been receiving for his work as a spy were not so large that Slack should have any trouble meeting them.

"Maybe it's Slicer himself who's holdin' out on me," Bart muttered. But that explanation didn't satisfy him. "No, it's Slack, all right. He told me I might have to wait fer my money." He brooded on his wrongs, only to burst out, "Dammit, it's Ripley an' Gibbs who've got Dan buffaloed! Why don't he do somethin' about them hombres?"

He knew Slack's cautious nature, and it infuriated him. Slack's penchant for betting only on a sure thing was an old story. "He'd let a rattler bite him before he makes a move!" Galey jerked out contemptuously.

His restlessness hurled him into the saddle and

away from the spot. So Slack had gone to Crazy Horse, had he? Bart saw no reason to question the statement. Hoping either to overtake Slack or meet him on the way back, he headed that way. Venom boiled up in his mind as he rode, the words he would fling at the other man marshaling themselves on his tongue.

But the longer he thought, the more certain he became that words would not produce the desired result. "What Slack needs is a fire built under him," he reflected bitterly. "Somethin' real to worry about! Maybe that 'd make him stir his stumps!"

Reaching Crazy Horse in the late afternoon, Galey repaired to the Golden Palace. He felt that he needed a drink to replenish the fires smoldering in him. He was still in the saloon when he saw Slack pass by on the street.

"What's he doin'?" Galey muttered to himself. Finishing his drink, he hurried out and trailed Slack to the Nevada Midland station. The urgency of his desire to face the other had faded now; when Slack emerged from the railroad office, Galey followed him back to the saloon, keeping out of sight. When Slack got his pony and turned toward the hills, Bart was not far behind.

For some miles he dogged the other warily. All the while a plan was forming in his brain. Failing light warned him that he had no time to lose if he meant to put it into effect. Circling to the protection of a ridge paralleling the trail, he twitched his rifle from the boot and slid out of the hull.

A rock gave him solid support for his gun. It was trained on the trail below. When Slack appeared, jogging along, Galey coolly took aim and squeezed the trigger. Slack's bronc whirled, dancing. A second later it started in the opposite direction on the dead run.

Galey stood up to watch, a grim smile wreathing his lips. He was no little pleased with himself.

"Mebby that 'll give Slack somethin' to think about," he mused aloud. "Wherever Ripley an' Gibbs may be right now, Dan 'll shore be askin' himself if they was behind that shootin'. If it pushes him to some decision that 'll be enough fer me!"

Remounting, he headed back in the direction of his own spread.

When Rainbow and Grumpy arrived at the tie camp in Singer Canyon it was to find Alf and Ed Raven there with half-a-dozen Mexican laborers, waiting to load the ties. Alf was the older brother; he raised his brows at Rainbow's explanations but did not demur, for he was not averse to the extra help.

Shortly afterward the engine arrived with the cars and, leaving them, chuffed away. The loading was begun. It was hard work, as Rainbow and

Grumpy soon learned; sweating without letup under the broiling sun. Only by setting the example could the *cholos* be persuaded to give their best.

At noon Rainbow found his muscles sore from the unaccustomed labor. Finished eating, he lit a cigarette and strolled away from the camp for a few minutes' relaxation. Below the camp the timbered canyon fell away steeply. Rainbow leaned against a pine, his gaze sinking into the green depths, when a familiar staccato bark smote his ears and around a bend in the railroad spur appeared the gasoline scooter, Sharon at the controls.

Pleasure relaxed the sober lines of Rainbow's face as he moved forward. The girl let the scooter coast to a halt and met him with a smile.

"The cars got here," she said. "Is everything else all right?"

The light in his eyes as he nodded said that it wasn't of her words alone that he was thinking. "One of the cars is loaded," he assured her. "We'll have the others ready on time."

Sharon stepped to the ground and stood beside him. She was so small that her trim auburn head came scarcely to his shoulder; yet the impact of her nearness was like a physical pressure on his senses. She had reserves of strength and a rich hunger for living, this girl. She said,

"I'm afraid this is a little out of your usual line of work, isn't it?"

"It is, for a fact," he admitted, smiling. "But that's nothing against it."

She was considering him thoughtfully. "I suppose anything is a relief from the constant necessity to pit yourself against dangerous men."

His headshake was brief. "It isn't that."

"No," she agreed unexpectedly. "It wouldn't be—for you. You are quite ready to meet anything the day brings, aren't you?"

It fitted into his private thought so patly as to startle him. The truth was, he wasn't as ready as she supposed. He hadn't, for instance, been prepared for anyone like her. Her level hazel eyes did something to him. To feel their inquiring weight was to watch the values of life changing. Things slid away which hitherto had seemed important, leaving in their wake an interest in Sharon Longstreet's concerns which outweighed them all.

"Some days bring strange surprises," he said lightly. She took the words literally.

"I'm afraid I never expected to be hauling freight down these hills again," she admitted. It didn't seem to occur to her that she was opening her most intimate thoughts to this man. "Since Lost Angel blew up there has been less and less demand for a railroad. It seems like a slap of fate that I should have lost the confidence of the cowmen who might have been able to help me."

A picture of Jim Goodnight flashed in his mind

at the words. Was it regret that Sharon felt? Her quiet, composed features told nothing.

"Maybe there's a better name for your trouble," he suggested evenly. She did not pretend not to understand.

"Slack? I don't think so. I fail to see how I can be blamed for the troubles of others. Perhaps the reputation Mr Slack bears on this range is unfortunate . . ."

He nodded. "Just who is Slack?" he queried idly. "A local product?"

"No, he drifted into this country as a puncher four or five years ago. I understand he hailed from Idaho. It was said that a little matter of swinging a wide loop was what persuaded him to leave his home range; but that is hardly enough to condemn him. Many men have gone far from an unpromising start."

"That's right." Rainbow's deft fingers, rolling a smoke, betrayed the depth of his thinking. "Slack has plenty of company there. You've got perfect confidence in him, I expect?"

The answer surprised him. "I wouldn't say that. If Dad taught me anything, it was to scrutinize my business dealings without exception. I am deeply involved with Dan Slack."

There was admiring approval in his regard. "Don't ever forget that," he said, "and you'll come out all right."

"I will if trying means anything," she agreed.

It was the precise expression of her character, but more, too. Sharon was such a girl as he had dreamed of but never expected to meet. Was it his own fate that had brought him here just at this time? He knew she looked on him with approval. Her regret for Jim Goodnight was not so great that she would not live her own life to the full.

The need was in him to let her know how he felt. Something held him back. What it was he could not have said; but he must make no mistakes. His voice was lazy.

"I expect those *cholos* had better get back to work."

Sharon turned at once. She was all business. "I'll have a word with Alf Raven before I leave."

They walked to the camp. Raven saw the girl; he got up at once and came forward. Leaving the two together, Rainbow turned to the men.

"Time's up, boys."

Grumpy sat staring at Sharon, his eyes alert. "So that's where Rainbow was," he thought. A little frown gathered between his eyes. "Did she come up here to talk to Raven, or was it Rainbow she was after?"

It wouldn't do to make snap judgments about such a girl; and yet, Grumpy had seen these things happen before. He knew the attraction of his partner's likeable personality. Rainbow was not proof against frank feminine approval. No man was.

"Someday," Grumpy reflected darkly, "his foot's goin' to slip. An' then where 'll I be?"

The work was started once more. The girl left; Alf Raven came back. For an hour there was only the heavy thud of the ties on the car floors, while Grumpy pursued his somber thoughts.

"What the hell, Rainbow!" he fired out at last, straightening his aching back. "I'd rather go back to punchin' cows if this is what Slack wants us to do." He clamped his lips over whatever else he had been about to say, at Rainbow's frown. But his scowling glances throughout the afternoon were eloquent.

The ties were not yet all aboard the cars by the time the sun dropped behind the flank of Superstition Mountain. Alf Raven shook his head and said, "In another two hours, mebby."

Rainbow nodded agreement. "We'll finish up before we knock off."

But it was nearly eleven o'clock by the time the last tie was tossed on the cars, and the slash fires which had afforded light for the work were allowed to die down at last. Some of the men were too worn out to stay awake for supper. Rainbow and Grumpy had never been as tired as they were when they crawled into the suggans supplied by Ed Raven. They sank instantly into deep sleep.

They might have been more wakeful had they been aware of the shadowy figure which stole into the tie camp during the small hours of the morning. It was Tim Bucktoe, and though he had every man in the camp at his mercy, he turned his back on them. It was toward the heavily loaded and securely blocked flatcars that he moved. Two cars from the rear end he slipped in and gave his attention to the coupling. It was a simple task to remove the pin fastening the two cars together. He succeeded without arousing anyone. A moment later, still carrying the pin, which he hurled into a ravine, he stole away as secretly as he had come, wolfish satisfaction stamped on his twisted face.

"When that train pulls apart comin' down the hills," the thought wormed through his twisted brain, "the windup 'll be some wrecked cars and torn-up track that 'll put a stop to this tie haulin' for good—and take care of those damn detectives at the same time!"

How well it would take care of them he knew only too thoroughly from experience.

When Rainbow and Grumpy were awakened in the early dawn by the unwarning scream of the high-pitched locomotive whistle, it seemed as if they had been asleep only a short time.

"Dammit all," Grumpy groaned, easing his cramped muscles. "Yuh go on an' go with the train, Rainbow, an' leave me here. I aim to do some more high-class ear wallopin'."

"Unh-uh," his partner vetoed the proposal flatly. "Hump yourself, old terrapin. You can do your sleepin' aboard the cars on the way down. In fact," he added, grinning, "I'm not so sure but what I'll do some myself."

The other muttered under his breath but made no strenuous demur. By the time they were ready for whatever the day might bring, the engine was hooked on to the string of cars. Alf Raven had a few words with Clem Rucker, the engineer, and the latter pulled the whistle cord.

"Climb aboard, Grump," Rainbow said crisply. They swung up on the last car just as it started to roll. From the tie camp there was a steady downgrade for almost a mile. The rocks and pines were soon flashing past at a good speed. But Rainbow and Grumpy had no interest whatever in scenery this morning. Grumpy had already stretched out on the ties and dozed off. Rainbow soon followed his example, the jars and jolts bothering neither of them.

Ahead in the engine cab there was considerably less indifference. Half-a-dozen times in the next five minutes Rucker craned from the cab window to peer back. "No dang sense to makin' the load so heavy," he groused to his fireman. "Dunno whether we'll be able to hold it back with this old girl so weak in the lungs of late!"

Half a mile below, just as the tracks reached the first windings of the canyon, they struck the first hump also. The locomotive took the slight upgrade with a snarl of drive-wheel flanges, the tie cars lurched drunkenly. Nervously vigilant,

Rucker looked back as they dropped over the crest and started downward again. Suddenly he gave vent to a yell.

"Jest what I expected!" he screeched. "The dang train's busted apart two cars from the end! Now there 'll be merry hell!"

Dropping his shovel with a clang, the fireman sprang to the step. He stared back. "My God, that's keno!" he groaned, white to the lips. Then he whirled. "Shove that throttle over in the corner!" he whipped out, fresh horror in his voice. "We gotta keep ahead of them loose cars an' no mistake about it! If they slam into us, goin' around one of these curves, it 'll spell our finish!"

Old Clem stared at him, his eyes like two burned holes in the frost-stubbled face. "Don't be thinkin' of yoreself! We got to save the engine for Sharon! We jest got to!" It was as though he was arguing with himself. "The tie cars 'll have to go to hell in their own way—an' them guards of Slack's aboard! There ain't no way in the world of savin' 'em!"

7

It was the hoarse bellow of the locomotive whistle, echoing through the canyon with a banshee wail, which awakened Rainbow and Grumpy. They sat up blinking. Grumpy made a grab for support as the flatcar screeched around a curve at a dangerous speed, and protest sprang into his face.

"Them damned fools up ahead are goin' too fast!" he rasped, staring at the rocky shoulders flashing past at a mad rate. Rainbow was thinking the same thing. He stood up to work his way ahead, when suddenly an exclamation burst from his lips.

"Good Lord! This car and the next have broken loose from the rest, Grumpy!" His voice was hoarse. "They're runnin' away from us!"

By now the runaway cars were hurtling downgrade a hundred yards to the rear of the rest of the train, entirely beyond control.

"There's the brakeman on the last car, wavin' his arms around," Grumpy jerked out. "What's he tryin' to yell?"

They could make out none of the wind-torn words drowned in the rumble of the locomotive exhaust and the rushing wheels.

"It's plain enough they can't do anything for us!" was Rainbow's terse answer.

"Mebby he's tryin' to tell us we'll slack down after a ways."

Rainbow shook his head. A glance down the canyon disproved that. For as far as the eye could see, the downgrade increased if anything. Already they were traveling so fast that to jump would have meant death.

"Not a chance! Our only hope is to set the

brakes on these cars. Hunt up a stick and we'll go to it!"

The first brake they tried refused to turn. It was no wonder; the cars should have been discarded long ago. A second brake took hold with a scream of protest. It did little good however. "Hell!" Grumpy burst out in exasperation. "No wonder! The block's busted on one side!"

Their eyes met as the gravity of the situation was borne in on them. "We'll have a try at the front end," Rainbow yelled.

It was all they could do to get from one car to the other. They had swung out onto the Nevada Midland main line now. The trucks jolted wildly over the uneven roadbed; on the curves the cars swayed so perilously the ties began to shift; ceaselessly the wind of their speed threatened to tear them loose. Grumpy's hat had long since been whipped away. At last they made the first car. Together they started to tighten down the brake on its forward end.

The blocks took hold with a grinding snarl. "That's doin' it!" Rainbow gritted as their momentum perceptibly slackened. "Once more, now!" They threw their combined strength against the sticks thrust in the brake wheel with a will. Suddenly something snapped. Grumpy sprawled headlong on the ties and Rainbow barely saved himself from pitching off the car. The brake chain had broken.

"That settles it!" Grumpy cried. "We'll take wing at the next curve! We're goin' faster 'n ever!"

The next moment they saw something which froze them and left them speechless. The first half of the train had gained only an extra hundred yards despite the best efforts of the loco-motive, rushing down the track with its exhaust thundering. Now as a final resort the brakeman was tossing ties off the last car as fast as he could.

"Good God!" Rainbow got out grayly. "They're tryin' to derail us to save themselves!" He couldn't blame them, nor could he fail to under-stand what it would mean for Sharon Longstreet if a wreck occurred which robbed her of her only engine. But the knowledge did nothing to solve his and Grumpy's dilemma.

Wooden faced, Grumpy watched in fascination these desperate efforts to toss their lives away. Tie after tie, flung off the flying car ahead, landed across the rails only to bound aside, end over end. More than one fell or was knocked between the rails, to be rolled over harmlessly. Chilled as he was by the horror of the thing, Grumpy felt the sweat whipping off his cheeks.

Nor were the ties the only risk they ran. The speed of the runaway cars had become terrific. Each time they struck a curve they threatened to leave the rails. The doomed men were so shaken up that their wits felt foggy.

It was bound to come to an end quickly. When it

did, it came so abruptly there was no time for reflection. On a sweeping curve jutting out into the lower canyon, the first car struck one of the tossed-off ties squarely. The wheels climbed the obstruction without even hesitating. The front end of the car lifted and left the rails to dive far over the embankment and into the canyon. The second car followed, tearing up the rails behind it. The cars struck once and turned over. With a shuddering crash the ties flew into space and rained into the depths like jackstraws. Trees went down; rocks flew. A twisted, splintered mass of junk, the cars and their freight roared down the canyon side in an avalanche.

Believing a wreck inevitable as the cars approached the curve, Rainbow and Grumpy had determined on a desperate measure, and just in time. Opposite a thick stand of cedars, they had taken their lives in their hands to leap from the hurtling cars, only a moment before the crash. Nothing but an impression of flying through space flickered in their reeling brains. With a splintering jar they landed amidst the thick branches of the cedars. The boughs broke their fall. Yet they were all but shaken loose from consciousness as they felt themselves dropping downward toward the ground.

Rainbow landed crushingly on his shoulder and rolled over. Ties bounded perilously near, but he was not struck. He sat up and made a grab for

Grumpy just as the other was about to tumble down the steep slope. Slowly they gathered their wits, staring about dazedly. Grumpy sighed his relief and made just one grim comment: "Reckon I'm stickin' to hosses after this!"

Skinned and scratched and torn till they resembled scarecrows, but otherwise uninjured, they crawled back to the right of way. For the space of a few yards it was torn up beyond belief.

"Well, here we are," said Grumpy ruefully. "An' that's shore somethin'!"

Within ten minutes they heard the locomotive coming back. It had reached a flat below and succeeded in stopping. The train backed up to within a short distance and stopped. Its crew came hurrying forward, white faced.

"Fer Gawd's sake!" the brakeman burst out. "Yuh mean to say yo're both still all in one piece?"

"You did yore damnedest to make mincemeat of us!" Grumpy flared at him.

Explanations were in progress and they were looking things over when a new sound brought them heeling around. The gasoline scooter was skimming down the tracks from the direction of Lost Angel, Sharon Longstreet and Dan Slack aboard. Rainbow ran up the track.

"Stop!" he cried. "There's been a wreck! The track is out!"

Slack caught his tone, if not his words. Abruptly his face went frozen. Sharon jammed on the brakes. The scooter coasted forward to a halt, only its front end dropping off the broken rail joints. The girl stared at the damage here, and then through the gaping hole torn in the trees down the canyon side.

"We heard the crash," she exclaimed. "What in the world happened?"

The story was soon told. They stared at one another. "How fortunate that you weren't both killed!" Sharon burst out, looking at Rainbow. She would have had difficulty putting into words how much she depended on this man. A secret feeling of numb helplessness was creeping over her in the face of Dan Slack's unscrupulous dealings. Sharon feared she knew not what. But she did know that only Rainbow stood between her and eventual ruin.

Slack was the one to put his finger on a point of vital interest to them all. "It's mighty queer what made that couplin' give away!" In his heart he was sure he knew.

"Too much weight in them cars," the grizzled engineer began testily. "I told Alf Raven as much!"

Sharon turned again to Rainbow. "What do you think might have caused the accident?"

"Frankly, ma'am, I don't know." He smiled at her, admiration for the way she was taking this thing plain in his eyes. "I suppose it could have just happened."

"There's no sign of a couplin' pin in the forward car," the brakeman put in. "The drawbar is all right. The pin must have bounced out."

For Rainbow's part, he was honestly bewildered as to what had caused the break. Again it was Slack who put in a decisive word, shaking his head. "The whole business was too pat to 've been an accident," he declared. "That coupling pin could have been out of there from the time you started. It 'll take you a whole day to clean up this mess."

"Thank heaven the locomotive was saved—and no one was hurt," Sharon exclaimed.

"You can take my word for it," Slack drove on shrewdly, "that those Indian Wells ranchers know more about this than they'll ever admit!"

"But that's impossible!" Sharon exclaimed quickly. Rainbow read her reluctance to believe that Jim Goodnight could have had any part in so treacherous a plot; but for once he personally felt obliged to agree with Slack. The Tuscarora Association members had already shown their teeth. Slack lost no time in calling attention to that fact.

"There's something in what you say," Rainbow admitted. "But nothin' can be done about it without positive proof." To change the subject, he said to Sharon, "I thought you went back to Crazy Horse yesterday, ma'am."

"Only to Indian Wells," she corrected him. "I

was in Lost Angel last night. It was just by chance that Mr Slack and I came down on the scooter this morning to find out whether the ties had gone through as planned."

Rainbow pursued the conversation for some minutes. The girl appeared in no wise averse. Grumpy noted that. The corners of his mouth drew down.

"One of these days he won't be nothin' but a cinder, playin' with fire the way he does," he muttered to himself.

Plans were made for the necessary track repairs before the train continued on to Crazy Horse. Nothing could be done about the ties that had plunged down the canyon. It was a blow to Sharon, coming at this time; Rainbow chalked that up against whoever had been responsible for the wreck.

He and Grumpy were back on one of the tie cars as they rolled down the hills. Grumpy's expression was glum as he stared unseeing at the passing scenery.

"Rainbow," he said out of a long silence, "ever since Slack spoke up 'bout the why-for of that accident, I been thinkin' he's dead wrong. Naturally he'd blame them cowmen, whether they did it or not!" He paused and his eyes narrowed shrewdly. "What if Slack pulled that pin on us himself? Mebby he's wise to us."

A reservation showed in Rainbow's choice of a reply. "Somebody is downright anxious to put us away, but you can see for yourself how close it came to there being no more Nevada Midland, along with us—and Slack needs that locomotive in his business." He shook his head. "It wasn't him."

"Reckon that's a fact," Grumpy admitted reluctantly. But he wasn't satisfied.

"There's that telegram I sent off to Matt Graham about Slack," Rainbow pursued thoughtfully. "There might be an answer waitin' for me now."

"We kin stop off at Indian Wells on the way back an' see," Grumpy proposed.

"I can find out before that," was the reply. "Telegrams for this range have to be relayed from the Western Pacific wire at Crazy Horse. I'll be able to learn there whether one went through. I may even be able to pick up a copy of it."

The train rumbled into Crazy Horse early in the afternoon. Rainbow and Grumpy dropped off. "We'll go get a drink while we're here," said Rainbow. He headed up the street.

"Hold on," Grumpy halted him. "We're right here at the station . . ." Rainbow looked at him inquiringly, and he added, "Ain't yuh goin' to ask about that telegram?"

"No, I'll go down to the Western Pacific office," Rainbow answered. He didn't say that he would rather his inquiries did not come to Sharon's attention, but such was the fact.

They had their drink and then strolled down to the railroad station on the transcontinental main line. Rainbow was soon in conversation with the telegrapher.

"I sent a telegram out to Matt Graham, the United States marshal at Carson City, from Indian Wells," he explained, showing his own credentials. "Can you tell me if there's an answer come through and whether I could have a copy of it?"

First making plain that it was an irregular proceeding, the operator said he'd see what he could do. There were some officials to be consulted. Rainbow succeeded in satisfying them. A search of the telegraph records for the past couple of days was begun.

A clerk came finally with perplexing news.

"There not only is no record of an answer to the wire you say you sent," he told Rainbow; "but we can't even trace the original telegram."

Rainbow told him what day it had been sent. "You'll find it all right. There can't be any mistake about its goin' through your office."

Further search was instituted, with no different result. The division superintendent said, "Sorry, Ripley, but there it is. It's plain the original wire wasn't cleared from this office at all; so it 'll be useless to hunt for a reply."

Rainbow had been doing some thinking of his own while he waited, but he said, "How would you explain this business?"

The railroad official shrugged. "If the telegram was never relayed to us, you'll have to look somewhere above here for the stoppage. I'll take care of it. I always thought Lafe Bailey, Miss Longstreet's relief operator, was damned careless. He was fired out of an S. P. tower two years ago for incompetence . . ."

"Do me a favor and let it go," Rainbow replied. "I've my own idea of what happened."

"Not by a damned sight!" the other retorted. "I'll look into this and no mistake about it. Abstracting or mislaying paid telegrams is a serious matter. Bailey will make a full explanation of this; he may even lose his job over it!"

"I don't," said Rainbow mildly, "want to have to bring pressure to bear on you, but . . ."

"You mean it's important to you that this doesn't get out?"

"That's it."

"Then that's another matter," was the answer. "It's against the regulations, Ripley, but I'll do as you ask this time."

Rainbow thanked him. A moment later he and Grumpy took their leave. Once in the open, the latter exploded wrathfully, "What in hell is behind this, Rainbow?"

"My telegram being stopped? Why, it means," said Rainbow thoughtfully, "that somebody is afraid I'll learn things he doesn't want me to know."

"An' that somebody is Mr Slack!"

Rainbow nodded. "It looks like it from here. But there's one or two wrinkles about this business I don't understand. If Slack is able to get hold of messages sent over the railroad wire, he's got a better grip on this range than I even dreamed."

"There's plenty to be found out 'bout that gent with a little tryin'," Grumpy declared harshly. "I felt it in my bones the second I laid eyes onto him!"

Clem Rucker had said he was returning north after taking care of the tie cars. The partners were in time to get a ride on the locomotive as far as Indian Wells. While the white-haired engineer pushed on to help with the track repairs, Rainbow and Grumpy dropped off at the station.

"Reckon we kin get broncs here," said Grumpy.

"Wait a minute first, till I go in here," Rainbow told him, starting for the telegraph office. Not understanding at first, Grumpy followed him.

The agent nodded as they stepped in the door. "I was wonderin' when you'd show up, Ripley," he said. "There's a wire here for you."

Grumpy's jaw dropped, but Rainbow showed no surprise as he took the paper. Scanning it briefly, he handed it over to Grumpy without a word. The latter's face grew red as he noted its contents.

"That what yuh wanted?" the agent queried.

"Yes," Rainbow answered. "Yes, that's it, all right."

Grumpy held himself in till they got outside; then he ejaculated forcefully, "By Gawd, Slack's stuck his neck out this time—signin' Matt Graham's name to a phony telegram!"

"That's right," Rainbow nodded. "But it may not be so easy to prove that he's the one who did it. Not that I need convincin' myself," he added. "If Slack made a real mistake anywheres, it's in tryin' to throw me off the scent by puttin' that in about his comin' from Arizona."

"Huh?" It had meant nothing to Grumpy, but he was quick to guess that Rainbow had learned something.

The latter told him about his talk with Sharon at the tie camp in Singer Canyon. "She said Slack came here from Idaho—that he had a darn good reason for gettin' out of that country. If I wasn't satisfied in my own mind about what he is, I'd telegraph up there for the whole story."

"I was wonderin' why yuh didn't get another wire off to Matt Graham while we was down below," Grumpy nodded.

"No need. If Graham tells us that Slack should be watched—or even that he's a crook—it wouldn't be anything we don't already know. There can't be enough to pin on him, or he would 've been picked up before this. Besides which, I want Slack to think his little game has worked perfectly."

Grumpy readily concurred. "No point in warnin' him we're closin' in."

"If we are," Rainbow said slowly. "Slack's proved to me that he's a cleverer gent than I ever expected. We've got a tough job ahead of us before he's rounded up, Grumpy."

"Wal, it won't be the first of his kind we've laid by the heels."

"Which don't make it any easier this time." Rainbow was thoughtful. "Of course, there's always the chance that he'll trip over his own rope. Meanwhile, we'll be doin' our damnedest to help him!"

8

"What now?" Grumpy queried as they finished supper and stepped out of the Indian Wells hash house. "We headin' back to Lost Angel?"

Rainbow shook his head. He had been rolling things over in his mind during the meal. "It 'll be sometime tomorrow before the torn-up track is repaired. Until then, Slack won't be worryin' about us. That gives us a few hours to work on somethin' that occurred to me."

Grumpy waited expectantly to hear what it was.

"We'll get broncs," Rainbow proceeded, "and ride back down to Crazy Horse."

"Hell, we jest come from there!" Grumpy was disgusted. To his surprise, the answer was a ready nod.

"That's just what I'd like anyone who spotted us down there to remember."

"Oh. Like that, eh?" It was enough for Grumpy. Without more words, he turned toward a livery barn, where he and Rainbow procured mounts. Swinging into the hull, the latter headed north out of town.

"We won't disturb anybody's mind about us," he said in explanation. "An extra mile's ridin' won't matter."

Once out of sight of town, they circled back and headed south down the hills. There was no hurry. It was drawing on toward ten o'clock by the time they neared Crazy Horse once more.

"Where to?" Grumpy asked.

"We'll go down to the Nevada Midland station," was Rainbow's reply. "I want a look at this Bailey."

"He's our man, eh?"

There was no doubt of it in Rainbow's mind. "If I'm as sure of where he is as I am of what he is, we'll soon be givin' him the once-over," he murmured as they left their broncs at the upper end of the railroad yard and moved toward the station.

Rainbow's calculations were only slightly out, for at that moment Lafe Bailey was standing on the dark platform at a corner of the building. A cigarette smoked in his fingers. A moment ago he had decided to step down the street to the nearest saloon for a drink. It was against the regulations, but an old custom with him. Just now he was persuading himself as usual that there was no harm in leaving his key for ten minutes. He had almost succeeded when, glancing back toward the glowing office window, he caught a flash of something which whipped him taut in an instant.

Between him and the brightly outlined frame of the window was the shadowy form of a man. Whoever it might be was making for the window with considerable stealth. Standing there, Bailey watched the other peer in the window cautiously, taking care that he was not spotted from within during the process.

Dull anger swept over Lafe and his jaws corded. "Damn her!" he grated under his breath. "Has she set a spy to watch me?"

The next moment a new thought hit him between the eyes. Sharon Longstreet would have fired him before she came down to this: it was something else. The shady transactions in which he was involved with Slack were never very far from his mind. There was that business of the phony telegram, for instance; suppose Ripley and Gibbs had somehow found out about that!

A cold chill ran up Bailey's spine. What should he do—warn Slack? Or was imagination running away with him? He didn't think so. At any rate, he was going to make sure of this if it meant clearing out. Neither of the range detectives knew what he looked like; the cagey thing would be to keep it that way.

Pinching his cigarette out between his fingers, Lafe tossed it away. He took a deep breath as his fingers touched the cedar butt of the Colt he carried in a shoulder sling. Turning on his heel, he started away in the darkness.

He had not gone half-a-dozen feet before a second shadowy form loomed up in his path. "Hold on," said a level voice with a rasp in it. "You're the station agent, aren't you? Where are you headin' for now?"

For a fleeting fraction of time Bailey was so rattled that he didn't know what to do—whether to throw his gun and make a break, or take a chance on bluffing it out. Then he got hold of himself.

"Yeh, I'm the agent," he said woodenly. "Steppin' down the street a minute to see a man. Yuh want somethin'?"

"Suppose you let it go for now and come back to the office with me," Rainbow proposed easily. "My business won't take long, but it's kind of pressin'."

Lafe hesitated. All doubt was gone from his mind; this was one of those damned detectives, all right, and the man at the window was the other.

"I reckon five minutes' wait won't do yuh any harm," he bluffed, still hoping to break away, and at the same time deeply curious to know what the pair might be after. "Make yoreselves comfortable an' I'll be right back."

It was the form of his concluding speech which warned Rainbow. Bailey not only knew that there were two of them; but ten to one he had identified them and mapped his own course of action. As Lafe started to brush by him, his hand closed over the agent's arm and he said crisply,

"Not so fast, not so fast! If you can't—"

Before he could get farther, Bailey galvanized into action. He was wiry. Fear lent him strength as well, but he was no match for Rainbow. The latter spun him roughly and gave him a shove toward the station.

"All right, get goin'! And remember I'm just one cat jump behind you!"

Bailey found himself complying, while he collected his scattered wits in a desperate effort to find a way out of his dilemma. Grumpy saw them coming. "Wal, dang my gizzard!" he grunted, and then clamped his lips tight, stepping into the office behind the others.

Once inside, Lafe whirled angrily on Rainbow.

"What's the meanin' of this?" he snapped. "Yo're pretty highhanded, shovin' me around!"

"You'll be shoved around plenty more before we're done with you," Rainbow told him cheerfully.

"What? What's that?" Lafe pretended furious indignation. "By God, we'll see whether—"

"Drop it, Bailey," Rainbow tossed at him curtly. His face hardened. "The game's up. There's no longer any need to cover things. Slack and the rest of his rustlers have been found out. We got wind of their next job in time. Before daylight tomorrow, they'll be corraled in the hills and the whole business busted wide open!"

Grumpy's jaw dropped at these astonishing words. He had been asking himself what Rainbow hoped to accomplish with the crooked agent, without finding the answer. So this was it. It was an old ruse, but a good one. Whether Lafe Bailey would fall for it or not was another matter.

As for Rainbow, he saw many things confirmed in the instant narrowing of Bailey's eyes. His reference to Slack's connection with the rustling had been a shot in the dark; yet it had told.

"Yeh?" Lafe snarled, his real nature coming to the surface. "So what, Ripley?"

"We'll let Lint Granger finish the story," Rainbow returned thinly. "You're nothin' but a cog in the machine, but just how a jury will look at it I couldn't pretend to say."

"Yuh wouldn't be tryin' to run a blazer, would yuh?" Lafe grated, as presence of mind returned.

"It don't look like we'd have to, Bailey," Grumpy retorted dryly, taking a hand in the game. "Yore goose is cooked. In fact, I might say it'll soon be hangin' high!"

Lafe cursed them venomously. It was evident,

however, that he intended to make no damaging admissions, if that was what Rainbow had hoped for.

"I dunno a thing yo're talkin' about!" he maintained doggedly. "Mark my words, if I ever git out of it, I'll make yuh both smart for this caper!"

Grumpy shrugged with a pretense of amusement, but the glance he shot Rainbow held a question. Aloud, he said, "Shall we take him over an' toss him in jail?"

"No, we'll wait till Granger comes down the hills with the others." Rainbow thought a minute. "We can lock Bailey in the baggage shed overnight." He relieved Lafe of his six gun as he spoke. "I'll put him in there. While I'm doin' it, Grumpy, you go get our horses."

"Okay." Grumpy failed to catch the portent of this, but he was unquestioning. Heading up through the freight yard, while Rainbow led his prisoner to the baggage shed, Grumpy located their mounts and turned back. He was still a hundred yards from the station when the pound of gunfire, the stamp of running boots and a harsh yell broke on his ears.

"Bailey's makin' a play!" he jerked out. "Gawd! If Rainbow let's him git away, the beans 'll be spilled for shore!"

Racing forward, he was in time to see Rainbow emerge from the baggage shed. He didn't look particularly worried. Grumpy hurled at him, "What in hell happened?"

Rainbow flashed a grin as he grabbed the reins of his pony and swung up. "Bailey elbowed me— knocked me plumb into a corner! I cut loose with a couple shots, but he got away."

He jammed the spurs in as he finished. They tore around the station toward the street. They were in time to see a shadowy form duck into an alley across the way; but when Grumpy started after with a rush, Rainbow halted him.

"Not so fast!" he grunted. "Give him a chance, Grump."

Grumpy turned a look of amazement on him. "Yuh mean yuh ain't *tryin'* to nab him?" he demanded. Rainbow laughed at him.

"Why do you think I let him get away, if I wanted him so bad?" he retorted.

Grumpy said "Huh!" but at last he understood.

"We'll give him time to get horseflesh under him," Rainbow proceeded easily, "and then tail along behind. It 'll be kind of interestin' to see where he goes!"

"That's drawin' it mighty fine," Grumpy muttered, shaking his head. "What if he gits to Slack, Rainbow?"

"We'll just see that he don't," was the grim answer.

They trailed Bailey to a tumble-down place on the edge of town which he called home. He had a bronc in the corral at the back. They saw him run out there with saddle and rifle, cinch up his pony and swing astride. A minute later he started away stealthily across the range.

The moon was out, but it was hidden from time to time by passing clouds. The intervals of light gave them ample opportunity to keep the fugitive in sight; at the same time they were able to draw up during the periods of darkness.

Bailey evidently had no inkling that his every movement was being watched, but he was taking no chances, sticking to the hollows and following the scrub growing along the dry water courses. A few minutes served to indicate that he was laying a course straight for the hills.

"He's makin' fer Slack as fast as he kin go!" Grumpy jerked out tensely.

Rainbow's nod was serene. "I expected that, but there's nothin' like bein' sure."

"But dammit, if he ever reaches him with that wild yarn of yores, there won't be nothin' about our doin's that Slack don't know! He'll come down on us like a rockslide!"

Rainbow didn't think so.

"It's the rustlers that Bailey 'll be worryin' about," he pointed out. "He'll try to get to them first. Slack won't be with them."

"How do yuh know that?" Grumpy challenged.

Rainbow delayed over his answer.

"Pin me down, and I'll have to admit I don't, for

a fact," he said. "But I don't entertain any doubts on the subject. If Slack is as sly as everything indicates, he'll make sure there's no direct hookup between him and the rustlin'. That crack of mine to Bailey was just a flyer. From his actions, it's pretty plain it was a bull's-eye. I haven't anything else to go on."

"So yuh think this buzzard we're foggin' will show us the way to the rustlers' hide-out?"

"That's it."

Grumpy mulled that over. "To be dead shore, we'll have to let him lead us right to it," he argued. "That means a showdown with them hombres or word 'll git back to Slack anyways."

"You've hit it," Rainbow nodded simply.

"It's takin' an awful chance," his partner averred soberly.

"It is, for a fact. But it won't be the first time," Rainbow said. "Am I makin' a mistake in believin' a crack at those birds is all we need?"

Grumpy snorted. It was all the answer he felt the question required. "The way yo're playin' yore cards oughta bring results in a hurry," he grumbled. "But I wouldn't give much fer our chances if we was to run into a jack pot where we needed help in a hurry. God knows where we'd go fer it on this range!"

Striking the hills, Bailey drove on like a man who knew exactly where he was going. It was harder to keep him in view now. The partners were hard put to it to make certain that he did not slip away, and at the same time keep under cover themselves. Grumpy continued to turn over the night's events.

"The way things are goin'," he said at last, "it looks like yuh hit the nail where it's flattest about a rustlin' job bein' planned fer tonight."

Rainbow nodded. "You got that, eh? It wasn't takin' much of a chance. Those gents are gettin' so bold that they're likely to be ridin' anytime. Come to think of it," he proceeded, "their success is so uniform that they must have inside information."

It was a new idea to Grumpy. "Yuh mean they've got a spy in the Tuscarora Association?" he demanded.

"One, or a dozen," Rainbow confirmed. "They seem never at a loss as to where to strike."

Grumpy would have made some reply, but at the moment Bailey altered his course, turning into a canyon which split the hills for miles. Rainbow murmured, "If I remember right, he's got no choice but to go straight on till he comes out on the Wishbone range."

"That's a fact! Yuh s'pose the rustlers are aimin' to git into Goodnight's stuff again, Rainbow?"

"We'll soon see," was all the answer he got.

They pushed on cautiously. The rock-walled canyon was deep in shadow. Neither was unaware of the possibility of an ambush; but Rainbow was confident that his reading of Lafe Bailey's mind had been more accurate than that.

"Shake it up!" he rasped. "We can't afford to let him out of our sight from now on!"

Ten minutes later the rhythmic clip-clop of horse hoofs on the rocky canyon floor wafted back to them. Near the canyon's head they ran into timber; Bailey had taken to the high places again. Grumpy looked about in the watery moonlight. "Goodnight's spread," he muttered.

Hastily they sought to draw up on their quarry. Bailey was heading across the ridges. In the mouth of a dry wash he had halted for several minutes. Rainbow paused to look around with care.

"This is where he expected to meet the rustlers," he exclaimed. "Several horses were here not long ago—there's fresh droppin's. Come on, Grumpy!" He jammed his horse the way Bailey had gone. "There ain't a minute to spare from here out!"

Putting their broncs through the pine scrub, they rode out on the crest of a swell just as the moon drifted out from under the clouds. It bathed the range in a lambent silver glow. They were high up. At their left the hills dropped away almost sheer. A quarter-mile away, and on a level with them-selves, Lafe Bailey rode along parallel with the brink.

Bailey was gazing into the valley below as if his life depended on it. Grumpy shot a look that way.

Suddenly a grunt escaped him. "Look!" he exclaimed. "There's some men hazin' a bunch of steers along! It must be the rustlers, Rainbow!"

Bailey had seen them too. He began to hunt feverishly for a way to get down to them.

"After him!" Rainbow ripped out. "They're the gents we've been lookin' for, but we can't let him reach them or get away, either!"

Jabbing the spurs in, they raced forward. Suddenly Bailey saw them. His efforts to find a way down the precipice increased to a mad pitch. There was a way down there: it lay halfway between himself and his pursuers. Too late Lafe spotted the trail. Putting his bronc into a run, he dashed that way until he saw he would never make it. He hauled in, the knowledge making him savage.

Jerking his rifle out of the boot, he threw it up and blazed away. It was Rainbow whom he had centered in his sights. The latter heard the snarling buzz of the slug. Another followed; there was a shock as if Rainbow's mount had misstepped, and a lead-colored mark appeared on his saddle horn.

"Let him have it!" Grumpy whipped out. "He'll blast us down if he can!"

Suiting action to the words, he unlimbered his six gun. His bullets, raising the dust beyond Bailey, were too much for the latter. Whirling his bronc, Lafe dashed away, hunched in the saddle till he showed as small a target as possible.

"Run him down!" Rainbow cried. "We've got the goods on him! Maybe we can wring some real information out of him now!"

Grumpy had his own opinion as to the proper fate for the renegade, but drawing his rifle, he began to throw lead at Bailey's horse. Slugs glanced off the rocks under the flying hoofs. Suddenly the pony broke. It all but threw Lafe. Yanking up on the reins, he strove to drive the animal to its old pace without success. He knew he was done then.

Before he could make up his mind what to do, the horse stumbled. Bailey was thrown over its head, to roll on the very edge of the chasm. Somehow he had managed to retain his hold on his gun. It spat viciously at Grumpy, who replied in a flash.

At that short range it seemed impossible that he could miss. But Lafe flung himself sidewise just as Grumpy fired. The next instant he was half over the edge of the cliff, his feet hanging, hands clawing for support. Even in that tense moment, Bailey made a grab for his rifle. He believed there was no drop of pity in these two and meant to fight like a wildcat till the last.

Grumpy whipped a shot which sent Lafe's rifle clattering. At the same time it kicked dirt into Bailey's face. Whether he believed himself hit, or the shock did it, his hands tore free from their support; with a yell of terror, Bailey slid over the brink and hurtled into space.

9

Grumpy flung an appealing look at Rainbow as Lafe Bailey abruptly disappeared from view. "Gawd! I never intended to do that," he got out hoarsely.

Rainbow was curt. "Can't be helped. Bailey practically insisted on it. Come on, Grumpy! There's nothin' more for us here."

They wheeled with one accord toward the trail down the precipice which Lafe had despaired of reaching. There was no doubt in Grumpy's mind what his partner intended. They were within striking distance of the rustlers. The circumstance carried its own challenge, regardless of what the odds might be.

Flashing a look into the valley, Rainbow saw the stock thieves trying to haze the steers along at a greater speed. In this vast, resounding quiet they had followed the fight on the cliff, gathering its portent if not the actuality of events. Rainbow saw at least four men; possibly there were more. Their efforts to prod the stolen cattle into a run were feverish.

"Dang it, I told yuh!" Grumpy burst out. "We're stackin' up against somethin' now. There must be half-a-dozen uh them wolves, Rainbow!"

"If we can get down there soon enough, they'll

think there's a dozen of us!" Rainbow tossed back grimly. "Just see that you don't break your neck on the way!"

It was all they could do to make haste down the narrow, twisting trail hugging the face of the cliff. Several times they came to a spot which at first glance appeared impassable. Somehow they managed to work past. Had the rustlers thought quickly enough to rush them while they were descending, their position might well have been hopeless. As it was, lead screamed toward them out of space; chips and fragments of rock rained down; the enemy's rifleshots cracked against the cliff.

Rainbow's jaws corded at the coolness of it. He and Grumpy had weathered such fire many times before; it was powerless to slow them up. If anything, it increased their need to come to grips with the rustlers.

Reaching the valley floor at last, they crossed the Nevada Midland right of way and raced toward the flats. Thick brush hampered their going, but at the same time it was protection in part. Rainbow had no idea whether the rustlers knew there was only two of them. He was depending on the hope that the others believed themselves discovered by the Indian Wells cowmen.

"Right at them, Grumpy!" he cried. "Make 'em think all hell's come down on their necks!"

He yanked his own rifle from the boot as he spoke. Five minutes later, whipping it to his shoulder, he blazed away; not once but several times. Grumpy followed suit, swinging aside so that a hundred yards separated him from his partner. That he was on the right track was attested a moment later when Rainbow motioned him farther away.

"Swing 'way around!" he called. "Close in on 'em from the side!"

His words were for the hearkening rustlers, in part, but Grumpy understood. The moon had dipped behind a mackerel fleece of clouds a few minutes before; shadows swam up out of the brush, half concealing steers and men alike. But the drifting scarves of dust were unmistakable. Steadily Rainbow and Grumpy closed in, the muzzle bursts of their guns stabbing the dark.

It was a fire that was returned hotly from several quarters. Death wheeled close without deterring the two in the slightest. For his part, Rainbow was determined to drive the marauders into the open once and for all, if it could be done.

A less determined attack might have turned out differently. As it was, the rustlers were convinced they had been jumped by a superior force. Rainbow saw one of them at the drag of the rustled bunch, hazing the steers forward madly and pausing to fling frenzied shots over his shoulder. A slug, singing past his face, changed his mind about sticking it out. With a yell he wheeled away, abandoning the cattle.

Closing in from the other side, Grumpy made it equally hot for another owlhoot. Like the first, he gave up and headed for distant parts, laying a heavy barrage of shots on his back-trail.

A third and fourth rustler, seeing their position and believing it hopeless, pulled out with scarcely less haste. Rainbow took after one of them, intent on nailing a rustler if only for proof of what had happened. The man seemed to guess his design, for he lined out in a businesslike fashion. Within a few minutes, they were a mile from the scene of the gun fight.

Rainbow was chagrined to note that if he was drawing up, it was not perceptible. He drilled on, steeling himself to carry this thing through to a conclusion.

He would have been astonished could he have known the identity of his quarry. It was Bart Galey. Usually too cagey to become involved personally, Galey had consented to ride this time with the rustlers in the belief that it was entirely safe. He cursed himself now for his folly.

He knew who it was behind him. At the first inkling of the fight on the cliff, he had leaped to the suspicion that Rainbow and Grumpy were responsible; but that they were alone hardly struck him as likely. Starting away with Rainbow hard on his heels, Galey had determined the other should never overhaul him, never learn who he was.

He was not long in finding out that of the two, his was the fastest horse. He could pull away from Rainbow at will. The knowledge emboldened him. Making for a rock-crested ridge, he crossed at a diagonal and quickly circled back. Within five minutes, Rainbow came driving past, following the scent of Galey's dust like a beagle. Bart waited, tense, till he was almost opposite. Throwing up his gun, he drew a bead on Rainbow and fired.

Had Rainbow been less wary at this game, the attempt to kill him might have succeeded. Before even the crack of Galey's gun reached his ears, the ripping tug at the brim of his hat warned him. When the next slug came, he had already dropped low on his pony's withers; the next second, Rainbow changed his bronc's course and charged straight at Galey's position.

It was too much for Bart. Though he whipped over another desperate shot, panic gripped him. Springing to his horse, he flung himself astride and fled.

Could Rainbow have lined him up in his sights at that moment, he would have cut the other down without compunction. Fate was with Bart this time, however. When Rainbow topped the ledge and came on, Galey was a deceptive form in the brush five hundred yards away.

Rage seethed in the latter as he rapidly drew beyond range once more. It was resentment directed at Rainbow; for though Bart cursed his clumsiness in bungling the chance to eliminate the other once and for all, he was not wholly deceived as to the cause of it. "Ripley's a devil!" he jerked out. "The trick that takes him by surprise 'll have to be a damned good 'un!"

For Rainbow's part, he was quick in deciding this chase to be hopeless. He and Grumpy had been forced to take what they could get in the line of horseflesh at Indian Wells; their luck had not been particularly good. Mentally apostrophizing that mischance, he turned back, asking himself what Grumpy's fortune had been.

That it was not much better than his own, he learned on returning to the point at which the rustled steers had been abandoned. There was Grumpy, waiting, as empty handed as himself. Rainbow's query was terse. "Nothin' doin', eh?"

Grumpy snorted his disgust. "If I'd had anythin' but this danged wooden sawhorse under me . . . !"

"Never mind. It's the breaks of the game." Rainbow sounded more cheerful than he felt. "Just what did we manage to scrape out of the heap, anyway?"

"One dead skunk, 'bout two dozen Wishbone yearlin' steers, an' a cloud uh rustlers' dust!" Grumpy answered him explosively. Rainbow grinned.

"Well, it's no new story with us, Grumpy. There isn't much we can do about it, except—" He broke off thoughtfully.

"Except what?" his partner growled.

"We can haze Goodnight's steers back on his range."

"Hell!" Grumpy showed a flash of returning spirit at the proposal. "Let him worry 'bout his own beef! He ain't give me cause to do him no favors."

"You've been riskin' your neck to run down the rustlers who got into his stuff," Rainbow retorted amusedly.

"But not on his account! Yuh know that, well's I do!" It came to Grumpy then, in a vague way, that he was being ribbed. His homely visage wrinkled into a twisted grin. "Aw, let's git goin', then, if that's our play. Dang yuh, Rainbow, yuh allus got an answer fer everything!"

Had the Wishbone steers not been run till they were tired, it would have been no easy task to round them up and start them back in the direction of Goodnight's range. Watching from cover, Bart Galey, who had circled back to keep tabs on the pair, could hardly believe his eyes.

"Damned if this ain't a break made to order fer me!" he breathed, a plan taking form in his mind almost with the words. "All them hombres have to do is stay with the steers long enough! I'll settle their hash an' no mistake!"

135

Wheeling his mount, Galey struck back into the hills till he was certain he could not be seen. Then he lined out for Goodnight's ranch. Less than half an hour saw him drawing near. The house was plunged in darkness; but this was an early hour of the morning. Bart drew up in the yard.

"Hello, the house!" he cried.

There was no answer, the place might have been deserted; but as Galey called again, a head was thrust out the bunkhouse door, towsled, with sleep-bleared eyes. "What yuh after, bellerin' 'round here that-a-way?" demanded the cook grumpily.

"I want Goodnight and want him in a hurry!" Bart hurled at him.

"He ain't here, Galey."

"Where is he?"

"I dunno where he is."

"What!" Bart bawled, with the vague idea that the other was having sport at his expense. "Damn you, Beefy; lay off the horseplay an' tell me where Jim is!"

"Tell yuh I dunno," Beefy insisted. "Bob an' the others rode over to Tas Johnson's Lazy Lightnin'; that's the last I heard of anybody, till you come bargin' up shootin' yore mouth off!"

He would have added more, but Galey didn't wait for it. He had learned all he needed to know. Turning away, he raced in the direction of Johnson's ranch. A tense question pounded in his brain as he rode. Would the men he sought be there? They had to be! His entire plan depended on the element of time; a couple of hours from now would be too late.

Old Tas's Lazy Lightning spread was not so far away that Galey could not cover the distance in short order. He was in luck: a buttery daub of light beckoned to him across the range, and the yard was filled with men when he pounded up. They wheeled toward him, the weariness of fruitless riding dropping away from them.

"Who is that?" Tas barked, pushing forward.

"It's me, Johnson—Galey!" Bart exclaimed. "Thank God I found yuh."

"Where the hell 've yuh been all night?" Johnson cut in on a note of censure. "We looked fer yuh, but—"

"I was doin' my own ridin'," Galey threw back; "an' mebby it's a damned good thing! I spotted some rustlers, Johnson. I know where they are right now!"

The news sent a shock through these men. Any who had felt impatience with Bart in the past forgot it now. "Spill it, Galey!" one of them ejaculated harshly. "Where are these birds, an' how come yuh didn't jump 'em yoreself?"

Quickly Bart told his story. He had been patrolling the range, as he thought, hopelessly; and was on the point of giving over when he spotted several men hazing a bunch of steers across the range. He didn't know who they were, or how many: wanting to make certain of the result, he had started for help without losing an instant.

"Wal, let's not lose any, then!" old Tas rumbled, his tone tightening. He turned to the cowmen. "Okay, boys. Stirrups, all of yuh!" And to Bart as he swung into the hull, "Lead out, Galey. An' don't make any mistakes!"

Bart said, "Don't worry. I'll take yuh to 'em in short order!"

Little was said as this grim-jawed band of men jogged out to bring justice to the sage. Fatigue had laid its brand on their faces an hour ago; but they brushed it aside. Not one of them but felt new life coursing through him at the prospect of locking horns with the evasive foe who had harried this range for so long. It would go hard with the men who sought to oppose them tonight.

Rainbow and Grumpy had driven the recaptured steers only a matter of three or four miles. Galey was able to judge their whereabouts with reasonable accuracy. They had almost reached the edge of Goodnight's range when the cowmen, with Bart and old Tas at their head, rode out on a swell and saw them below.

An angry buzz ran through the ranchers at the sight. Previous disappointment tonight had keyed them up to a sharp readiness. "There they are!" a man rasped tensely. "By God, they ain't gittin' away from us this time!"

Shoving their broncs forward, they started down.

Rainbow was the first to observe their approach. He hauled in for a better look and Grumpy noted the action. Sweeping a glance toward the rise, he took in the situation in a flash.

"That's Goodnight's crowd!" he jerked out. "We'll have some explainin' to do now, Rainbow!"

Rainbow was thinking the same thing, his face hardening in lean lines. "We will, for a fact."

"Yuh waitin' for 'em?" his partner demanded.

The answer was delayed momentarily. "We haven't a thing to fear, if we tell exactly what happened," Rainbow began.

"Hell!" Grumpy was scornful. "We may never have the chance to speak up! That bunch ain't got a bit uh use fer us, after what's happened. An' if it's a case uh run, our broncs ain't wuth a damn!" he reminded, cursing their luck under his breath.

"Don't go off the handle!" Rainbow warned him sharply. "I'll hail them before anything happens."

As it turned out, however, he never got the chance. While he was still waiting, watching the oncoming riders narrowly, the guns began to pound as the ranchers opened fire. Lead droned overhead. It was more than enough for Grumpy.

"I'm leavin'!" he bit off. "It don't matter who we are; them gents 'll down us first an' ask questions afterward! I don't want any uh that in mine!"

Rainbow was not many seconds in coming to the same decision. All too clearly the cowmen were in no mood for parley. Believing they had caught the rustlers red handed, they were bent on making short work of the matter.

"Punch wind!" he rapped to Grumpy. "There ain't any other out!"

Pulling away from the steers, they headed for the hills at the best pace they could get out of their mounts. It was none too fast. Within a matter of minutes, the pursuers were hard on their heels, closing in with the ruthlessness of wolf hounds. Slugs whined uncomfortably close. Grumpy ducked as a bullet clipped his ear, and Rainbow received a graze on his thigh.

The latter flung a glance back. It was not for himself that he feared so much as for the horses. If one of them were downed now, or even lamed, it would be well-nigh disastrous. Their only hope was to fade into the folds of the high hills, where they might throw off pursuit by trickery.

Striking the hills at last, Rainbow's fears were scarcely relieved. Minutes passed; and while the fire from the rear continued unabated, it grew no worse. He began to hope then. Fagged as his and Grumpy's ponies were, it came to him that those of the cowmen must be in a similar condition or it would have been all over by now.

Steadily they climbed to higher levels, Rainbow leading the way up winding water courses which confused their pursuers. They came out on the high range, and here, except for stunted brush, the going was open again. The cowmen were strung out for a mile behind them, only one or two near enough to be within effective range. These continued to throw slugs.

Heading for the timber, Rainbow was telling himself that if they could make it, they would get away, when without any warning Grumpy's bronc folded up under him and the little man was flung half-a-dozen yards. He scrambled up as Rainbow wheeled toward him, blood streaming down his face from cuts and scratches, but otherwise uninjured.

"They got my bronc!" he gasped.

"Climb on behind me!" Rainbow ordered sharply, holding his horse with iron hand. Grumpy didn't stand on ceremony. Scarcely had his weight settled behind Rainbow's back before the pony sprang forward pluckily. But the load was too much. Rainbow needed no telling that at this rate the game was up.

Instead of making for the timber, he raced over the open, a new plan twisting and turning in his brain. "Where yuh goin'?" Grumpy yelled in his ear. "They'll pull us down out here in five minutes!"

"We're not far from where we were foggin'

Bailey," Rainbow answered him. "His bronc should be somewhere near by."

Yet he almost despaired of locating it, when rounding a brush patch near an outcropping ledge, they nearly ran into the horse. Grumpy made a sound in his throat that was close to approval. "Yuh shore got yore wits about yuh at times, Rainbow!" he conceded.

It was no easy task to capture the spooky bronc, but by deft maneuvering Rainbow managed it. Grumpy crawled into the saddle. "Now it's plumb up to us!" he exclaimed.

"This way!" Rainbow called lowly.

Doubling behind the outcrop, they let a pair of pursuers drive past without awareness of what they were doing. But more were coming. Rainbow rasped, "Make for the timber!"

Somehow they reached it at last. Once under cover of the trees, the pursuit was no longer so close that they found no way to turn. Rainbow knew that this range would be combed for miles, until daylight and beyond; but by shrewd management he and Grumpy soon lost themselves in the Calicoes, with no sign of the cowmen to the rear.

"Wal!" said Grumpy finally. "Purty warm work fer a couple old leather burners like us. An' in results," he added ruefully, "it netted us the grand sum of exzactly nothin'!"

"Never mind." Rainbow was sententious. "We came mighty close to bein' chalked up in the red this time. Crawlin' out from under that is somethin'." He gauged the hour by the look of the paling sky. "Reckon it's about time we were gettin' back to Lost Angel, Grumpy."

Breathing their broncs while they had a smoke and talked things over, they swung up and headed that way.

10

The first carload of Slack's tailings went down the Nevada Midland the following day. Rainbow and Grumpy were riding the right of way a few miles below Lost Angel. Clem Rucker waved to them from the cab as the train passed.

Following recent events, it was a quiet day for the partners until, late in the afternoon, they spotted two horsemen jogging down the tracks toward them. Grumpy tightened up in a flash. "Who kin that be?" he bristled.

Rainbow's gaze narrowed. "One of 'em looks like Slack," he murmured.

It was Slack; and the man with him was Slicer Cully. They drew near so purposefully that before a word was spoken, Rainbow knew there was something on Slack's mind. The latter wasted no time in coming to the point.

"What in hell is the matter with you two?" he rasped in a severe tone.

Rainbow scrutinized him levelly.

"Nothin' to speak of. What are you drivin' at?" he gave back.

Slack jerked out, "There was a man killed by the locomotive today, on track yo're supposed to be guardin'!"

If he expected to surprise Rainbow and Grumpy, he succeeded amply. Grumpy said "Huh?" his jaw dropping, and Rainbow fired a quick question: "Who was it?"

"Lafe Bailey!" was the answer. "He was hit down in the cut, where the track swings under them cliffs—all banged up and his bones broke! It's damned queer yuh don't know nothin' about it, Ripley! Yo're supposed to be ridin' the road; an' yuh didn't even know there was a man on it!"

"We can't be everywhere at once," Rainbow pointed out thinly.

"No. But yuh could split up and cover twice as much ground!" Slack shot at him.

"And get knocked off? Anybody tryin' to wreck the track won't be showin' up alone, Slack; you know that." Rainbow shook his head decidedly. "Nothin' doin'!"

"Well, that's sense—" Slack began with a trifle less assurance. Before he could go on, Rainbow thrust in,

"Bailey. Where 've I heard that name before? Wasn't he the relief agent at Crazy Horse?"

Slack nodded reluctantly. "That's him."

"Then what was he doin' above Indian Wells?"

It was a question for which Slack had sought an answer in vain, and his failure worried him. Discreet inquiries had informed him that he was mistaken about Ripley and Gibbs having anything to do with the bushwhack shots fired at him: they had been working hard at the tie camp in Singer Canyon at the time. But Bart Galey had got word to him of the rustling, and the part the pair had played in the adventure. Their success in breaking up the steal and in avoiding the trap Galey had laid for them had him more worried then ever about them.

"Nobody knows," he answered Rainbow's question. "Bailey was supposed to be on duty at the time he disappeared. Miss Longstreet has asked Lint Granger to investigate."

Grumpy thought, "Yo're danged right it was her! *You'd* never be doin' it, Slack!" Aloud, he said, "What was Bailey doin', walkin'?"

"That's queer too!" Slack said explosively. "It don't make sense; but if he had a bronc, it ain't showed up."

"Mebby he was ridin' the cars on the way up this mornin'," Grumpy hazarded, "an' fell under the wheels."

Slack brushed this aside like a piece of idle chatter. "I ain't discussin' Lafe Bailey's actions with yuh," he told Rainbow, his face reddening; "but why yuh let it happen at all!"

Rainbow shrugged. "If a man can't keep out of a train's way, I wouldn't know what to suggest," he retorted dryly.

Slack had more to say, but it all boiled down to the fact that he was angrier than he dared admit. He guessed shrewdly that Bailey's presence in the hills had something to do with the rustling, the fight for the steers having occurred near where Lafe had died. He would never know now what message the bogus agent might have been carrying. Nor could he tax Rainbow and Grumpy with their part in that night's activities without explaining how he came to know more about it than other men.

"This track guardin' is a serious matter," he warned severely. "I ain't payin' yuh for nothin' else. After this, see to it that yuh keep yore nose to the grindstone!"

Rainbow nodded. "You're the doctor, Slack." But watching Slack and Cully ride on a minute later, there was a speculative glint in his eyes.

Grumpy shook his head. "That was shore a fluke," he muttered. "Bailey landin' so near the track that way!"

Rainbow said thoughtfully, "It must be hell, havin' to bottle up what Slack's got in him, without bein' able to spill what he wants to. We'll have to watch that hombre, Grumpy."

"Yuh think he knows about our doin's?"

"I do. Some, anyway, and he's been doin' some

large guessin' at the rest. There's no other reason for his bein' so wrathy. He wants," Rainbow continued as if to himself, "to be sure of where we are and what we're doin'. It looks as if we'd have to give a pretty good imitation of fallin' for it, for a while."

There was some talk that night in Lost Angel about Lafe Bailey's mysterious death, but it was not till the following day that Sukey Withers gave Rainbow a piece of information which bothered him no little.

"Miz Longstreet ast Lint Granger to look into the matter," said Sukey, "an' the sheriff's been questionin' the engine crew, so I hear. Rucker claims he dunno nothin' about it; denied he'd wiped any blood off the cowcatcher. It made Lint mad as a hornet. Says there ain't no two ways 'bout how Bailey was killed, an' no frog-hoppin' ole juniper like Rucker kin make a fool outa him!"

"But Granger wouldn't arrest Rucker?" Rainbow put in the query quickly.

"Hard to tell. Clem's a salty old nubbin; he may fire off a broadside yet that 'll force the sheriff to act."

There was more, but that was the gist of Withers' news. Rainbow told Grumpy about it later.

"It don't look so good," he admitted soberly. "I never counted on havin' to tell what we know about Bailey's death in order to clear Rucker."

"Why do it, anyway?" Grumpy demanded. "Let

Rucker take care of hisself; he's old 'nough!"

"And where would Sharon Longstreet be if we did that?" Rainbow retorted. "She depends on old Clem. Probably there isn't another man in the country who can run that tinpot locomotive and get out of it what he can."

Grumpy looked at him slowly and said "Hmm." It summed up all he was willing to put into words, but his concern was of another order now that he perceived the direction of Rainbow's thoughts. He knew the other would not hesitate to jeopardize them if by doing so he could help the girl.

"Why not go tuh Granger privately an' tell him what yuh know?" Grumpy queried finally. "That 'd persuade him to lay off old Rucker."

Rainbow shook his head.

"Not till I've decided there's no other way out," he returned. "We could never get Lint to consent to silence; he'd insist on goin' straight to Slack about this business of the telegrams. It 'd be his duty to do so, I expect. And that would tip our hand."

"That's so." Grumpy's face was long. "What 'll yuh do then, Rainbow?"

"We'll wait and see what happens."

Knowing the reason for which they were hired, Granger rode out to question them. Rainbow told the lawman simply that neither he nor Grumpy knew anything about Bailey's being struck by the train.

"It's dang queer!" Lint declared. "Nobody knows a thing, but Lafe is dead fer all that. I could forget a lot of things if I only knowed how he got where he was found!"

"Slack mentioned that he was supposed to be on duty in Crazy Horse at the time." Rainbow nodded. "Miss Longstreet was up the line seein' about track repairs. If Bailey 'd stayed where he belonged, he'd probably be alive this minute."

If Granger was impressed by this attempt to make him question Bailey's motives, he failed to show it. "Yuh didn't see Lafe up this way that day, Ripley?" he questioned flatly.

For answer, Rainbow lifted his brows humorously, letting Granger put his own construction on that.

"I hear you're thinkin' of takin' Clem Rucker into custody," he suggested diffidently. Lint made an impatient gesture.

"I want *him* to think that," he pointed out, "but what good would it do? If he hit Bailey, he never knowed it. I thought at first," he confessed, "that Rucker was holdin' somethin' out on me, but . . ." He shook his head.

Rainbow and Grumpy exchanged glances. It told them all they needed to know. Rainbow's relief was for Sharon; but if Grumpy thought he meant to forget his concern for the girl, he soon learned of his mistake.

Unsatisfied, Granger left them to their work of

149

patrolling the track. It was the beginning of a dull, if exceedingly busy period for them. Rainbow saw to it that whatever their opinion of Slack might be, they shirked no part of their duty to Sharon Longstreet. Early and late they were in the saddle and riding continuously.

"Danged if yuh ain't more thoroughgoin' than I ever knowed yuh to be before!" Grumpy growled suspiciously. "Ever since the day Slack piled into us, yuh been foggin' us back an' forth without a letup! We couldn't take no more care uh that train if we was to lead it on a string. An' the hell of it is, we ain't seen a thing outa the way so far!"

"You ought to be glad your work is simplified that way," Rainbow grinned at him. But Grumpy was not to be thus easily put aside.

"What the hell!" he vented his explosive disgust. "This is a hot job fer a couple of gents like us! We come into this country to snag some rustlers, an' instead of followin' up our leads, like we had our growth an' knowed what we was doin', here we are, ridin' fence fer a phony hombre who wants to keep us outa the way an' is makin' a pretty fair job of doin' it! We been sidetracked, I tell yuh!"

He was not being funny; the words were spoken in dead earnest. Nor did Rainbow put him off as he expected him to. Instead, he reflected for some moments in silence.

"You're right," he admitted slowly. "While I

expected to go to some pains to throw Slack off the track about us, I never intended to forget those rustlers for a second. There's two or three angles I've been turnin' over in my mind. One of them is to learn, if possible, by what method Slack keeps tabs on the activities of those cowmen."

"How kin yuh find that out?"

"Why, by going to the cowmen themselves about it."

Grumpy snorted incredulously. "That's sense, ain't it? There ain't no gettin' in touch with them hombres, Rainbow."

"Why not?"

Grumpy showed his surprise at the question. "Why, dammit all," he exclaimed, "didn't they give yuh a flat warnin' against comin' back—an' dang near brain me with a pool cue in the bargain?" His perplexity was plain, and his indignation as well.

"That was because they believed we were throwin' in with Slack," Rainbow argued reasonably.

"Do yuh think yuh kin persuade 'em otherwise at this late hour of the day?" Grumpy snapped scornfully.

"I can try."

"Unh-uh." Grumpy was decisive. "Yuh kin try, yes; but, Rainbow, yuh won't git nowheres with them hotheads—there ain't no use even givin' it a whirl!"

He might have saved his warning. Rainbow had no intention of trying to get anywheres with those stubborn, headstrong men who had already made plain their stand.

"If you're talkin' about Bart Galey," he grinned, "I'm willin' to agree. But Jim Goodnight and one or two others are an altogether different breed." He was thinking aloud now. "There's that old rawhide, for instance; what's his name?—old Tas Johnson." He fell silent, reflecting.

Grumpy watched him narrowly, a furrow between his eyes. "What yuh figgerin' on now?" he queried suspiciously.

"Not figurin'. I'm decided," was the unexpected answer. And when the other waited for more, "We're goin' to Tas Johnson, Grumpy, and lay our cards on the table. If we can persuade him to dicker with us, swell. There ain't any other way."

Grumpy grunted his skepticism. "Yuh figger to keep it a secret from Goodnight an' them others, then?"

"And from Slack and the railroad crowd—in fact, from everybody but Johnson and ourselves!"

Grumpy's eyes began to gleam. "That means a little night ridin', I reckon."

A nod was the reply. "Tonight. Maybe I've wasted too much time as it is. I don't want old Tas to feel I've taken too long to think things over. But we'll see."

Since they had formed the custom of occasionally arriving at Lost Angel long after dark from their patrol work, it attracted no particular attention when they failed to show up for supper on this night. Dusk found them still far down the right of way and striking out across the range in the direction of Tas Johnson's Lazy Lightning. They were in no haste.

"Reckon we better be keepin' our eyes peeled over this way," Grumpy muttered uneasily. "Them cowmen won't be welcomin' no night visitors with open arms."

It was so true that Rainbow half expected they would be challenged sooner or later by cruising punchers; he held himself in readiness to fade promptly and effectively into the surrounding landscape in such an event, for discovery by anyone but the man they sought to reach would spell ruin to their chances of success.

Grumpy was equally alive to the possibilities. So wary were they that by nine o'clock they pulled in on a grassy ridge crest to look down on the gleaming lights of Tas Johnson's little ranch house in the hollow below.

"Johnson's still up—he may even have visitors," Rainbow murmured. "We'll wait a while."

It was well they did. Half an hour later several men emerged from Johnson's tumble-down shack and moved off into the shadows. Presently the sound of corral bars being let down came to the listeners; then the stamp of hoofs and a steady rhythmic beat as the riders drew off across the range, faintly silhouetted by the starlight.

"Just a few minutes longer," Rainbow checked his partner's impatience. When the lights in Johnson's place abruptly went out, he was satisfied. "He's alone," he said.

They started down there, keeping the broncs to a noiseless walk. Neither needed any warning of the danger in what they were doing. To be spotted, to have their purpose misread before they could make it clear, might mean swift disaster. Rainbow led the way. A hundred yards from the house he swung down from his horse.

"We'll leave 'em here in the edge of the brush," he breathed to Grumpy. They stole forward on foot.

Johnson's house was plunged in the complete, oppressive silence of the high desert. The place might have been deserted, so entirely lacking were any signs or sounds of occupancy. Rainbow moved up on the rickety board porch and knocked.

Silence.

Rainbow tried again, still without result. Grumpy, waiting in restless suspense, began, "Louder, Rainbow. He must 've gone off to sleep orready."

But a new thought had come to the latter. What if old Tas had slipped out to follow those other riders after dousing his light? It was possible. These rangemen were obviously so concerned about their predicament that they would overlook no slightest opportunity of doing something about it.

Rainbow was just turning away from the door, convinced that were he to break in, he would find the place deserted and Johnson nowhere about the place, when a jarring voice from the corner of the house arrested him in his tracks.

"Who are you, an' what do yuh want?"

It was a rasping challenge; but Rainbow was relieved to recognize old Tas's belligerent tones. He said, "It's Ripley and Gibbs, Johnson. I've come for a long talk with you."

"Have, huh?" There was no letdown of tension in that response. "Wal, in the meantime shove out hyar where I kin see yuh, an' don't make no quick moves, either of yuh, or yuh've had yore last long talk this side o' hell!"

11

Doing as they were bid, Rainbow and Grumpy slowly closed the distance between themselves and Tas Johnson. The old man stuck to the corner of the house. Finally he growled,

"Orright, that's far 'nough! I'm satisfied yo're who yuh say yuh are. Name yore business, Ripley, an' I'll decide whether we got anythin' to talk over or not!"

Rainbow frowned. He had not anticipated any such unremitting suspicion on the part of the other. Moreover, he was at a clear disadvantage, trying to talk across the muzzle of a drawn gun.

"It's about this rustlin', Johnson. Why not go in the house and make ourselves comfortable?"

"You ain't makin' yoreselves comfortable 'round any place o' mine—or welcome either— till I've changed my mind 'bout yuh plenty," Tas grated.

"How can you do that before we've talked it over and you've heard our story?" Rainbow retorted.

The answer was unbending, hostile silence. Rainbow tried again, "Because we didn't do the obvious thing in Crazy Horse, Johnson, some of your boys jumped to conclusions. They were hasty, and for that reason they were dead wrong. Correctin' that mistake is what I'm tryin' to do now."

Old Tas fingered the edges of that gingerly with his mind. "So there was a mistake made, was there? It wouldn't be yore takin' up with Dan Slack, by any chance; an' findin' out yore mistake after it's too late?"

"Everything we did was according to direct intention," Rainbow assured him. "And that's just as true right now."

Johnson studied his tone narrowly. "Why come to me with this?" he snapped suddenly. "Jim Goodnight's the man for yuh to tackle if yuh got anythin' that needs sayin'—"

"That's where you're dead wrong," Rainbow caught him up quickly. "Goodnight's all right; but his responsibility to all those men warps his judgment." He did not say that the latter's attitude toward Sharon Longstreet had confirmed him in this opinion, but such was the case. "After Goodnight, you know why we haven't gone to any of the others. If there's a leveler head in the Tuscarora Association, I decided it was yours. That's why we're here now, Johnson, and for no other reason."

For a long moment old Tas maintained silence; but his sensibilities were touched. He had long been of this precise opinion, in secret, himself. At last he grunted.

"Huh! Wal, that don't make yuh think I'm any easier to pull the wool over than any o' the others, does it?"

"Not at all. If there's any wool being pulled, Johnson, it's over the eyes of the men who need to be fooled for a purpose."

"Whut purpose might that be?" Tas rasped thinly.

"Why, for the purpose of rounding up these rustlers Grumpy and I came here to run down," Rainbow told him. "Did you really believe we're stayin' here for any other purpose?" He laughed the idea to scorn. "If it was work as gunmen we were after, we could have got it without traveling so far from Cheyenne—and been able to ask for just as good pay, and maybe better, to boot."

Johnson rasped his stubbly jaw thoughtfully. "Somethin' in that," he admitted, no longer concealing himself so carefully. "But, Ripley, tell me this: why in time did yuh have to take the bull by the horns like yuh done?"

Rainbow quickly explained the first meeting with Slack, and how suspicious it had appeared. It was almost as if Slack were determined to keep them from accepting the Tuscarora Association's offer. "We decided to let him get away with it and see what would happen," Rainbow concluded. "Does that explain to you why we had to let Goodnight and you and the others make up your own minds about us?"

Old Tas's keen mind was probing every angle of the situation cautiously.

"I reckon we ain't none of us got any use fer Slack," he growled. "But jest where do yuh reckon he fits into this rustlin' business?"

"I don't know," Rainbow confessed frankly. "But I'm just as interested as you are, and twice as curious. It made me decide to find out."

"Wal, now." The old rawhide's tone had undergone a gradual change, until distrust was almost wholly missing. Tas said, "Come inside, Ripley.

I'll talk this thing over anyway, an' glad to."

They entered Johnson's littered kitchen. Rainbow dropped a hand on the man's arm as he struck a match.

"I don't want a soul but you to know we've been here," he warned. Tas met his eyes with a flashing glance in which there was questioning at first, and then quick understanding.

"Okay." He put out the match. "Jest wait till I make shore of the winders."

He stumbled about in darkness, curtaining the windows with care, and finally lit a lamp. There was a glint of mingled enjoyment and anticipation in his pupils as he turned to Rainbow and Grumpy. "Have a seat. An' tell me some more. My ears are pinned wide open."

Rainbow's first concern was to convince him of their real intentions. He lost no time setting about it.

"This whole business of the mine tailin's and the railroad has got somethin' funny about it," he declared. "Dan Slack knows you cowmen have got too much on your hands to worry about him much. Still he insists on havin' expensive guards and payin' their salary himself."

"An' what's the answer?" Tas queried.

"Well, some mighty funny things 've been happenin'." Rainbow told about the cave-in at the Lost Angel hotel, and the accident in the mine. "And did you know about the wreck on

159

the railroad?" he wound up, his glance falling on Johnson's face with seeming casualness.

"Uh—yeh; by golly, I did hear 'bout that. What was the cause of it, Ripley?"

The words were enough to satisfy Rainbow that Johnson, at least, knew nothing of its cause. He shook his head.

"We don't know. But you can see how all these things fit together."

Old Tas nodded slowly. He got an inkling of what was in Rainbow's mind as well, for he said musingly, "O' course, there's Bart Galey—an' Tom Wilder—some of them fellers. They're purty redheaded when it comes to Slack an' the railroad. But all this don't help much about the rustlin'," he ended shrewdly.

"No. That's what's been bothering Grumpy and me. It's why we've come to you, Johnson. Will you work with us?"

Tas grew wary in a flash.

"In what way?"

"We aim to do somethin' about these rustlers," was the prompt and frank reply. "We can't—without lettin' Slack know what we're up to—unless we've got some means of knowin' exactly what's goin' on all the time."

"So it's information yuh want, huh?" The old fellow's wooden manner told how significant he found the proposal. Were Rainbow and Grumpy in fact the spies he had at first suspected them to be, they could not more satisfactorily have gained their ends than by this request.

"Forget it, Johnson!" Rainbow exclaimed sharply. "We can work by ourselves in the dark, if it comes to that—but where would it get us? Any farther ahead than the rest of you have already succeeded in getting?"

"Yo're right," old Tas confessed grudgingly. "Jest what do yuh want to know?"

"Everything! But mainly, we're interested in the movements of these stock thieves: exactly where they strike each time, and everything that's found out concernin' their getaway. All this mysteriousness about where the steers go is interestin' to me. If we can find that out, we'll be in line to learn a whole lot more in short order."

Tas signified his agreement. For an hour they talked the situation over, making their plans.

"We'll have to meet at night," Rainbow pointed out, "and in a different place each time. We can appoint the place each time we get together; and if for any reason we miss each other, it 'll be the last-named place every night till we do meet. I don't need to tell you how important it is," he drove on, "that not a soul but ourselves knows about these meetings, Johnson."

Tas assented. "It's pretty plain somebody's keepin' an eye on us," he said. "Yuh think it's from inside?"

Rainbow wasn't saying. "Those are all things

that will come out in the wash. What I'm concerned about right now is the things we don't know. Suppose you tell us what's been goin' on the last week or so."

Johnson told them all he could. When he was done, Rainbow and Grumpy were in possession of considerable information. It didn't make the problem any easier of solution.

"Don't let a thing escape you," Rainbow warned Tas. "Our ability to get anywheres depends on our knowledge of every move in the game."

"What 'll yuh do now—go back to ridin' the railroad?"

"Yes, we've got to seem to be doing the same things right along. But we'll find time for a little extra work on the side. Your business is to be just as suspicious of everything as we are. And we'll meet you again, two nights from tonight—where?"

Old Tas thought a minute, then named a rendezvous not far from the edge of the Wishbone range. "In the meantime I'll be keepin' tabs on you two, along with everything else," he warned. "You better be able to explain the first phony move in this hand we're playin' out together!"

Rainbow nodded cheerfully. "That's okay with me, Johnson. We'll hold up our end. If you'll do the same, that's all we ask. Maybe now it won't be so long before we get some action on these stock thieves," he wound up.

There was no more to be said. Tas put out the

light before Rainbow and Grumpy slipped out. Soon they were in the hull and pulling away toward the railroad and Lost Angel.

"Suspicious old coot," Grumpy grunted, after some minutes of musing silence.

"Sure. But wouldn't you be too, in his boots?"

Grumpy turned that over. "Reckon I would," he admitted.

In the morning they returned to guarding the right of way. Late that afternoon they were riding the line as usual when Rainbow, in the lead, drew up to study something on the ground. A dozen horsemen had crossed here. The knowledge pulled both up sharply. Several cars of Slack's tailings had gone down the line half an hour before without any trouble; Clem Rucker had waved to them from the engine cab. Nevertheless, the circumstance of this strange horse sign, which was reasonably fresh, needed explaining.

"Somebody smellin' around," Grumpy suggested suspiciously.

"Hard to say." Rainbow was thoughtful. "But I'd like to know just who made those tracks and what they were doin'."

"We'll foller a ways an' see what we find."

No attempt had been made to break the trail they followed. It struck through the hills boldly, and they soon found themselves far beyond railroad property. Grumpy pulled up finally to scan their surroundings. His voice was throaty and tense.

"We must be shovin' deep into Goodnight's Wishbone range by now, Rainbow."

His answer was a nod. But Rainbow did not haul up. Twenty minutes later he stiffened suddenly at sight of a dozen horsemen a mile off. The men were coming this way. He and Grumpy had already been seen.

Grumpy tightened up, and his words were curt. "That's Goodnight an' his crowd!" he muttered warningly. "They act like they was spoilin' for trouble!"

The ranchers were. They were the same men with whom Rainbow and Grumpy had had their brush in Crazy Horse. Jim Goodnight rode at their head. A bunch of steers had been run off of Tas Johnson's Lazy Lightning spread only last night, and they were trailing the rustlers, or trying to. A while ago the sign of the stolen steers had faded out, as it always did. It made them savage with desperation. If things went on as they had been going, it would mean ruin for them all.

Only by jamming Bart Galey aside did Jim Goodnight keep to the fore as Rainbow and Grumpy drew near. Goodnight said,

"You better explain what you're doin' on this range, Ripley!" His eyes flashed and it was plain he was holding himself with a tight rein.

Rainbow's voice was level. "Maybe I don't have to tell you there was an accident on the railroad the other day, Goodnight."

"Those tie cars?" The other nodded curtly. "I heard about it."

"Since then we've been followin' sign pretty close. It's what we're doin' right now."

A silence fell, and Goodnight's face got red. But it was Bart Galey who burst out angrily, "What in hell are you drivin' at?" He edged forward, his hand on his gun. "Damn yore soul, Ripley, I'll run you out of this country singlehanded if I have to!" Goodnight waved him to silence.

"The railroad property ends quite a piece back," he said pointedly. "You're on Wishbone range now."

It was Rainbow's turn to flush, his jaws hardening. "We both seem to be doin' some trespassin', Goodnight. Hereafter, you keep your men off the Nevada Midland right of way!"

Goodnight's lips thinned. "Is that a warnin'?"

"It's an order!" The words rang clear. "I don't need anybody to tell me that some of your crowd knows plenty about the accident to those tie cars, and I don't think you do! It's your game to put Sharon Longstreet's railroad out of commission!"

The tension built up in a flash. The cowmen muttered, shifting restlessly. Goodnight's next words came with a rush. Secretly as concerned for Sharon Longstreet's welfare as ever, sudden jealousy of Ripley's interest in her shot through him like a flame.

"I'll believe Sharon thinks that when she says

so to my face! As for you, Ripley, remember this: I'll take better care of what belongs to her than you ever will!"

For a long moment their eyes clashed. Only the hope that something might yet come of this held Bart Galey and the others in check. Grumpy's unwinking regard was trained on them, waiting for the first move.

Rainbow seemed at length to satisfy himself of something. Deliberately he turned his bronc. "Come on, Grumpy," he murmured. "We'll be on our way."

"Hold on, here!" Bart Galey jerked out truculently. He whirled to Goodnight. "They can't get away with this! Yuh heard what he accused us of!"

The others seconded his sentiment; even Tas Johnson glared at Rainbow and Grumpy as if he distrusted them deeply; but Goodnight silenced his men in short order. "Ripley said his piece," he rasped flatly, "and he got his answer! That closes the matter—for now!"

It was with frank reluctance that Grumpy turned his back on these belligerent men and jogged away beside Rainbow. Fighting rawhide that he was, he wanted little excuse to carry the gauge to them. Only mature judgment kept Rainbow from feeling the same way. But the words of which he unburdened himself ten minutes later showed that he could think soberly as well.

"You may be right about Slack after all, Grumpy. Goodnight knew nothing about that wreck; what he said convinced me of that." He reflected a moment, his brows knit. "Of course that still leaves Galey and the other hotheads to consider."

"Reckon I'd have considered 'em on the spot, with the business end of a six gun, if I'd been doin' it!" Grumpy grumbled. Rainbow shook his head.

"No you wouldn't. Startin' a fuss with all of them would be a fine way to bring up at the short end of a rope. You know that as well as I."

Grumpy did, but he was not in a mood to admit it. A moment later he said, "I'll say old Tas Johnson put on a fine job of actin' back there—if that's what he was doin'. Glared at us as if he hated our innards!"

"Good thing he did," Rainbow came back promptly. "That's just what I told him to do."

"Then yuh don't think he's changed his mind about us again?"

"Since last night? No, I don't." Rainbow's tone was serene. "If you're lookin' for trouble as usual, Grumpy, you won't find any this time, I'm afraid. If Johnson had given us away back there—spilled the beans and sailed into us all spraddled out— that would 've been somethin' to worry about. Until somethin' like that happens, you'll have to find a better reason to make me think we've had all our work for nothin'."

12

Things were so quiet that night in Lost Angel that it seemed the camp might never have been the scene of a great excitement. Rainbow improved the occasion by getting better acquainted with Sukey Withers. The store was quiet an hour after supper; Slack's men were playing cards in the old store where they took their meals and even the usual hangers-on had drifted over to watch. Seated on the counter over which Withers sold his liquor and tobacco and an occasional pair of boots, Rainbow began with casual questions.

At first indifferent, Withers soon swung with enthusiasm into a narrative of Lost Angel in its heyday. He had seen it all; no part of the feverish gold excitement which had built this camp in a few short months had passed him by.

"You'd think from all yuh hear that the Buckskin was the biggest mine round hyar. T'wan't," said Sukey. "Mebby 'twas the steadiest payin', but purty small pertaters alongside some I've seen. There was the Ophir, now. Seven hunderd thousan' dollars taken out of 'er in three weeks! By two brothers. McDonald, their name was. Or take the Big Bonanza . . ."

His reminiscences flowed on. Gradually Rainbow gained a picture of a roaring camp not inferior to Virginia City or even some of the California strikes in their day.

Switching the talk to the Nevada Midland, Rainbow elicited information which deeply interested him concerning Sharon Longstreet's father. Colonel Tom Longstreet, as he was called, had been a dyed-in-the-wool pioneer in more ways than one. As a boy he had freighted across Indian country and the desert, building a comfortable fortune for himself before he was thirty. Then had come an adventure in Oregon, where he had met the girl who was to be his wife—daughter of a westward-moving Missouri farmer who had driven his own covered wagon from Westport over the long trail following the Platte, the Sweetwater and the Snake, to fat acres in the shadow of the Cascades.

That girl had died at Sharon's birth, and Longstreet, selling out a thriving stage line in the far northwest and leaving that land of bitter memories, had drifted to Nevada in search of new worlds to conquer; the language of a man on his lips, and companioned by a sunburned, whiplike girl who might have been born a boy.

Rainbow followed closely the story of the Nevada Midland's building. Sukey Withers had been Longstreet's right-hand man in those days. Appointed marshal of the hell-roaring camp, he had maintained order in his rough fashion, mastered and domineered through it all by just one person—Sharon. Sukey still idolized the girl; still told himself he was watching over her best interests. It was what had held him in Lost Angel during the dead years. For someday, he averred with unshakable conviction, the camp would come back; the mines would reopen to pour out their endless streams of gold and silver; and then Sharon would need someone, a man or two like Sukey Withers and Cyclone Bradley, say, to stand beside her and back her up.

Rolling himself in his blanket that night, Rainbow's head was full of Sharon Longstreet. The last image to float across his fancy before he dozed off was her soft face, as vividly real as if she stood before him in the flesh. She had a strange drag for him, in no wise lessened by the fact that she was a person of her hands; that she knew how to do things, to make a go of it when it seemed there was no going on.

Nor did the fact that Jim Goodnight had broken with her, it seemed irreparably, in any wise diminish Rainbow's interest in the girl.

If he was still thinking of her the following morning, however, Grumpy received no inkling of it. "Shucks, Rainbow," he grumbled as they made ready to ride in the early dawn. "This is a dang wild-goose chase fer a couple long-haired cow waddies like us to be on! Why not take a day off to give to our own affairs?"

Rainbow shot him a look. "You don't mean a

day off to take it easy in, by any chance?" he queried dryly.

It was so near the mark that Grumpy's visage reddened and he began to argue heatedly. Rainbow cut him off. "We've marked out our trail," was his ultimatum, "and we'll follow it. For now, anyway."

Dan Slack had spent the night in Lost Angel. He met them in the street as they were starting out. "Boys," he greeted, with an affable wave of the hand, "how's everything goin'?"

"Wal, yesterday—" Grumpy began, but Rainbow cut in smoothly, "No excitement to speak of, Slack. We seem to be gettin' a break since the tie cars went down the canyon."

Slack nodded. His beady, unwinking eyes regarded them steadily. "Glad to hear it. It won't always be that way. But what's this about yesterday?"

He was looking at Grumpy. Before the latter could speak up, however, Rainbow said, "Why, we ran across some horse sign that had us wonderin'. Lost it after a little ways. There was nothin' out of the way."

"Don't be too shore of that!" Slack cautioned him soberly. "It would be dead easy for some bull-headed cowman to shove a few sticks of dynamite under the rails and blow out a section! That's exactly what I'm guardin' against, Ripley. I hired you to take the unexpectedness out of our troubles."

171

Rainbow nodded. "That's what we spend sixteen hours a day thinkin' about."

"Then yuh better make it twenty-four!" Slack returned curtly.

Grumpy's features darkened. He stared at Slack angrily and was on the point of a biting retort, when Rainbow headed him off. "That's right," he said equably. And to Grumpy, "We'll be shovin' off, I reckon."

Grumpy allowed himself to be overridden then; but they were scarcely beyond earshot before he burst out, "He's got a gall, talkin' to us that way! 'Better make it twenty-four hours,' he says. What's he mean by it?"

"He's got a legitimate kick," Rainbow surprised him by answering reasonably. "No sooner than he hired us, things started to happen; I'm surprised he hasn't made a crack about it before this. It's one of the few things that make me suspect he may be hooked up with it all, somewhere."

Grumpy had never thought of this before. He grunted as the impact of it hit him. "Why, say; that is a fact."

"You get it now, eh?" Rainbow's tone was thin. "Maybe it occurs to you there's some meanin' in the rest of what he said."

"Yuh mean about the dynamite under the tracks?"

"That's what I mean!"

Grumpy said "Hmm!" and turned that over thoroughly.

"His sayin' a thing like that may be just accidental," Rainbow drove on, "but I'm not inclined to give him an inch. What if a hole did turn up where the track ought to be?"

"Yuh said yoreself that Slack needs that locomotive too much in his business to wreck it," Grumpy argued.

"And maybe I've changed my mind since then," Rainbow caught him up.

"What yuh drivin' at now?"

"I may be wrong," Rainbow said slowly, "and I hope I am. But it wouldn't surprise me if Slack was to turn on Miss Longstreet all of a sudden."

"What for?" Grumpy demanded, amazed.

"He'd be pretty likely to hide his reason well," was the answer, "but it would be a good one. And don't look so disgusted! I've yet to see the time I was absolutely satisfied about Slack's intentions toward anyone but himself. He's been doin' a lot for Sharon; givin' her freight to carry and hirin' us—"

"And gettin' wrathy because she wants to accommodate the Raven brothers!" Grumpy inserted. It brought Rainbow up short.

"That's true. She lost time, cars and money to pay for those lost ties," he pondered. "Funny this is the first time I ever looked at that business from any angle except our own. Why, Grumpy," he discovered, "if Slack could have been sure that accident would turn out as it did, it would be a cast-iron motive for him to have caused it!"

Grumpy was watching him shrewdly. "Where's that leave us?" he queried. But his own thoughts were busy, for a moment later he added, "There's one thing we got left that we ain't done."

"What's that?"

"Havin' a look around up at that tie camp in Singer Canyon!" Grumpy gauged the effect of his words. "Let's ride up there right now an' have a look around."

Rainbow shook a decided negative. "I've been thinkin' about just that," he admitted. "We'll do it—but not now—not after what Slack said about the dynamite. That sounded too much like a build-up for an 'I told you so!' to me. We're ridin' the tracks today, and ridin' them careful! If there's anything we miss seein', it 'll be because we can be in only one place at a time."

They did as he said. But watch as they would, they saw nothing out of the ordinary. It was no child's play to stick to the thankless task, while the glare of the sun seemed to gather and concentrate along the ballasted right of way; when all the time speculation beat at them with its tiny insistent hammers, urging them to be elsewhere and more profitably employed.

"Swell chance of our bein' able to do anything about it, if the track was goin' to be blasted," Grumpy gave it as his opinion, late that afternoon. "With Slack behind it, as yuh suggest, he'd be dang shore we was elsewhere when it happened!"

"I don't know," Rainbow clung to his doubt. "We might be somewhere else, but we could hardly get beyond hearing of a blast that would do any real harm, in these hills."

The words were hardly out of his mouth before both of them drew in with a jerk and sat straining their ears. From far away had come a dull, thunderous rumble. It lasted only a couple of seconds and their eyes met in mutual questioning when it was over.

"Reckon we *could* hear a good, rousin' blast this far from the Buckskin," Grumpy hazarded dubiously.

Rainbow scanned the bulky, cotton-white scrolls in the sky. "It's a cinch those clouds aren't heavy enough for a whisper of storm," he muttered in a worried tone. "That was a blast an' no mistake!" He shoved his bronc forward in the direction from which the sound had come. "Shake it up, Grumpy! We're makin' sure of this!"

Grumpy's disgust at the necessity was large.

"We're meetin' Tas Johnson tonight," he reminded. "It's only a few miles from here too. But no, we got to fog to hell an' gone up the line— an' then traipse back ag'in!"

He would have added more, but Rainbow's silence warned him that this time, at least, no argument would avail. Following the railroad track, they covered several miles. Grumpy was on the point of a salty "I told yuh so!" of his own, when Rainbow, in the lead, stiffened to stare ahead fixedly.

"What is that, along there in the cut?"

The westering sun was so low that its glare filled their eyes; but a moment later they made out what it was that had attracted Rainbow's attention.

"Jumpin' Judas!" Grumpy ejaculated. "There's a hunk uh track gone that 'd swaller a dozen cars!"

Drawing near, they saw that his words were true. At a point between cutbanks where the sound of the explosion would be baffled and thrown into senseless echoes amongst the hills, a dozen sticks of blasting powder had been thrust under the track and set off. For the space of twenty yards, the roadbed was torn up and pitted; the rails themselves little more than snarled lengths of twisted iron.

Grumpy looked the spot over and said "Huh!" in a puzzled voice. Rainbow lost no time in turning back down the track a couple of hundred yards, where he affixed to a rail the warning torpedoes he carried in his saddlebag for just such an emergency. He came back with a thoughtful expression on his face.

"Wal," Grumpy grated, "who was it this time? Slack or them cowmen?"

Rainbow rasped his chin. "It could 've been either one," he decided soberly. "Those ranchers were rarin' to go yesterday. 'Yuh heard what he

176

accused us of!' Bart Galey said. A child could have guessed he was just itchin' to accommodate. On the other hand," he continued in a puzzled tone, "Slack as much as told us we could expect just this. How would he know, unless—"

"Yeh, how?" Grumpy echoed sourly, and added, "I don't s'pose there's much doubt where Slack 'll lay the blame!"

"Well," Rainbow began. "There's no time to lose. One of us will have to make for Lost Angel with word for Slack."

"An' meanwhile, you'll be doin' what?" Grumpy hurled at him with supreme disgust, seeing in what quarter the wind lay. Rainbow grinned at him.

"Why, I'll be meetin' Tas Johnson as we planned," he said smoothly. "We can't miss up after what's happened. If Slack asks where I am, I've gone to Indian Wells to get word to Miss Longstreet."

Grumpy found no choice but to start on his errand. He did so a few minutes later. Rainbow made a complete circle around the spot where the rails had been blasted, found no tracks and swung back into the saddle. With his last glimpse of Grumpy, receding in the distance on the way to Lost Angel, the sun dipped behind the far flank of Superstition Mountain. Shadows swam up out of the east.

A mile away in the hills, a man crouching behind

a rocky ledge watched all that went on below. It was Slicer Cully. He knew it was Ripley and Gibbs down there; his blowing up of the track had been designed to draw them here, and it had succeeded. He had made sure they would be unable to trail him. A grim smile cracked his sinister visage when Grumpy pulled away; a few minutes later, when Rainbow started in the opposite direction, Cully stood up, nodding his bullet head.

"That 'll keep them hombres busy fer a spell," he muttered. "Now if me an' the boys can fool Goodnight's crowd the same way, we'll drive off a sizeable bunch tonight without a skimp of trouble!"

He swung up on his bronc and started back to join the rustlers.

Turning his mount's head back down the hills, Rainbow rode steadily through the evening and was still far from his objective when dusk cloaked the land. An hour after dark he judged himself to be nearing the Wishbone range. Later he spotted a landmark named by Tas Johnson. Setting a course by that, he was soon at the appointed rendezvous, a blasted and riven sentinel rock rising high above the surrounding country.

Johnson was not there. But Rainbow was slightly ahead of time. Rolling a cigarette absent-mindedly, and then breaking and scattering its contents to the breeze when he was on the point of striking a match, he went over in mind the things he wanted to discuss with old Tas. The night was vast, still, seemingly empty. Rainbow had barely reached the end of his cogitations when a voice roughened with reserved suspicion said,

"So yuh showed up, did yuh?"

Rainbow whirled. He didn't need that tall, lanky shape outlined against the faint horizon stars to tell him that Johnson had come.

"Sure I'm here. Did you think I wouldn't be, Johnson?"

Tas grunted, "Hard to tell. But I reckon yuh got brass 'nough to do anything yuh want, Ripley."

Rainbow studied him narrowly. He didn't exactly like that tone. "Don't tell me you've been changin' your mind about this again," he said.

"It's dang queer," said Tas cagily, an edge to his voice, "that a bunch uh my Lazy Lightnin' stuff should be hazed off the very night we had our powwow! Where was you an' yore pardner when that was goin' on?"

Rainbow stared at him. "You mean that's what you were doin' yesterday—trackin' some rustlers who got into your own stuff?" A prickling sensation ran up his neck at the back, and he began to understand things better.

"I don't mean nothin' different!"

Rainbow said slowly, "That's bad. Just tell me exactly what happened, Johnson, and what you learned."

179

"I shore wisht I could satisfy myself about you!" Tas burst out explosively. "It's dang funny yuh turned up the other night, jest when yuh did an' of yore own accord!"

The words vibrated with uncertainty. Rainbow's answer was short. "It was damned lucky, I should say. If I'd turned up at your place any time since, I wouldn't have been very likely to find you home."

"No," Tas growled in his throat, "yuh wouldn't at that. Where's yore pardner?" he broke off with sudden suspicion.

Rainbow told about the dynamited track, adding that Grumpy had gone to Lost Angel with word for Slack. Johnson nodded grudgingly. "Reckon I heard a whisper of that rumble, 'way here. Dang me," he drove on forcefully, "yuh got an answer every time, Ripley! It allus seems to be a good 'un, too. Yuh shore got a way about yuh. When I'm off by myself I git all sorts uh suspicions about yuh; but when yuh start to talk, yuh got me with yuh right off."

"Any man would be cagy at a time like this," Rainbow told him easily. "I don't blame you a bit."

"Huh!" Old Tas was entirely mollified. "Lookin' at it that way, I reckon yuh got reason to be suspicious of folks yoreself. Things 've shore been goin' against yuh since takin' over here. Got any idee who blasted the railroad track?" And at Rainbow's prompt negative, "Wal, that puts yuh right in the same class with us, then—with one more mysterious affair to chalk up."

"There's something twisty about this whole setup," Rainbow admitted, "that I haven't got the straight of at all. Soon as I do, things will begin to drop into place and I'll produce results in a hurry."

His quiet tone carried conviction. Tas peered at him keenly, then nodded his endorsement. "Reckon yuh will. Meanwhile—"

"I'm still waitin' for the story about your rustled stuff," Rainbow inserted gently.

Johnson quickly supplied the deficiency. According to his tale, the rustlers were getting bolder. One of his two punchers, both of whom had been riding guard on the night of the rustling, had been jumped unwarningly—attacked from the brush, gun whipped and left lying stove up and unconscious on the ground. The other had been run several miles by a trio of killers. In the meantime, a bunch of Tas's Lazy Lightning stuff had been cut out and hazed away in almost leisurely fashion.

Rainbow was following the narrative closely. "None of the rustlers were spotted, I suppose?"

"Unh-uh."

"So you turned to the other cowmen for help. Find out anything at all?"

"Not a thing," Tas confessed. But he hesitated as he spoke. On Rainbow's pressing him, he added, "I may be a dang fool, Ripley, but I think I know where them steers went! Goodnight as much as advised me to forget it. I did, then—but it keeps comin' back."

"Out with it," Rainbow grunted.

There was a deep rocky canyon, a veritable gash of Thor's giant hammer, in the rear flank of Superstition Mountain, into which Tas had reason to believe his steers had been driven. It was a blind box canyon only a few miles long, he admitted. It sounded crazy on the face of it that rustlers should shove their heads in a trap. Although he had passed it up while he was with the other ranchers, Johnson had later gone back to examine that canyon. He had found nothing; but still he was far from satisfied.

Rainbow reflected briefly. "Would you care to take me there now?" he queried. "There 'll be a moon later."

"Shore, I will!" Tas was only too willing. "Let's get goin'!"

Without more ado, they turned their ponies and started off through the velvety night.

13

A few miles to the north the dark bulk of Superstition cut its silhouette against the luminous night. To the east the sky was tinged with silver— the moon would make its appearance shortly above the serrated range behind which it hid.

"What," Rainbow asked his companion, "did Goodnight have to say about your returning to this canyon for a look around?"

"Reckon Jim don't know it," was the reply. "I ain't seen him since the afternoon we met you."

"Where's he keepin' himself?" Rainbow queried quickly.

"Reckon he's follerin' some trail of his own. I ain't had time to find out." Old Tas's tone was grim. He went on, "It's one thing to be givin' yore neighbors a hand in time of trouble, Ripley; but when it's yore own stuff that disappears, yuh git down to business an' no foolin' around about it!"

After a silence, Rainbow pursued, "You don't blame me for the tone I took the other day with Goodnight, Johnson?"

" 'Bout the railroad wreck?" said Tas. "Wal—I reckoned yuh was workin' some slant uh yore own."

"I was. Whoever was responsible for the wreck and for me and Grumpy almost gettin' killed, it wasn't anything Goodnight knew a thing about."

"Did yuh think he did?"

"I didn't know," Rainbow answered simply. "My system is that once you prove a thing, you can be sure of it."

"But it don't go beyond Goodnight, in this case—is that it?" old Tas probed shrewdly.

Rainbow wasn't ready to answer that question, and he evaded it smoothly. "Outside of you, I don't know the rest of his crowd well enough to say a word. But we're drawin' close to the mountain, Johnson. Where is this canyon you were talkin' about?"

Tas led the way across a treacherous malpais toward a darker splash of shadow on the flank of Superstition. "The' ain't a clump uh brush or blade uh grass in the canyon," he murmured, "nothin' but rocks an' sand an' mebby a few snakes. Coffin Canyon, it's called. Few folks comes here unless they have to; an' there's dang few reasons fer that."

Unconsciously he had lowered his voice. Rainbow caught the gathering tension of it. Nor was it wholly a tribute to the spookiness of the hour or the gloomy suggestion of this isolated spot. Definite menace reached out silently to push against him. Its feel was unmistakable, and its cause just as obscure.

They had not yet reached the far edge of the malpais when the moon, an enormous globe which glowed orange, lifted above the rocky tips of the far mountains. It bathed their surroundings in a weird illumination which brightened as the orb climbed beyond the thick layer of atmosphere. Now Rainbow could see plainly the ragged opening of Coffin Canyon.

A few minutes later they threaded ledges and rock heaps within the portal. Rainbow was busy scanning the place. "Ever spot cattle sign here?" he inquired.

"Shore—drifters. But wait 'll yuh see, Ripley."

They rode into the canyon. Here shadows gathered around them like rustling curtains; the eery hoot of an owl sounded from the crags. Rainbow stiffened at that, then relaxed. Night riders often imitated that call for reasons of their own; but there was no duplicating the real thing. This was—for it fluttered out over the canyon a moment later with a dry fluttering of wings, disgusted at being disturbed.

Old Tas cocked a bleak eye at the night flyer, muttering into his mustache. A few minutes later he pulled up at a point nearly half a mile beyond the canyon's mouth and with a wave of the hand indicated a rough circle of rocks which Rainbow recognized at once as a possible corral.

"Have a look at that!" he rumbled.

Rainbow pushed forward. Then he dismounted, his interest deepening with every passing moment. The rock circle *had* been used as a corral, and recently, he discovered; there were droppings inside not more than two or three days old.

Rainbow was still pursuing his investigations when some muffled sound from down the canyon drifted to his ears. On the heels of it, old Tas hissed from outside the gate, "Psst!"

Rainbow reached his side in half-a-dozen noiseless strides. "What was that?" he whispered.

"Riders comin', I think," was the answer. "Hold on a minute."

"We better pull away from here while we're doin' it!" Rainbow returned grimly. "Bein' jumped in this place by a bunch of rustlers is just the opposite to what I want!"

Tas's assent was wordless. Both knew they had little time to spare. But even as they started away, the thud of hoofs grew in volume and a deep murmur of voices reached their ears.

The canyon at this point was incredibly rough, its floor broken by humps, upthrusts of rock, boulder patches. Rainbow and Tas succeeded in reaching cover before they were seen; but they had scarcely hauled up, intent on crawling to some rocky point of vantage, when a harsh exclamation sounded from the corral:

"Watch out, boys!" it warned. "There's somebody down in here!"

"What yuh mean?"

"Them tracks—they wasn't here an hour ago! There may be half-a-dozen guns trained on us right now!"

Questions and answers crackled back and forth with the snap of whips. A tension built up to which the feeling Rainbow had experienced before was as nothing. He was not yet absolutely certain who the men back at the corral were; but some instinct cried danger, and Tas's reason for bringing him here warned of rustlers.

Johnson was a salty old juniper. Standing arrested, his jaw squared, he shot a questioning look at Rainbow. "Shall we jump them skunks an' skin us a hide or two?" he growled.

He had his answer the next moment. Someone below had taken charge decisively: a bull voice which teased Rainbow with familiarity, but which he couldn't quite place.

"Spread out, boys, an' comb the rocks!" it snapped. "There ain't but two of 'em. Smoke 'em out!"

There was a scrape and whirl of hoofs. Rainbow said hurriedly, "It's two against five or six. This is no place for us!" He whirled his pony and started away, Johnson following.

Tas was just opening his mouth to speak when a gun crashed. The slug screamed off the rocks beyond Rainbow; a second shot roared, then more, the echoes slamming back and forth in these rocky confines.

Rainbow threw his Colt and sent a string of slugs backward. For the moment it discouraged pursuit, while old Tas jammed his mount over the rough going; but it also advertised their where-abouts beyond question. Jamming in the spurs, Rainbow caught up with his companion. "Where to?" he jerked out.

"There ain't nowheres to go!" Tas tossed back raggedly. "We're caught like rats in a trap, Ripley! We're bound to be cornered—unless we climb the blasted walls!"

Behind them they could hear the gathering

clatter of pursuit. Men cried to one another; further firing awakened the dead echoes of Coffin Canyon. But the fugitives had quartered across the canyon floor, momentarily losing the enemy. Rainbow grunted, "Keep on up the canyon! We'll hit on somethin'—we've got to!"

The following instant a harsh yell shattered the taut silence. "There they go! This way—this way!"

Old Tas drew in with a jerk, his bronc sliding on all fours. "That was Bart Galey's voice!" he exclaimed. "Hell, Ripley—if that's the boys out there, we're runnin' away from nothin'!"

Rainbow soon disabused him of that opinion. "Not so as you could notice it!" he ground out, grasping Johnson's bridle and hurling him forward. "Keep goin', Johnson! That may be the cowmen, as you say; but I can't see in it any reason for our bein' found together!"

Slugs droning around their heads made a swift change in Tas's own view of the situation. He began to swear; and his belief that the pursuers were his friends, who had mistaken himself and Rainbow for rustlers, did not prevent him from flinging a warning shot or two over his shoulder.

As for Rainbow, he gave all his attention to putting distance behind him. It was impossible to strike a good speed. The shadows flung by the rocks were deceptive; again and again the horses stumbled, only to be saved from a nasty fall in the nick of time. Leading the way, Rainbow did not neglect to cast anxious, questing glances over the broken, precipitous walls. Suddenly he reined down to stare at a slanting fissure running up the south wall.

"What yuh thinkin' of?" Tas demanded.

"I'm askin' myself if we can climb that."

"Nothin' like tryin'!" Johnson whipped out. He honestly didn't think they could; but there was little point in hanging back for that reason. It was certain that nothing better was likely to offer anywhere in the rugged length of Coffin Canyon.

Jamming the broncs that way, they were soon at the foot of the fissure. It was little more than a razoredge running upward along the cliff face. Rainbow shot one keen, inquiring look over its length and then applied himself to the immediate present.

His bronc took the ledge with misgivings at first, but climbed as if it seemed to know the need for haste. Johnson stayed close to his heels. Before fifty yards had been covered, however, both horses balked. Gritting his teeth, Rainbow slid out of the hull and began to lead the way upward. His confidence was enough to persuade the pony to follow.

Steadily they wormed on toward the top. They were in full view of the canyon floor now. Suddenly a man yelled down there; a rifle crashed. Granite dust sprang from the cliff face at Rainbow's feet. The next shot was closer.

"God!" old Tas burst out hoarsely. "This is a piece uh damned foolishness, Ripley! We'll never make it to the top! If we get stuck before we're knocked off by a slug, we kin never turn around!"

"We ain't turnin' around this trip," was the curt response. "Backin' up ain't my style!"

Tas said no more. There was little attention to be spared for anything but the going immediately underfoot; but in the stolen glances Rainbow took in the direction of their pursuers, he managed to make out at least five men, several of whom were pinning their faith on their rifles, pounding away steadily; while two others raced to the foot of the fissure and started to climb up in pursuit.

"They're determined to finish us and no mistake about it!" Rainbow reflected, seeing that. Halting, he rasped to Tas, "Take a crack at those gents tryin' to follow us, just to sort of discourage 'em, Johnson. I can't do it from here without shootin' too close to yore head."

Tas managed to get a clear view down the ledge and began to shoot. The measure of his earnestness was attested by the sudden outcry which greeted his efforts. Tas grunted.

"Got one of their hosses," he muttered; "an' dang near got them. Damn their hides, what do they mean, lightin' into a man this way before they even make shore who they're shootin' at?"

Rainbow said nothing; but it was beginning to

sink in even for Tas that he might have been mistaken about the identity of those men.

Had it not been for the deceptive light, the tricky angle of fire and an occasional rocky spire which afforded cover for a ways, the two could never have hoped to complete this hazardous climb. As it was, lead whined about them in a lethal hail and more than once the broncs received grazes which furrowed the hair.

Once the knife-edge track they were following threatened to peter out. Only by proceeding with the utmost caution, inching forward while the horses tested each foothold, were they able to cross the dangerous point in safety. After that the going gradually got better, a gully opening out which led all the way up to the rim.

"I'll hand it to yuh, Ripley," old Tas exclaimed gruffly, "yo're the first gent I ever heard of found a trail out of Coffin Canyon!"

"Yeh. Well," Rainbow answered, "we're not out of it yet, Tas."

"Yuh mean they may circle back an' come foggin' at us again?"

"Somethin' like that." It had not escaped Rainbow, from the savageness of the attack on them, that their lives would not have been worth a moment's purchase had their luck been any less good, or had he thought slower than he had done.

"By God, anybody that comes at me in the open,

after this, better come a-smokin'!" Johnson ejaculated angrily.

The first sign that Rainbow had come close to the truth in his prediction was a bullet which struck the rocks near at hand as they threaded their way over the high shoulder of Superstition, and whined away into space. The crack of the rifle came faintly, whipped away by the breeze.

"Which way 'd that come from?" Tas barked. Rainbow swept an arm toward the west.

"Somewhere over there!" He struck in the spurs as he spoke. "Let's go, Johnson! This 'll be an even break—for us, if not for the hombre behind that rifle!"

A crisp fusillade broke out as they started off, seeming to indicate panic in the marksman. But they were undeterred. Soon they drew near the would-be assassin.

Try as he would, Rainbow could get no glimpse of the man. But suddenly Johnson's pony faltered. It almost threw Tas. He caught himself somehow, hauled up angrily swearing. Rainbow drew in and wheeled back.

"Are you hit?" he rifled.

"No! It's my bronc, Ripley—must 've been nicked back there in the canyon. Keep a-goin'!" Tas was harsh. "I may be outa this, but you've got to nail that coyote!"

Rainbow saw that he was right. Johnson's horse might get him out of the rough country with careful nursing; but it would show no more speed tonight. Kneeing his bronc forward, Rainbow drove on. "See you at the same place—in two or three days, Tas!" he flung over his shoulder. The next moment Johnson dropped out of sight to the rear.

Rainbow had no fears about the old man's being able to take care of himself in the open despite the condition of his horse. He gave all his attention to the unknown he was bent on running to earth. That the other had turned to run was evident. The firing had broken off abruptly. A moment later Rainbow glimpsed the fleeing rider, streaking off through the stunted brush. He flung looks over his shoulder and must have spotted his pursuer; but he was too far in the lead for identification. Moreover, he seemed bent on making sure he was not overhauled.

There was an excellent chance that he might succeed; for the climb up the ledge from the floor of Coffin Canyon had taken the edge off Rainbow's mount. The latter refused to give up, however, getting every ounce of speed and strength he could out of the animal. Even so, he was chagrined to note his quarry steadily drawing away. Within ten minutes the man had got out of sight, and Rainbow gave up all hope of over-hauling him.

But he could track the man down, run him to his burrow, and that he determined to do. The moon was good for several hours yet. But for a long time Rainbow traced his man by the scent of the dust he had raised. He looked back only once.

"Maybe it's just as well you dropped out, Tas," he murmured his thought aloud. "It looks like this would be a long chase and a hard one!"

When the last dusty tinge was gone from the steady night breeze, he still had an occasional hoof mark or broken sage clump to guide him. For a long time Rainbow had noted that the way led generally southwest; he asked himself what lay in that direction and was unable to answer. There were no ranches that way—of this he was sure. He remembered talk of a back-trail store and saloon called Owyhee Crossing, which he had never seen; perhaps that was where the man ahead was going.

An hour later he broke into a little-used freight trail and nodded to himself.

The hour was late when Rainbow drew near the little collection of tumble-down buildings called Owyhee Crossing, but lights still threw a buttery glow from the saloon. Several hip-shot broncs dozed at the tie rack outside. He ran a critical eye over these; they told him nothing. Had his man driven on through this place?

Rainbow swung down and made for the saloon. Time was, he had heard, when it had possessed an unsavory reputation. Drifters, down-and-outers, even an occasional owlhoot, had hung out here if rumor was not at fault. With the rustling on the

Indian Wells range, cowmen were reputed to have cleaned the place out; but the original owner was still in possession, the spot was still isolated. One look inside would help Rainbow form his opinion of the setup.

Reaching the door, he pushed in. There were half-a-dozen men in the place: a threesome seated at a table in a shadowy corner, the bland-faced bartender, a sleepy-eyed swamper lounging against the wall. The one man who appeared to have just entered, standing before the bar with his elbow hooked on its edge, a glass before him, was Bart Galey.

14

Rainbow's eyes narrowed in a flash as they settled on Galey. He moved forward, not unaware of the sudden silence which thickened the atmosphere in this place. Turning with forced casualness, Bart met his gaze. His very stillness gave the effect of a start. Then, with a malicious twist, his lips parted,

"It's you, eh?"

Galey was a burly, knot-muscled block of a man. Bleak-eyed, his jaw square, jutting beyond an ugly iron-lipped mouth, he could have given pause to anyone not looking for trouble. Just now, Rainbow was.

Ignoring the bartender's restless expectancy, Rainbow moved close to Galey, pushing sidewise against the bar, all his attention fastened on the other. Bart noted this warily. His response to it came in a rasping bluster.

"Yuh got a gall, Ripley; ridin' this range like a damned nighthawk! What yuh after here?"

Rainbow's answer was soft only in tone.

"I'm after you, Galey."

As near as a man could simulate swift surprise, Galey did. His eyes widened, then pinched into inscrutable slits through which he drilled Rainbow with cold fury.

"So it's me yo're after," he drawled sarcastically in the electric pause. Rainbow guessed that a good half of his hostility was designed for its effect on these other men. "Suppose yuh jest say why!"

There was menace here, but not all of it was concentrated in Galey's taut form. The blank-faced trio at the table waited with a dreadful alertness for Rainbow's reply. He didn't keep them waiting.

"A dozen sticks of black powder were shoved under the Nevada Midland tracks today and touched off," he said thinly, "and, Galey, I think you did it!"

It threw a genuine jolt into Bart. Whatever he had expected, it had not been this.

"Huh?" he floundered. Catching himself then, his lip curled. "Yo're crazy, man! What do I care about the Nevada Midland, one way or another?"

It was almost jaunty; but Rainbow caught a flicker in his eye which said that Bart was thinking swiftly. Clearly it was he whom Rainbow had trailed across the range; just as clearly he had expected the latter to spring his attack from that angle. Now Rainbow's quick change of front had thrown him into uncertainty; he didn't know where he stood or what might be coming next.

"We'll take that up later, Galey! You planted that blast and destroyed the track!"

Galey's harsh laugh was half a sneer.

"How about provin' all this?" he proposed insolently.

"It don't need any proof," was the level answer. "When I pick up a set of tracks at the wrecked rails, and they lead me directly to you—"

"It's a lie!" Galey flamed, before Rainbow could continue. His wrathy indignation was real. "I never rode here from the railroad tracks at all!"

"Then where did you come from?" Rainbow shot out. Wholly unforeseen, the question threw Galey completely off his stride. He stumbled over his words.

"Well, I—I wasn't nowhere near the Nevada Midland! It ain't up to me to prove that! It's up to you, Ripley, an' yuh can't do it!"

"I can prove that you made the worst mistake of your life," Rainbow snapped back. "And I'm doin' it!" With the words he whipped over a short-arm jolt that sent Galey heeling back.

Bart caught himself with a bellow. His visage a mask of rage and hatred, he crouched, gathering himself for the attack. Tensing to meet that rush, Rainbow flashed a raking scrutiny over the other men. He was asking himself whether they would move to Galey's aid, but decided against it. They were keyed to watchfulness, but there was no indication that they would close in.

Still he wasn't satisfied. Only the sudden conviction that Galey *had* had something to do with the track blasting persuaded him to force matters—plus the fact that not two hours past Bart had made a determined attempt on his life. To bring Galey to book at the end of a six gun would be overstepping himself; but there were other ways of teaching a man a sharp lesson.

Galey's bull charge he evaded by side-stepping; chopping at the other's jaw on the instant. Bart flung past, reeling. But the only result was that his face went a deeper red, the deadly glint in his beady eyes a trifle wilder.

"I'll smash you, yuh sneakin' hound!" he ripped out.

His next rush was more wary. Rainbow found himself caught with his back to the bar, trading blows with the rapidity of gunfire. And there was dynamite in Galey's fists. Wherever one landed it left an aching numbness.

Rainbow gave as good as he got. Only by the exertion of sheer strength could he force Bart back until he had free play for his feet. Galey attempted to close with him and was met by a blinding barrage of slugs which left him momentarily dazed, groggy.

The watching men saw that. They were with Galey, it was clear from their encouraging exclamations; but something held them in bounds. One did jump up from his seat excitedly. Instead of rushing in to swarm over Rainbow, he aimed a kick at a spittoon. The vessel skidded across the floor, spilling its contents just as Rainbow made a rushing follow-up.

His boot slipped. Bart was quick to respond. Checking himself, he aimed a pile-driver blow at Rainbow's head. Rainbow tried to duck and cover. In a flash he found himself on the floor. Galey kicked viciously at his head, missed, and unable to control his blazing fury, landed on Rainbow's prone body, spraddled out like a springing cougar. They rolled over and over, locked in combat.

First Bart was on top, then Rainbow. His antagonist knew no rules; whenever he saw the chance to jam Rainbow's head against the bar rail, he did. After the second blow, the latter's brain reeled in threatened darkness; he fought instinctively, desperately.

There was a bitter drive in his determination. By

sheer strength he flung Galey from him, struggled to his knees. Bart scrambled up and plunged, breath whistling hoarsely. Caught in a viselike grip, he was thrown half the width of the room.

Rainbow staggered up then. He was giddy, his clothes ripped; blood ran down his cheek. But his fighting spirit was untouched. Galey let out a roar and charged, only to meet a swing from the shoulder that flung him farther than before. Chairs, a table, crashed over at his fall. His head thudded on the floor. He struggled up tigerishly.

This time Rainbow was standing over him. Bart got one look at that forbidding, rocky face and sank back.

"Get up!" the crisp order grated on his ear. Bart started to comply. But instead of reaching his feet, he plunged suddenly at Rainbow's knees. It was a tactical mistake, for Rainbow's falling body landed squarely on Bart's back, knocking the wind out of him.

Rainbow spared no more words and no more pity on the man. Scrambling erect, he fastened an iron grip on Galey's shoulder; jerked him up. A smashing blow sent Bart smashing down. Again Rainbow was on him, dragging him to his feet. Galey was so far gone that he was unable to keep his balance.

"Lay off, Ripley!" a man cried angrily. "Yuh licked him! Do yuh wanta finish him?"

It brought Rainbow to himself. Letting go of

Bart, he whirled. Bart fell back with a sodden thump, bloody, half conscious.

"He got what he deserved!" Rainbow jerked out. "Does anybody else want a taste of the same?"

Standing there, chest heaving, he stabbed them with cold eyes. He had lost his gun in the fight, had nothing but his fists and his wits. Nevertheless, there was that in him which held these men. Hard faced, they gave back stare for stare, but made no hostile move.

"Hell, yuh don't even know for shore that Galey did what yuh claimed he did!" one protested. "Yuh may 've been hired to look after that streak of rust, but don't go too far!"

Rainbow made sure they were keeping hands off, then turned and bent to pick up his gun. He straightened with a jerk at an involuntary movement of the bartender. That individual froze, eyes widening.

"Just be mighty careful what you do till I walk out of here," Rainbow told him wickedly.

"I ain't mixin' with this!" the man exclaimed nervously.

Rainbow jerked a nod. "Be sure you don't," he grunted. As for the others, he gave them a final chilly appraisal. They glowered but offered no interference as he turned toward the door.

"I might have a word to say about that cuspidor," he tossed back, "but I'll let it go. If there's ever a motion from this direction I don't like the looks of, I'll take the matter up without askin' any questions."

On the heels of that warning, he stepped out. At his bronc's head he waited a full minute, but the door remained empty. Swinging up, Rainbow cut around the buildings just to make sure and headed across the brush.

Ten minutes later he reined in beside the little creek which had given Owyhee Crossing its name, to wash up. Feeling better then, he rolled a smoke and headed in the direction of Lost Angel. It was a long ride, but he was in no hurry. Idly he wondered how Tas Johnson had made out—if he was home by now. It seemed likely. As for Grumpy, Rainbow was able easily to picture his partner's reaction on learning all he had missed. But a companion thought lingered in his mind which he finally put into words.

"I'd sure like to know how Slack takes the news of that wrecked track," he mused. A moment later he shook his head. "He'll be wrathy, of course; Slack's a wise coon. It might not tell me a thing."

As matters turned out, he was on the spot when Dan Slack received the news—or almost immediately afterward, at any rate. Jogging into Lost Angel's thrice-empty, dreaming street in the early morning, he was startled as he passed the hotel to hear human voices raised in argument. Slack and

202

Grumpy were standing together in the vacant brush lot beside the hotel; Rainbow reined that way, getting down and strolling forward.

He nodded as Slack turned to face him, but the latter neglected to return the greeting.

"Ripley, Gibbs tells me that a piece of track has been ripped out!" he exploded testily. "Dammit, man—that's what you were hired to prevent! Good God! Are yuh worth anything at all? How long ago was it I warned yuh just that might happen?"

His vehemence had Grumpy hot under the collar and breathing with difficulty. Plainly he had started to tell Slack off and was inwardly cursing the chance which had brought Rainbow on the scene before he was finished.

As for Rainbow, he looked from one to the other, a worried frown furrowing his brow slightly, and nodded.

"Yeh, you did, Slack. That's a fact," he admitted. "But don't tell me you just found out?"

"I went down the hills yesterday," Slack rasped, "and just now got back. Gibbs says he got word to Indian Wells last evenin'. I don't know what's the matter with that girl—she could 've notified me then!"

"Likely she didn't want to worry you," Rainbow inserted. "Murphy's busy makin' repairs, I expect?"

"He is; but yuh don't need to throw up a smoke screen of talk, Ripley! What the hell were you doin' yesterday when that blast was set off? Why wasn't yuh there to prevent it?"

Rainbow's eyes narrowed and he hesitated. Then his smile flashed out. "Reckon you've got an honest kick there," he said mildly. "The fact that we were makin' sure of the track a few miles away don't help a bit. We fell down, all right. The fact that I did somethin' about it after the track was wrecked don't help any, either."

"What's that?" Slack queried, caught. "What did you do about it?" Grumpy likewise bent an inquiring regard on his partner.

"When we saw how things were," Rainbow explained, "the same thought crossed my mind that's probably in yours right now: I thought of those cowmen. There was a bright moon last night; I found some tracks." He didn't think it necessary to say where he had found them. "They led me to the Owyhee Crossin' trail, where I lost them. But in the saloon at the Crossin', I found Bart Galey."

"Yes. And . . . ?"

"Why, I couldn't twist nothin' out of Galey, Slack. Naturally he wouldn't admit a thing. So I gave him a beatin' that 'll lay him out a few days and make him remember a whole lot longer."

Grumpy's jaw dropped; an odd look, half of regret, half of accusation, came into his eyes. Slack was studying Rainbow's features thoughtfully.

"I see," he said ponderously. Then he tightened up again. "Likely enough Galey was responsible; but as yuh say, that don't help a particle. I still say—"

"Would you tell Lint Granger about this?" Rainbow queried quickly, with pretended uncertainty. Slack snorted scornfully.

"Hell, no! What can the sheriff do—especially if yuh can't prove anything? Yuh should 've shoved lead at Galey, made it a real warnin' for his crowd!" He ground the words out in such a fashion that there was little doubt what he would have done, had he faced Bart Galey at Owyhee Crossing.

Rainbow nodded, impressed. "Maybe I should 've, at that. I was afraid I'd get in trouble that way; you wouldn't have even us to guard the railroad, Slack, if that happened."

"That's so." Slack appeared struck by the thought for the first time. He drove on sourly, "Although what good yuh are to me if things go right on happenin' behind yore back, I can't see! Can yuh promise me you'll do better from here out?"

His tone, if not his words, might have been construed in more ways than one. Grumpy growled in his throat, his bronze deepening; he stared in bewilderment as Rainbow put on a meek expression.

"You're payin' us big enough money, Slack," said the latter almost humbly. "There ain't anything we can do but buckle down and produce results."

"You better!" was the grating rejoinder. "I don't mind sayin' I'm considerable disappointed in you two. From yore reputation I expected more of yuh. If yuh can't do better, I'll have to—"

"You won't have to replace us," Rainbow assured him hurriedly, to Grumpy's supreme disgust. "I'll guarantee there 'll be no more dynamitin' done; we'll make sure of that!"

"Yuh got one more chance to do that," Slack said flatly. "I won't accept no more excuses, Ripley!" Turning on his heel, he strode off.

Grumpy stood staring after him, rage in his swelling jaws. "Damn it all, Rainbow!" he burst out. "I never thought it of yuh! What did yuh have to go suckin' up to him that way for?"

Surprisingly, Rainbow grinned at him. "Why, I've heard that butter 'll catch more flies than vinegar," he returned.

Grumpy's answer was a wrathy snort of disdain. "Mebby yo're right at that—if flies is what yo're after," he retorted stingingly.

Rainbow said no more. Getting his breakfast, he took his time but showed no inclination to get any sleep. "Get up your bronc, Grumpy," he said finally. "We'll be goin' to work."

"I suppose after Slack's call-down, we'll jest about be livin' on them railroad tracks," Grumpy grunted.

To his surprise, Rainbow shook his head. "Right now we're goin' up to Singer Canyon for that look around."

It satisfied Grumpy. Striking the Nevada Midland, they rode beside the tracks to a point from which, by cutting across the hills, they were able to reach Singer Canyon quickly. The Ravens and their crew were back in the timber, cutting pine; the partners had the camp on the spur to themselves. They made for the tracks.

"Here's where the last car stood," said Grumpy. They started to examine the ground systematically all about the spot. They found nothing till Rainbow bent over a track he found in the dust, frowned and began to follow it with some curiosity. Seeing him thus occupied, Grumpy came forward to look. A grunt escaped him.

"The man who made these tracks had a draggin' foot," Rainbow pointed out. "I don't recall any of Raven's *cholos* who was like that."

"No." A moment later, Grumpy added, "It wasn't made by a tie cutter at all, Rainbow! Here's his sign, strikin' off this way. He was headin' out fer some'eres!"

Swinging into the hull, they started to follow the trail. It led off across the range in the general direction of Lost Angel. Several times it faded out on the flinty ground, and once they lost it altogether, only to pick it up half an hour later. It disappeared for the last time within half a mile of the Buckskin Mine. Pushing on, they soon saw the mouth of one of the upper drifts, its heap of tailings tumbled down the mountainside.

Their eyes met when the significance of this dawned on them. "By gravy, there's somebody in that mine an' no mistake about it!" Grumpy exclaimed gruffly. "Remember what we found under the hotel? An' there was that business of the dump car, too!"

"And with his lease on the Buckskin and his men in there, Slack could 've known a lot about any one of those things," Rainbow concurred levelly. "But, Grumpy, it don't make sense! With one of his crowd almost killed there in the mine, and that track torn up that he needs. No, it brings us back every time to the same startin' point: Slack couldn't be behind all this!" He was frankly nonplussed by the results of his own reasoning.

"One thing is shore," Grumpy summed up shrewdly. "There's some hidden stake in this mine, Rainbow, a whole lot more important than tailin's! Aside from his row with these ranchers, Slack's up to some game of his own; there wouldn't be so much worryin' done 'bout us if he wasn't! But what's he drivin' at?"

They could find no immediate answer.

15

Dan Slack was talking to Con Murphy in Lost Angel's deserted street when several old men stepped out on the sagging porch of Sukey Withers's store. Slack noted them looking off across the hills. Glancing that way, he saw nothing at first. But a few moments later an old desert rat appeared on a high shoulder, driving two laden pack burros before him. He was coming this way.

Getting the last details of the condition of the Nevada Midland track, Slack only absently attended the arrival of the prospector. Withers, Bradley and their cronies were waiting for the latter. They greeted him heartily and took him into the store. Done with Murphy and about to turn away, Slack was caught by the sounds of jubilation coming from that direction.

He paused. His glance sharpened as it rested momentarily on the burros standing drowsily before the store. A thought clicked in his brain.

"That old rat's one of the bunch Withers has attracted here by his wild yarns of the camp openin' up again," he mused. Then he frowned. "There may be somethin' in it, at that. There's still gold in this country. The vein Bucktoe located in the Buckskin proves it."

Slack's frown deepened. If there was going to

be a fresh strike in this country, he intended to know about it. Moreover, were gold to be found, these grizzled old junipers could be depended on to locate it.

While Murphy walked off in the direction of the railroad right of way, Slack answered his impulse by heading for the store. He had come a long ways since his arrival on this range by the employment of ceaseless vigilance. And it would have been plain to the most casual that activities of considerable interest were going forward in the store.

Strolling in out of the blinding sunshine with his heavy, confident step, Slack was instantly aware of the blank silence which fell. The old-timers were gathered around the newcomer at one end of the counter. It was the latter who swept something off the counter with a lightning gesture and pocketed it before he turned to give Slack a furtive glance.

"Rye," Slack nodded to old Sukey. Sipping his drink and drumming absently on the counter with his fingers, he gave a good imitation of concentrating on his own affairs. Meanwhile his thoughts raced. Had the newcomer located a rich prospect? The elaborately casual small talk of the prospectors said yes. So did the ore samples which had disappeared in that old fellow's pocket, not too quickly for Slack to identify them for what they were.

But it became evident that he would learn

nothing by the simple process of eavesdropping. Whatever had made these rawhides so jubilant a couple of minutes ago was definitely smoothed over in his presence. Gritting his teeth, but with no outward evidence of his irritation, Slack finished his drink, paid for it and walked out.

As long as he was in sight of Withers's dirty store windows, he presented the prospect of his indifferent, retreating back; but a hundred yards up the street, Slack stopped, rested his shoulders against a crumbling wall, rolled a thoughtful cigarette and gave himself up to contemplation. There was not much he could arrive at, but that little was of definite interest.

"The old devil's found somethin' good," he reflected. "He's let his cronies in on it, but it stops there. Well, I'll find out what it is!"

There was a number of ways of learning, but Slack was a man of direct methods when they could be made to work. Without letting it be known, he watched Withers's store till he was sure Sukey was there alone. Then Slack went down there.

Sukey nodded to his order for another drink but offered no conversation. Slack stood at the counter awhile in silence. Abruptly he opened up, "Who were those old fellows in here a while ago, Withers? I can't place them myself."

Sukey mumbled something about their being friends of his.

"Oh. Prospectors, eh?" Slack seemed to have just arrived at the conclusion. And at Withers's grunt, "Reckon they're wastin' their time. Nothin' for their kind around here."

Sukey shrugged. He didn't appear anxious to discuss the subject.

"Would you say so?" Slack persisted.

"Ain't no tellin'," Sukey evaded easily. He was aware that Slack had referred to his faith in Lost Angel more than once as a "damned pipe dream," and he had no use for the man.

Slack laughed unpleasantly. "I suppose if a man gets an idea in his head, there's no budgin' him from it. But—" He broke off.

Sukey waited in frank disinterest, and Slack saw that he was to be prodded into no revelations through indignation. He began to toy with the situation more reasonably.

"Still, I expect some of these old junipers know more about quartz in a day than I'll ever learn. All jokin' aside, do yuh think they'll have any luck here?"

"Shore, I do!" Sukey answered explosively. He began to turn the color of a cock's comb. "Dammit, Slack, you've heard me declare myself often 'nough!"

"This prospector who drifted in today," Slack pursued speculatively, ignoring the other's contemptuous tone. "Thinks he's found somethin', don't he?"

"Hoke Waters?" Sukey was wary in a flash. The heat went out of his face and his eyes avoided Slack's. "What makes yuh think that?"

"Why, I spotted that sample he thought he shoved in his jeans so neat," Slack chuckled, with an appearance of frankness. "I can't say I take it as serious as he does. At the same time, of course, I'm interested in such things. What did that sample amount to, anyway?" he added like an afterthought.

It was Sukey's turn to exercise guile. "Didn't amount to much," he grunted.

"There was a lot of noise in here over nothin' as I came up the steps," Slack observed. It warned Sukey that Slack had indeed taken note of a good deal more than he had at first been ready to admit; the fact made Withers all the more cagey.

"Shucks. The boys was hurrahin' Hoke a mite. Wa'n't nothin' else to it," he averred.

Defeated at every turn in his effort to pry information out of old Sukey, Slack perforce allowed the subject to drop. But his suspicions were all the more inflamed by this determined secretiveness. Instead of letting the subject slip from his mind as he would have done ordinarily, he turned over the remaining ways by which he could hope to learn the truth.

The notion of having Hoke Waters trailed back to his prospect was abandoned at once both because of its clumsiness and because it entailed too much delay.

"I could go right to work on the old juniper himself," Slack mused darkly. But he was not sold on crude methods when an element of chance entered into their use; and his distrust of half-a-dozen such men as old Hoke and Sukey Withers was great.

He decided to canvass the possibilities more thoroughly before coming to a decision. The delay only sharpened his need to know what these old codgers thought fit to hide from him.

Hoke Waters had commandeered a tumble-down shack on the edge of camp. Here he settled down to hold court, smoking his short pipe contentedly in the sagging doorway while his burros browsed the brush near at hand.

Scouting the situation until he was forced to conclude that the old desert rat had no intention of leaving his belongings unguarded, even for a short time, Slack that afternoon found Hoke, Cyclone Bradley and a couple of other oldsters in the midst of a heated debate before the shack. And this time Slack did not make the mistake of breaking it up by showing himself.

"They're talkin' about the strike Waters made," he muttered, biting his lips with vexation.

There was no means of approaching them from the direction of the street. Only the brush remained, and Slack's eye roved that way, glazing with speculation. A moment later he nodded to some thought of his own.

Leaving the street, he worked down between two abandoned shacks till he was in the brush. Then he began to crawl toward the arguing prospectors. They were so absorbed that Slack was able from time to time to steal a look, his face flushed from the unaccustomed effort of this method of travel; his ears on the stretch. At last he was as close as he dared go through the thinning brush without danger of detection—and still he could catch only an occasional word.

His disappointment was keen. It seemed to him that fate was deliberately placing obstacles between him and what he wanted. A moment later he revised that impression. Perhaps after all it was only his daring that was being tested.

Some yards away a thick tongue of brush ran out, considerably closer to his objective. There was more than a chance that if he could reach that, he would be able to hear everything.

Cautiously Slack started to circle. A few minutes later he was working out through the neck of brush extending into the cleared space. Each time he paused to listen, the murmuring drone of voices at the shack grew louder. "Another dozen feet and they might just as well write me a letter," he told himself grimly.

Before he got that far, however, a sound halted him which at first he failed to recognize. It was like a body slithering through the sagebrush near at hand. Crouching, Slack maintained utter, breathless silence and immobility while he waited. Still the sound drew nearer. The fear flashed in his mind that he had been discovered; but still that drone of talk went on uninterrupted a dozen yards away. He couldn't understand it, unless Hoke Waters and his pals were preparing a sudden surprise for him which he would find extremely distasteful.

The next moment something like a grunt breaking on his ears whirled him around. Relief washed over him with a sudden burst of sweat. Instead of a shrewd-eyed desert rat glaring at him accusingly, Slack found himself staring at one of Hoke Waters's curious burros, wearing a bland expression of tolerance and waggling ears that might have been attached with ball bearings.

Slack puffed out his cheeks and got his breath. Everything was all right after all. But a second later he was glaring at the burro disgustedly.

"Don't stand there starin' at me and floppin' them damned elephant ears!" he muttered under his breath. "Hell, I might's well be wearin' a cow bell as have you taggin' me!"

Whatever the burro thought of the situation, it evinced no inclination to relinquish its interest. When Slack crawled a few feet, the animal pushed through the brush to a position from which it could watch more clearly. It was maddening.

Giving vent to his temper, Slack snatched up a fragment of rock and hurled it. The missile struck the burro's ribs and resounded like a low-pitched drum. Instead of showing resentment, the brute swiveled its ears and rolled back its eyes with every indication of blissful contentment.

"God!" Slack breathed. He didn't know what to make of his situation. Just as he was getting where he could really hear something, this had to happen! Worse than that, the talk at the shack broke off and Hoke Waters was heard to say clearly,

"What's Jinny scentin' out there in the bresh?"

"A bull snake, or a rattler," another hazarded in answer, with unconscious irony. "Leave 'er be, Hoke, she kin take keer of herself an' you too."

"So you say!" Hoke snorted, bristling. "Why, dang it all, Jinny's the most valyble half uh this yere pardnership! Jest step out there, will yuh, Lint, an' see what's bewitchin' that jackass?"

The man addressed growled under his breath and took half-a-dozen steps. Then he paused.

"Shucks! 'Tain't nothin', Hoke," he protested. "Yo're gittin' worse 'n an ole woman 'bout them canaries uh yores!"

"Am, huh?" Hoke snapped, the hackles rising. "Nemmine 'bout me an' them jackasses. Bein' afraid yo're goin' to be give an order is what's gripin' you, yuh cantankerous ole cuss!"

Slack did not hear the conclusion of the

argument. At the first word, a shock coursing through him, he started to crawl away hurriedly on all fours. Not if he could help it was he going to be discovered here. Even the excuse of an intended practical joke would be hardly likely to appease these old fighting roosters. Far from being willing to tangle with them, Slack didn't even want their attention called to himself, for sooner or later things might happen which would be awkward to explain away if his connection with them were learned.

Waters's burro trailed him a dozen yards before, dropping into a dry wash, Slack started away at a better speed. Not until he had won once more to the safety of Lost Angel's street did he relax; and even then his relief at the harmless conclusion of the adventure was tinged by chagrin that he had failed to overhear a word on the subject which by now held a position of utmost prominence in his thoughts.

Moreover, Slack had grown impatient of half measures. He put in the remainder of the day busying himself at the Buckskin, and an hour after supper made an almost elaborate affair of departing for Crazy Horse. Men watched him ride across the range, heading down the hills through the orange glow of sunset; they did not see him turn back when the gray shadows began to pool in the hollows and slowly swim upward, running together and thickening till they engulfed the land. An hour after dark, with the brilliant stars shining remotely, Slack drew near the camp once more.

Tethering his bronc in the brush, he circled the street and took in the setup. Things were about as usual, except that the buzz of talk at Sukey Withers's store was strangely animated. Slack hunted for Hoke Waters, found him present and nodded curtly to himself. "Why didn't I think of this in the first place?" he wondered as he headed for old Hoke's shack.

The place was plunged in deep gloom as he approached. But Slack had studied the layout that afternoon; he had no trouble finding the door and slipping inside. Listening intently, he satisfied himself that the shack was empty except for himself and started to rummage around. But at this point his luck broke down again; he had trouble laying his hands on what he was looking for.

"Where does the old fool keep his samples?" he thought. Feeling under a bunk for the heavy burlap sack which should have been there, he failed to find it. The meager heap of Waters's belongings in a corner of the room yielded nothing either.

Slack's face tightened in ugly lines at the reflection that Hoke might be carrying such samples as he possessed on his person. A moment later he shook his head.

"That can't be the answer. These old buzzards

are always knockin' off a chunk to carry away. I'll have to look somewhere else."

He was both cheered and vexed by the possibility that the prospector's samples had proven so rich that he had taken extra precautions in hiding them. Dared he risk a match? Something told him to refrain; yet so strong was his urge that he had one ready in his hand when a sound struck his ears which brought him up tense. What was that? The next moment it came again. Slack darted to the door, nerves jangling.

At the sound of stumbling boots and creaky, querulous voices all doubt was removed. Thank heaven these crotchety old birds were always haggling over something as long as they were together!

Despite his warning, Slack was not quick enough to cover all sound of his hasty retreat as he made around the corner of the shack and ducked into the brush.

"What was that?" he heard Hoke Waters raise his cracked tones sharply. "Somebody snoopin' around yere?" He rambled on, venting dark threats.

Whoever he had with him was not so troubled. "What? I didn't hear nothin'."

"If yuh hadn't been listenin' so hard to the sound of yore own voice," Hoke jerked out fiercely, "yuh would 've heard plenty!"

The answer was a snort. "Wal, if there *was* anythin', it must 've been a dog smellin' around.

Suke's got one of the critters hangin' round the store. Hell, Hoke, yo're all spooked up!"

Listening from the brush, Slack cursed under his breath even while his nerves were quieting down. A close shave, that time! And still he was without the sample he had to have. The harder it was to procure, the more definitely he decided that he had to get it.

For an hour he watched the shack in which a candle stuck in a bottle burned yellowly, while the two oldsters pottered about. Slack had never been so savagely impatient with the ways of the old. Their time was their own, of course, but they were enough to weary the devil himself before Hoke's visitor finally ambled away. Hoke stuffed his pipe, smoked it to the heel sitting in the doorway, and with a sigh, knocked it out, got up and blew out the candle at long last.

Slack was so close that he heard the old man's little moans of comfort as he stretched out in his blankets. He waited half an hour longer to make sure Waters had fallen asleep. This time, stealing in like a shadow, Slack determined he would stay till he laid hands on a sample, if he had to choke the knowledge of its whereabouts out of the old duffer.

As it turned out, there was no need of that. Exploring the head of the bunk with slothlike caution, within a foot of Hoke's face, after every other corner of the shack had offered a blank,

Slack felt his fingers come in contact with the roughness of broken rock. It sent a shock coursing over him, for the fact that an ore sample was as jealously guarded as this was ample proof of its value.

Carefully he lifted a chunk of quartz the size of his two balled fists. Standing there, testing Waters's quiet, even breathing for the first hint of wakefulness, he stuffed the sample into his shirt. He might have urgent need of both hands before he got out of here, and such an eventuality was not going to find him wanting. The sample once out of the way, he drew a deep breath. Nothing to keep him here any longer.

With the stealth of a cougar, he reached the door and slipped out. No need to worry about tracks: the ground here was packed hard. Five minutes later Slack reached his pony, swung up and headed down the hills at a space-devouring rack.

It was long after midnight when he jogged into Crazy Horse. Few lights burned except in the saloons. Slack forced himself to go home and rest; but the first streaks of dawn found him astir once more, and the proprietor of the little assay office near the Humboldt House found Slack seated on his step when he came to open up.

"Give me a report on this right away," Slack grunted, handing over the sample. The other hefted the chunk, shot him a surprised look and nodded without comment.

Later in the morning Slack listened wooden faced while the assayer told him that ore as rich as this sample would run better than one hundred and fifty dollars to the ton. Paying his fee, Slack folded the report and thrust it in his pocket. Thereafter, he was busy for some time around Crazy Horse; and though he strove to appear his usual impassive self outwardly, a close observer would have said that he had recently reached an important decision about which he intended to do something. He was still in the same exultant frame of mind when he headed once more for Lost Angel.

"The camp *is* comin' back!" he thought. "There 'll be rich pickin's for the lucky ones; and here's where I declare myself in on the ground floor!"

16

"Come on, Grumpy." Rainbow's tone was decisive. "We're trailin' that sign right to where it's goin' if it can be done!"

Returning to the last traces of the dragging foot, they quartered the ground thoroughly. Soon they were cutting wider and wider circles, without finding anything. Suddenly Grumpy straightened to stare. "What kin that be?" he queried, pointing.

They were high on the flank of Superstition Mountain, and it was toward a little cup on the slope that he was gazing. There was a patch of green amidst the brush. Without more words they pushed over there, to come out on the edge of a little garden. Its existence here was a surprise. No one was in sight, but in this cultivated patch of soil the prints of the dragging foot were thick. A plain trail led toward what looked like a cave in the rocks.

"This is the answer to our puzzle," Rainbow nodded his conviction. "Find the man who tends this garden and you've got the gent who wrecked the train!"

"If yo're right, we may git a slug square between the eyes while we're standin' here chinnin'! Let's move down the slope a ways!"

From the main entrance of the mine Dan Slack, Slicer and several other men saw them there, high up, without recognizing them. "Who is that?" Slicer rapped out tensely. "An' what are they after?" His tone said that it could be nothing good. Slack stared long and then grunted, "We'll see about this!" He started up, the others following.

Rainbow, keeping a wary eye on his surroundings, spotted them coming. The sun glinted on gun barrels; those dour faces were tight and cold. Steadily the climbers drew near. No shots were fired, but Slack's steely eyes were inscrutable as he came within hail and recognized Rainbow and Grumpy.

"What are you boys doin' up here?" There was

more than angry suspicion in his tone. "This ain't railroad property!"

Ignoring the implication, Rainbow said nothing till they met. Then he explained about the meeting on the Wishbone range and his conviction that Goodnight had nothing to do with wrecking the tie cars, adding how they had returned to Singer Canyon only to find a set of tracks which had led them here.

"You were hired to guard the railroad, Ripley, not to ride around the hills to suit yoreself!" Slack broke in angrily.

Rainbow's gaze hardened. "That's right," he conceded, "but maybe it's a good thing we did, or we would never 've found out what we have. Slack, there's somebody in that mine!"

A chill flashed over Slack while Rainbow reminded him of the suspicious things that had been happening. He managed to say dryly,

"Have you *seen* anybody in the mine?"

"No."

Slack seemed relieved. "Thought so," he commented. "Haven't any other proof, have yuh?"

If he expected another no, Rainbow disappointed him. "We found a garden up the slope here a ways."

Slack didn't know what to make of that. "Let's have a look at it," he said, trying to dissemble his surprise.

They were soon there. Slack's lip curled at sight

of the flowers. "Pansies an' sunflowers!" he grunted. "This is the doin' of them old desert rats down in Lost Angel."

"What about this trail to the rocks?" Grumpy struck in. "That hole may lead right into the mine!"

Slack disposed of this shortly. "It's either Withers or Bradley or one of the old codgers they've brought in with their wild yarns," he insisted. "Likely he keeps his hoe in the cave, or there may be water in there; it's plain he got some from somewheres." His face was dark. "Whatever the answer is, I don't want nobody foolin' around up here! I'll make that plain enough right now." He turned. "Slicer, you and the boys grub this stuff out of the ground. Throw it in a heap here!"

Rainbow's brows drew down at the needlessness of it, but he said nothing. Slack muttered his umbrage against the Lost Angel worthies as the garden was speedily and systematically uprooted. Slack seemed to feel that he had done away with Rainbow's suspicions along with the plants, for he did not refer to them again.

Another pair of eyes watched that wanton destruction, unguessed by anyone. They belonged to Tim Bucktoe, crouched in the shadows at the mouth of the mine vent; and their pupils blazed with unbridled wrath and hatred as Bucktoe witnessed the ruin of the one thing that meant anything to him. His face twisted and his huge hands worked. Only a deep-seated sense of wariness prevented him from rushing out there.

When Slack and the others started down the mountain, Bucktoe did go out. His mouth had a dangerous set and he made hoarse sounds in his throat. Picking up a wilted flower from the heap, he looked at it bleakly. The impulse came to reset these plants, but he knew its uselessness. All of them would die.

"By God, Slack 'll pay for this!" he grated. "Someday, somehow, he'll pay for it!" If he could have reached the other in private at that moment, he would have torn him apart with his hands.

Turning abruptly, he lurched toward the mine vent. Fury hurled him downward through the darkness, making for the Buckskin's main tunnel. He knew ways of avoiding the guards there; and even with cold calculation returning, he meant to have things out with Slack at the earliest possible moment.

A secondary drift let him out on the rocky slope a few hundred yards from the mine tunnel. So swiftly had he traveled that he was in time to see Rainbow and Grumpy going over the trail toward Lost Angel. Slack and Slicer Cully watched them out of sight, and then at a sign from the latter stepped into a wooden tool shack which Slack had had erected near at hand. Bucktoe's eyes narrowed at that. A moment later he was flitting across the slope from rock to rock till he found himself near the rear of the shack. Drawing close like some noiseless, distorted shadow, he put his ear to a crack in the boards and listened.

"You'll have to keep a closer watch on Ripley and his partner, that's all," Slack was saying to Slicer in a tone of finality.

"We'll have to do more 'n that to 'em!" Cully threw back. There was deep uneasiness in his tone. "God, Dan, don't yuh realize things are tightenin' up on my boys every day? Galey tells me the ranchers 've brought in trackers; I damn well know they've got gunmen on the range. An' then yuh had to go hire these two detectives!" He was savage. "Why didn't yuh make it two wolves an' be done with it?"

Slack tried to placate him, but for once Slicer cut him off short. "Don't give me none of that stuff!" he rasped angrily. "I'm tellin' yuh—if things don't change mighty quick, the steers are jest goin' to stop comin', that's flat!"

Silence. Then, from Slack, "I know. I can promise you things will be better before long, if you'll just hang on. I was practically forced to agree to hiring Ripley and Gibbs by Sharon Longstreet," the lie slipped off his tongue glibly, "but I'm figuring right now on a way to get rid of her. In fact, I've already got somethin' started."

"How yuh mean?" Slicer demanded, caught.

Slack hesitated over his reply. He had thought things out since his last meeting with Tim

Bucktoe. The latter's grinding domination was slowly and steadily forcing him to the point of revolt, and at last he believed he saw a way clear. It entailed doing away with Bucktoe, which would take some doing, but the advantages so far outweighed the risk that he could not afford to hesitate. Not only was there a nice profit in rustled stuff, but here was the Buckskin Mine with its rich new vein. Whenever he thought of that last, Slack's rapacity threatened to run away with him. It looked like he was sure of a good thing all to himself, if he handled it right.

"I'll just take over the railroad, lock, stock and barrel," he said coolly. His tone said that he knew how well enough. "There's goin' to be fat pickin's here, if the camp opens up again—freight receipts and the like."

"Wal . . ." Slicer was unappeased. "It sounds long on talk, to me, and short on the results. But I'm willin' to wait and see."

"It won't be long," Slack assured him smoothly. Bucktoe waited for no more. Sensing the breakup of the conference, he stole away before there was any chance of discovery. Shortly he was back in the mine. He lost no time in reaching Lost Angel, where once more he chalked up the symbol on a Chinatown poster which would call Slack to him.

Later Slack saw that summons, and a swift frown raced across his brow. Now that he had taken the first furtive steps toward independence, it irked him to be at Bucktoe's beck and call. Prospecting for some means of eliminating the other safely and surely, he had all but blurted the truth out to Slicer Cully there in the tool shed and would have been hard put to it to explain why at the last minute he had not. Even now he wanted to ignore Bucktoe's call; he actually walked past the mouth of the alley with that intention. But something warned him to go slow. It would be fatal to tip his hand too soon. Turning back, he made his way into the alley and sounded his owl hoot.

From the promptness with which Bucktoe pounced out at him, even before his lips opened, it was plain he had plenty on his mind. His first words confirmed it. "Well, Slack, you managed to put in a busy day an' no mistake!"

It was an ugly snarl. Slack stared at him while a secret pang shot through his vitals. Was it possible the cripple had somehow divined the recent trend of his thoughts? For a moment that possibility held him in its chilling grip. Then he relaxed. He was safe; how could Bucktoe have possibly found out anything, cut off as he was from communication with anyone but himself? For the moment, so great was his relief, the other's next speech only served further to allay his fears.

"I was up there on the mountain watchin' when yuh ordered that garden torn up. That was my garden, Slack, the one thing I valued, an' yuh tossed it away like an old boot! I'll never forgive yuh!"

Slack started, and his face changed. "No! *Yore* garden?" He was incredulous, voluble. "Why, I was shore it belonged to one of them old rawhides down in camp! I'll swear—"

"Yuh needn't!" Bucktoe cut him off harshly. "Talk ain't goin' to make up for the damage yuh done. There ain't no use in tryin' it!"

He appeared to gather driving force, and his words became explosive. "Yuh know I can always tell what yo're thinkin', Slack. I can read it in yore face. Right now yo're turnin' over the chances of grabbin' the Nevada Midland away from that girl! It'll be a good thing, yo're thinkin'—especially if the camp opens up again. You'll grab it, have it all to yoreself. So you figure. Am I right?"

Slack's graying face was answer enough. Bucktoe drilled him with his pale eyes and slowly shook his huge head. "You'll never do that, Slack. Don't yuh try! I told yuh once that railroad was mine! Double-cross me, an' I'll sqush yuh the same as I'd step on an ant!"

It was like a pronouncement of doom. Slack was crushed. It left him panicky as well. By what devilish ingenuity did Bucktoe manage to learn these things? There was something uncanny about it that sent a shudder over Slack.

"I was aimin' to talk it over with yuh," he muttered. "Why should the girl have all the gravy if the road turns out to be makin' a little money?" He explained his plans.

Bucktoe studied him cagily, devils of hatred and contempt in his pupils. "That sounds better," he murmured deliberately. "Jest see that yuh go on lookin' at things that way. I've decided," he went on, "to take over the railroad myself. You'll manage the details. It won't be hard. All yuh have to do is clamp down on the girl. The way things are, she'll be forced to turn everything over for satisfaction of debt."

He mistook the glint in Slack's eyes for one of attention. For some minutes they discussed Slack's course of action; and before they parted the latter understood exactly what it was he was supposed to do.

Slack's face was flinty as he continued on down Lost Angel's street toward Withers' store. Old Sukey was there, holding forth as usual to Cyclone Bradley and half-a-dozen other men. Rainbow and Grumpy were with them. All Slack's old authority had returned by the time he stepped in the door and paused in the middle of the floor. The silence which followed his arrival he arrogated to himself.

"Withers," he began heavily, "yore garden up on the Mountain was called to my attention today. I had it rooted out, and I'll do the same for any other garden I find up there. That's a warnin'! I reckon it goes for all of you gents, and we might's well be plain and clear about it: I don't want no trespassin'. I leased that Buckskin property, and I don't aim to have no body foolin' around up there! If I'm forced to, I'll use sterner methods to prevent it! Is that understood?"

Sukey heard him out, staring his amazement. "Garden?" he said blankly. "I dunno nothin' about no gardens!"

Slack was well aware of the fact, but he was carrying this thing to a conclusion for the benefit of Rainbow and Grumpy. "Never mind the excuses," he grunted shortly. "It was either you or one of yore cronies that was so busy up there—it don't matter who, this time. Jest see that it don't happen again, that's all!"

Rainbow stared at him in silence. He could not help reflecting how little use he had for this man's methods. And he liked the man himself no better. But if Slack was involved in any activities that were actually outside the law, Rainbow had not as yet discovered what they were.

Incensed at Slack's cool arrogance, Withers and Bradley and the others were beginning to fire up. Their leathery skin reddened and there was a dangerous glint showing in their faded eyes. In another moment they would blast him in proper style. Slack saw what was coming. He started to head it off by turning away, but before he could take a step there sounded the quick rush of hurrying feet on the steps outside and a second later Sharon Longstreet appeared in the door.

She was breathless and visibly excited. Paying no heed to the rest of the men in the store, her gaze remained fastened on Slack. Her tone was clear and purposeful. "Mr Slack, it has just reached me that you've decided to make some changes in your arrangements for shipping tailings from the Buckskin—or so the W. P. freight agent tells me."

Slack appeared surprised to see her, but his answer was smooth. "That's right, Miss Longstreet."

Her direct gaze did not waver. "It seems strange that they should have heard about it before I did," she said plainly, "since I am chiefly concerned. May I ask what the change in your plans amounts to?"

"Why certainly. I didn't want to say anything to you till I knew it was unavoidable. The fact is I'm intending to close down—stop shipping altogether." Speaking under direct instructions from Tim Bucktoe, Slack yet managed to make it sound like the result of sober deliberation. "I expected a better return than I've been getting. The best thing I can do is to take my licking and like it."

At the first word of a change of plans Rainbow and Grumpy straightened up with a jerk. It was their earliest intimation of anything like this. They listened with deep interest and mounting suspicion.

Sharon was obviously taken back by the disastrous significance of Slack's words. White faced, she exclaimed, "But you can't do that! If you stop shipping it will leave me in a terrible hole! The basis of our agreement was that you would be working all summer. I still owe the money you lent me to repair the track at this end of the line."

"I know, and I'm plumb sorry it had to work out this way," Slack returned suavely. "But there it is. Of course, I'll do all I can to help yuh. For instance, I'll be willin' to consider a settlement of yore debt instead of demandin' the money. The Nevada Midland is so run down it ain't worth much any more. It 'll always be a load on yore back. Nobody else would want it, but I'll consent to take it off yore hands." Watching her reaction narrowly, he added, "I might even be able to give you a few hundred dollars extra and beyond the debt."

Sharon gasped at the effrontery of the preposterous offer, but it was Rainbow who spoke up in a deceptive drawl, "A joke is a joke, Slack; don't carry the thing too far." And to Sharon, "Miss Longstreet, he hasn't any real intention of stoppin' his shipments. You can ease your mind." His words were quiet, but there was a challenge in his smile as he turned to Slack.

Slack whirled on him with unexpected fury. "Keep yore suggestions to yoreself," he rasped.

"I've already had an example of yore reasonin' today, and I don't think much of it!"

Rainbow's face went flat and hard. "It don't make sense, Slack—wantin' to buy up a railroad that you claim is worthless."

"I don't know that it means anything to you!" Slack ground out. "Yuh put yore nose in altogether too many things that don't concern yuh, Ripley!"

"This concerns me," was the frosty answer. "You'll never take the Nevada Midland away from Sharon Longstreet as easy as that! I've met up with some smooth crooks in my time; but for sheer downright gall, you've got 'em all stopped cold. If I called you a coyote, I'd have to apologize to the next one I met!"

Sharon flashed him a look at once grateful and apprehensive, and the listening old-timers jerked their chins down in stout concurrence with his sentiments. As for Slack, he glared biliously for a second before he exploded,

"Ripley, yo're fired! You and Gibbs can get out of Lost Angel as quick as yuh please."

"An' leave you to play yore rotten game with a free hand, is that it?" Grumpy threw at him harshly. "I guess not, Slack! Now that we know what yo're up to, we'll shore stay. An' what's more, we'll stop you cold!"

Rage tightened Slack's beefy face at the turn things were taking. This pair had been a thorn in his side from the minute he had laid eyes on them.

Driven and harried as he was on every side, he had grown desperate. Things threatened to come to a head with crashing swiftness now.

The men here were aware of his thought even as it flashed in his brain. In the tense silence which fell, their eyes waited for the lightning drop of his hand which would spell a gunplay. Sharon was white to the lips.

But Slack was not so far gone that he was lost to all caution. It had never been his way to risk anything less than a sure bet. And the odds were heavily against him now. Slowly he relaxed as the tautness ran out of him.

"Do what yuh please, then," he grated. "No one is interested in yore actions. Somethin' can be done about it if yuh get too nosey!"

He strove to put a bold face on it as he turned away, but it was a backdown that fooled nobody. Rainbow shrugged and turned to Sharon. She had a tense smile for him as she started for the door. It was all the invitation he needed. He and Grumpy followed her outside and the three walked back through Lost Angel's deserted street in the direction of the railroad. Rainbow and Grumpy were leading their ponies.

"Do you think he will really do as he says?" Sharon asked Rainbow with ill-concealed anxiety.

"Slack? If he's sure he can gain by it, he will," was the grim reply. "But I wouldn't worry too much about that. We slowed him up a little; I don't think he'll move till he's turned it over some more. In the meantime, we're goin' to stick around."

"Please be careful!" she exclaimed impulsively. "Your lives are in danger, I'm sure of it. And yet—" Her voice broke slightly. "I have no one else whatever to depend on. But for you, I might already be ruined! You must know how grateful I am—"

"Shucks, ma'am," he cut her off. "We'll see you through and glad of the chance. We've got a stake in this ourselves. Don't you worry about us; we'll get along fine."

He went on in this vein, seeking to restore her shaken confidence, till they were near the tracks. Her gasoline scooter was waiting there. Sharon stepped aboard, ready for the return to Crazy Horse. Rainbow was holding her with a lightly spoken jest for the pleasure of watching her smile, when the swift clatter of a madly driven horse whirled them around. They recognized Bide Jennis, old Tas Johnson's brother-in-law, who ran a little spread over on Bone Creek. He was one of the men whom Rainbow and Grumpy had met on the Wishbone. Seeing them, he reined this way and drew in with a jerk.

A glance told that Jennis was boiling with excitement. His face was flinty, his glance sharp. Sharon exclaimed instantly, "What is it, Bide? Is there something wrong?"

"I'll say there is!" Jennis bit the words off. "Two days ago we was huntin' the sign of one rustled bunch, ma'am, when we run plumb onto some more of the rustlers at their work! There was lead thrown, and two or three of the boys got nicked."

"Jim?" Sharon demanded. "Has he been hurt?" The words seemed dragged out of her, and she waited for the answer.

"No. I was with him; Goodnight didn't get so much as a touch," Jennis assured her. "But later we parted, and—" He paused, reluctant to voice the rest of it, but forged on,

"Ma'am, Goodnight ain't been seen since!"

"Bide!" she whispered anxiously. "You mean—?"

He nodded stonily. "Jim's disappeared! We've hunted high and low, and he ain't nowheres on the range."

"What could have happened to him?"

"Well, if the rustlers got hold of him, he could 've been shot and tossed down a hole in the rocks," said Bide bluntly, not pulling his punches. "We didn't get to see who they was. Whatever happened, somebody figured to put Jim away! We think—"

"Yes?" The girl's query was tense.

"We think," Jennis continued thinly, his steely gaze swiveling suddenly to cover Rainbow and Grumpy, "these two gents here had somethin' to do with it!"

17

A dead silence fell, and in this thin-drawn moment Sharon's gasp was plainly heard. Before she could speak, Rainbow beat her to it.

"So you think Grumpy and I had something to do with Goodnight disappearin', Jennis?" He had not moved, and his voice betrayed nothing.

Bide nodded, watching them narrowly. His answer was soft only in tone; its meaning cried a flat challenge. He said, "That's what we think, Ripley!"

Sharon exclaimed, "But that's nonsense! Why should Rainbow and Grumpy be interested in getting Jim out of the way?"

"Reason enough," Jennis gave back hardily. "I reckon yuh ain't heard 'bout the threats passed the very day Jim disappeared, ma'am. But there wasn't no love lost on either side!"

"Threats?" she said.

Swiftly Rainbow explained about the meeting on the Wishbone range. "I expect we were both hasty, but I swear there were no actual threats, unless by Bart Galey," he added, "and neither Grumpy nor I have seen Goodnight since."

"That's all easy to say, Ripley," Jennis retorted. "But who's to know what orders yuh got from Dan Slack."

"I can tell you the answer to that," Sharon declared quickly, in a relieved tone. "Not ten minutes ago Mr Slack discharged Rainbow for calling him a crook and a coyote!"

Bide's jaw dropped. He looked both mystified and interested, while Sharon explained what had taken place in Withers' store. "I'll be damned!" he said under his breath at the end. And then, "Ripley, you've had us all guessin'! What in hell *is* yore game in this country?"

There was still a reserve in his tone. Rainbow said, "We came here to run down a bunch of rustlers—and that's what we're doin', Jennis. It was pretty plain that the methods you men were usin' wouldn't get us anywhere. We decided to play our own hand and let you and Goodnight and the others think what you would. When we got this offer from Slack, I thought it was suspicious. The shrewdest move was to accept, of course. We haven't learned anything," he admitted, "but Slack is a crook. He's proved that!"

Before he had spoken a dozen words the tension eased. When he concluded, Bide shoved his bronc forward and thrust out a hand.

"I've got to apologize to you, Ripley—you and yore pardner. I reckon we all have. You've satisfied me that yo're on the level."

Even Grumpy was grinning as they shook hands. Sharon spoke up.

"Rainbow, will you go with Bide at once—help

him and the others to find Jim?" Her anxiety was unmistakable. To her surprise, Rainbow shook his head.

"I'm afraid we can't do that," he gave back reluctantly. "Grumpy and I are playin' this hand out our own way. We'll do what we can to find Goodnight, but I can't guarantee just how soon we'll get results."

He didn't elaborate on his opinion that there was much more to be done than finding Jim. There could be nothing gained in admitting to Sharon his conviction that unless drastic steps were taken, and soon, the Nevada Midland, her only liveli-hood, would be swept away. Slack had his plans laid and his grip was steadily, ruth-lessly closing. If Rainbow found himself unable to halt the latter, there would be no one to stand between the girl and her ruin.

Sharon hesitated. Her willingness to assent at all was the measure of her trust in him, for she was wholly unable to hide her great anxiety for Goodnight. "Very well," she said. "If it must be that way, it must. I will run down to Indian Wells, get a pony there and ride to Tas Johnson's Lazy Lightning." She turned to Jennis. "You say the other ranchers are there now? I'll undertake to square Rainbow and Grumpy with them, if you have any trouble making them listen." And to Rainbow again, "If you find you need any help, then, you can get it."

Rainbow's eyes thanked her. Once again, however, he shook his head. "It's good of you," he said, "but you won't have to bother. Tas Johnson knows all about us." And to Jennis, "Just tell Tas the time has come to speak up. He'll put you right about Grumpy and me."

Bide looked at him in surprise. "You mean there's an understandin' between you an' Johnson, Ripley?"

"That's right. Tas knows about every move we've been makin', and why."

Jennis shook his head in bewilderment. "Danged if yuh ain't a wise one, Ripley!" he said humbly. "I see it all now. But yuh shore kept the rest of us in the dark!"

"It seemed the best way," Rainbow smiled faintly. "But you know now what to do. We better all get goin'!" He reined his bronc around and Grumpy followed suit. Saying so-long with raised hands, they jogged away.

"Rainbow," Grumpy began after some minutes of thought, "what's yore idear of what happened to Goodnight?"

"I couldn't say."

"It wasn't them rustlers that got him," Grumpy proceeded positively. "They'd have knocked him off where they found him an' let him lay!"

"Reckon so."

"But this hombre in the mine, now—what if it should be this Tim Bucktoe yuh was tellin' me about? It was Goodnight's father who was responsible fer his accident," Grumpy reminded. "Mebby he's snagged Jim an' is holdin' him in the Buckskin."

"It's just barely possible that's what happened," Rainbow conceded. "There's more than one reason for our bein' interested in that mine, any way you look at it!"

"What 'll yuh do, then?"

"We'll ride a circle around here," was the deliberate answer, "and see what we can find."

It suited Grumpy, although what they proposed was far from easy, entailing as it did a climb high on the shoulder of Superstition Mountain. Soon they were high above the valley. The view from here was vast, including vistas of the Calico Hills and the distant desert. But they were not interested in scenery; they kept their eyes glued to the ground. It was Rainbow who made the first discovery.

"Look here," he directed sharply, pointing to something on what might be taken for a faintly defined trail through the brush. Pushing forward, Grumpy saw the traces of old cattle droppings. Instantly his interest was aroused.

"Huh! Somebody's been foggin' steers along here. It's a cinch they wouldn't drift this high of their own accord."

Without a word Rainbow fell to following the faint trail. Grumpy was not far behind him. And now they divided their attention between the ground and the rocks and brush to the fore. Neither would have been in the least surprised to run onto a hidden brush corral. Instead, the trail led steadily downward, until they were once more on the valley's floor. Half an hour later they drew up within a hundred yards of the rocky mouth of the Buckskin Mine. "Wal!" Grumpy exclaimed in a significant tone.

But they were due for an even greater surprise. In the deepening twilight they saw four men ride out of the mine tunnel on saddle horses. Slicer Cully was at their head.

"Get in the brush!" Rainbow snapped. "We ain't lettin' those gents spot us!"

He spoke none too soon. Scarcely had they concealed themselves when Cully and his men turned this way and struck out briskly. They rode by so close that their muttered talk could be heard. When they were gone, Rainbow murmured, "We'll just make sure where they're goin'!"

They started after. It was not ten minutes before they thought they had lost the men altogether; only the fact that the others had been seen was assurance of the fact that they were near. Rainbow and Grumpy picked them up again presently. The difficulty of keeping them in sight at all was proof enough of the secretiveness of their movements. All too plainly Cully and his companions rode in fear of discovery.

Rainbow drew in at length. His tone was crisp. "There goes your rustlers," was what he said.

Grumpy merely nodded, gazing through slitted eyes after Slicer and the rest. "Gettin' the deadwood on friend Slack at last," he commented grimly. "We follerin' them buzzards?"

Rainbow's hesitation was of the briefest. The way had led back up the mountain again; just now they were on a shoulder from which they could see afar. "No, we're stayin' right here. There's no tellin' which way the cat 'll jump." He reflected a moment and then added, "I'd give somethin' to know what Slack is doin' right now—"

At that moment, Slack was pacing the narrow confines of the tool shed before the Buckskin Mine. His restlessness was deep. The ease with which Tim Bucktoe manipulated his movements as he chose had become so galling that it was like the exposed nerve of a tooth which he could not leave alone. Bitterest of all was the knowledge that his hope of possessing the Nevada Midland all for himself bade fair to fall through. Worse still, Bucktoe had in some diabolical fashion become aware of his plans just at the critical moment. It would be harder than ever, if not impossible, to catch him off his guard.

Yet it had to be done. The increasing drive of that necessity flung Slack this way and that in the grasp of his fear and hatred. At last it came to him that thinking about it would get him nowhere. "There's no use dependin' on Slicer or anyone else," he gritted. "I've got to finish that wolf myself—do it the only way it can be done! A slug in the back 'll stop Bucktoe for good. That way nobody 'll know."

Spinning on his heel, he caught up a repeating rifle leaning against the wall of the shed and turned to the door. Soon he was climbing the steep flank of Superstition. The sweat that beaded his jowls was not all the result of his nervous haste; there was a fever in his brain, a terrible itch in his trigger finger.

Night was falling by the time he drew near the cup on the slope containing Bucktoe's garden. Like an animal he stole through the brush till he overlooked the spot from a rocky ledge. Cautiously he peered down. As he had hoped—he was afraid vainly—Bucktoe was there even now, moving about in the cultivated patch. Most of the wilted, drooping plants which Slack had had uprooted he had reset in a vain effort to save them; at present he was carrying water, portioning it out, fingering the limp leaves regretfully— utterly engrossed in his occupation.

Stealthily Slack raised his rifle and trained it on the unsuspecting figure. He did not fire immediately, however. His nerves were jumping so badly that he scarcely dared trust his aim. There was some malign yet potent force in the character of Bucktoe which struck into him even from this distance. Grimly he steeled himself to shoot before the other became aware of his danger.

The crash of the rifle echoed up the side of Superstition with metallic, fading reverberations. Slack stared transfixed across the sights at his would-be victim. But Bucktoe did not drop as he had expected him to. Instead he whirled, his deformed body making him look like some unnatural monster preparing to leap. Without a second's delay his six gun cracked; granite dust flew from the ledge behind which Slack lay.

Slack knew an instant's panic then. True, the light had not been good; his nerves were frayed and jumpy; yet it seemed to him that there was a devil in that man down there in the garden which protected him, rendered him indestructible. Slack fired again, then several times in rapid succession, without apparent result. Bucktoe not only replied with interest, but he started this way like a charging bull.

It was too much for Slack. A yell of terror was jerked out of him. Without taking thought he rolled over, gained his feet and started thrashing down the mountain side through the brush. Within a minute of the time of his first shot, he was in full flight. Another minute put him well beyond range of Bucktoe's small gun, but still he drove downward in mad haste, hounded by a nameless fear. Something told him his enemy would guess his identity unerringly. Bucktoe might even have recognized him. Not yet did Slack take time to reflect what the inevitable consequences would be, but their portent overshadowed him.

Scarcely half a mile away, Rainbow and Grumpy heard the scattered shots. Whirling to peer in the direction from which they had sounded, they asked themselves what it meant. Grumpy evinced astonishment. He exclaimed, "That can't be them rustlers—"

"Be quiet!" Rainbow cut him off. In the silence which ensued they caught a crashing and crackling in the brush. Hastily moving to a better vantage, they saw a man on foot, plunging down the mountain. Grumpy's jaw dropped. "What the hell!"

"That's Slack!" Rainbow rapped, recognizing the other's shape. "Somebody's been smokin' him! But who?"

In the fading light they watched Slack out of sight but waited in vain for any pursuit. Rainbow prospected the idea of climbing the slope to learn what they could in that direction, but finally he gave over. "Too late for that. We'll stay where we are," he decided. "We're here for a reason that still holds good."

Wait as they would, they learned nothing more. Time passed. But Rainbow's patience endured. There was a late moon. Even that was beginning to fade into the darkness which preceded dawn, when at last they were rewarded. Suddenly Rainbow jerked alert and murmured one word, "Listen!"

What they heard was the thud of hoofs on rock. Creeping to the edge of the brush, they looked out to see upwards of a dozen steers being hazed along in charge of four riders whom they had no difficulty in recognizing. They were Slicer Cully and his men. When they passed, Rainbow and Grumpy fell in behind. This time they had no trouble in keeping up; for the direction was plain enough, and it led straight toward the Buckskin Mine.

Just as the sky started to pale toward the east, the partners watched from cover while the rustled steers were hazed into the mine tunnel.

"So that's the how of it," Grumpy grunted his comprehension. "They're holdin' the overbranded stuff in the mine while it's healin'—there's likely ten miles of gallery in there, an' plenty of room. But they must be drivin' the stuff out some other way when it's ready to move, Rainbow."

The latter nodded. "We've sure got somethin' to go on now," he said. "Our first move 'll be to get into that mine!"

"There 'll be guards down there," Grumpy exclaimed. "An' this time they'll savvy what we're after!" He didn't have to say what that meant.

The answer was a shrug. "We've got to get into

the mine," Rainbow said plainly, "and that's what we'll do."

Waiting only long enough to give the rustlers a chance to get out of the way, they pushed forward. Slack was nowhere in evidence. Dismounting at a little distance, they made boldly for the mine entrance. An armed man stepped forward as they neared, barring their path.

"Stay where yuh are," he warned roughly. "I had special orders that yuh was to be kept off of Buckskin property, Ripley! Yuh better head the other way!"

"Where's Slack?" Rainbow queried easily, to distract the other as he pressed close. "We want to talk to him."

"I dunno where he is," was the surly response. "Stand back, now! Don't yuh come no nearer or I'll—"

He never finished it. Before he was able to bring up his rifle, Rainbow lunged toward him swiftly and his fist lashed out. It caught the guard flush on the point of the jaw. The man staggered back, caught himself.

The next instant he flung forward with a rush. His gun had been knocked out of his grasp, but he still had his fists. Snarling his fury, he closed in with a roundhouse swing. Rainbow parried it. At the same time he loosed a short, chopping blow that rocked his adversary. The man's guard came down, exposing his head. A second blow, into which Rainbow packed everything he had, picked the other up and flung him ten feet, to land heavily on his back. By an instinctive reflex he started to struggle up on an elbow. But that last blow had been too much; he sank back, to move no more.

"Get on inside!" Rainbow snapped to Grumpy as voices were heard behind them in the open. But it was already too late. They had been seen. Several of Slack's men, coming from the direction of Lost Angel, raised a sudden shout and pounded this way. The next moment a gun banged, the slug struck the rocky wall at Grumpy's side and whined away viciously.

"Come out of there, Ripley! We got yuh now!"

Instead of complying, Rainbow and Grumpy sprang for the protection of the shadows deeper in the mine. Crouched behind a protecting shoulder of rock, they watched as these men closed in, effectually cutting off their chances of escape from the tunnel's mouth. Rifles began to bark. Grumpy answered briskly, then turned a rueful look on his companion.

"Now we're in a swell jack pot," he grumbled. "With half-a-dozen of Slack's gun slingers out in front, an' four of his rustlers behind us, things 'll soon be gettin' plenty hot!"

The words were prophetic. They were scarcely uttered before the guns started to pound outside and the slugs probed seemingly into every cranny

252

and corner of the tunnel. Rainbow and Grumpy found their position untenable and they fell back. It was some distance to the first lateral drift. They dared not pause till they had reached it. But there Grumpy stubbornly stuck, firing at every gun flash of their attackers.

"You better be sparin' of them cartridges," Rainbow warned. "There's no tellin' how soon we'll be gettin' out of this!"

It was good advice. A moment later they caught Slack's heavy tones as he gave orders from the tunnel mouth. "Smoke 'em out of there!" he cried harshly. "Cut 'em down! We ain't takin' any chances with them hombres!"

The firing increased. Lead droned through the tunnel with a lethal song. There was always the danger of being struck by flying chips of rock from the walls. No sign had as yet come from the rear to advertise the fact that Slicer Cully and the other rustlers knew what was afoot, but not for a minute did Rainbow forget them.

When things got so hot that it seemed they could no longer hold out without being hit, they fell back still farther. Rainbow recognized the desperateness of their case; for while the mine was wholly strange to them, Slack and his men knew it thoroughly. The circumstance might tell heavily against them in the end. Too, there was the fact that somewhere back in here the rustlers lay in wait, and neither neglected thought of the strange man they believed to be hiding in the mine. Darkness hampered them; they had no means of lighting their way save the few matches they carried, and the sparing shots they fired were more in the nature of warnings than anything else.

Time dragged by. With a lull in the shooting they started to crawl back toward the mine entrance. They had not gone a dozen feet before a renewal of the attack drove them back farther than before. Rainbow hunted for some means of escape until at length he was forced to confess himself lost. Grumpy was muttering curses of exaspera-tion under his breath, when suddenly Rainbow's grasp closed over his arm.

"Huh?" he grunted.

"Listen to that, Grumpy!"

In the silence which followed there came to them the hollow bellowing of cattle, drifting through the rocky corridors from afar.

"Good Lord!" Grumpy breathed his relief. "They're on another level! That explains why we ain't been attacked from the rear. From the sound, there must be somethin' goin' on! Why, Rainbow, I'd swear they got a couple hundred head down in here!"

Rainbow's nod was grim. "We know where they are now. But it won't help us any if we can't get out of here!"

18

Crawling ever deeper in the mine to a position of momentary security, Rainbow and Grumpy fell to counting their remaining cartridges and to a discussion of their chances. Though they had apparently solved the secret of the Buckskin, their position seemed hopeless.

"What about the way they're drivin' the steers out of here?" Grumpy queried. "If we kin only find that we got a chance."

Rainbow assented. "We'll have to find it," he said simply.

They started off. But if they had believed the bellowing of the steers would guide them they were doomed to disappointment. Echoing in every gallery with lingering overtones, the sound was so deceptive that they were utterly unable to determine its direction. There were so many shafts, guarded for the most part with flimsy boarding, that they found it impossible even to make certain on what level the steers were being held.

Occasionally they heard Slack's men calling to one another. Now and then a fusillade of shots rattled down the drift in which they had taken refuge. A shot or two in reply was enough to discourage any rushes. Once they heard Slicer

Cully rap out an order; the flickering light of a lantern or candle splashed down a shaft from an upper level. It told them that the rustlers had joined the hunt.

"Wonder if Goodnight really is down in here some'eres," said Grumpy suddenly in a lowered tone. "He was no fool. Mebby he hit on the same thing we did—an' the same thing happened to him. They may even 've knocked him off!"

It was a possibility, and one to which Rainbow's thoughts were later to leap with dramatic understanding.

Their own movements were more and more curtailed. Twice they sought by crawling to other levels to work back past Slack's men toward the mouth of the mine. Both times a hail of lead at a critical moment warned them that all means of egress had been closed off. The only way open to them was back into the mine. They could work deeper and deeper as they were doing, no more.

The time came when Grumpy started to take in the extra notches in his belt. The dread of slowly starving to death was more real to him than the fear of being shot down. Rainbow assured him that imagination was working on him; they had not been in the mine for more than a matter of twelve or fifteen hours. Fortunately they found an occasional trickle of water by means of which to allay their thirst. By taking turns they managed to snatch a little rest.

But if they had hoped to outwait Slack, they were slated for signal failure. His patience was even shorter than theirs, but his persistence was endless. More than once they heard him haranguing his cohorts angrily. One time the talk was so close that every word was distinguishable.

"You've been throwin' it into me for days to do somethin' about Ripley and Gibbs," Slack hurled at Slicer Cully. "Now they're cornered and yuh got a free hand! Why don't yuh wade in and smoke 'em down?"

"Yeh?" Slicer was vindictive. "Why don't I bed down with a couple of rattlers?"

Slack cursed him with heat. Suddenly Slicer cut him off, his tone jarring with a new note of menace, "Lay off the rough stuff, Slack! What's eatin' yuh, anyway? Them hombres are penned up; they can't make a play. But yo're as spooked as if everything had gone to hell!"

"I ain't trustin' that pair a minute," was Slack's grating answer. "As long as they're alive, they're dynamite!"

"Reckon I feel that way myself," Slicer grunted. "But dammit, Slack, I still think yo're coverin' up somethin'!"

As a matter of fact, Slack was. There was a double fear riding him; and if he bore down in emphasis to Slicer on one side of it, that did not make his secret dread rest any lighter. He was unable to get out of his mind the fact that Tim

Bucktoe was somewhere in the mine. It was inconceivable that Bucktoe did not know what was going on; and if it was even more likely that sooner or later he would take a hand, Slack did not have to ask himself on which side that would be. After what had happened on the mountain side last evening, Bucktoe would shoot him down on sight.

The danger he ran had Slack on tenterhooks every moment he spent in the mine. Yet he feared to leave lest while he was absent Rainbow Ripley and Grumpy Gibbs should somehow slip away. At the same time there was the faint hope that Bucktoe might get caught in a cross fire and be wiped out. There was an element of desperation in the thought that all three of the men who threatened his safety and his prosperity were even now in the Buckskin and yet just beyond his reach.

While his best efforts in the past had failed, he determined that this time not one of the three should escape.

Common intelligence told him that he must move before the enemy had time to join forces. He pretended a harshness that was not his as he rasped to Slicer, "Talk won't help us. I want Ripley and his partner hunted down and finished, and I want it done now!"

"Suppose yuh take a hand yoreself, if yo're in such a sweat!" Slicer flared, his tolerance worn thin.

Slack was silent for a minute. "By God, I will!"

he burst out, tensely. "Round up two or three of the boys. I'll put an end to this business in damned short order!"

The voices grew indistinct as the men moved away, but Rainbow and Grumpy had heard enough to warn them of what was coming. Hastily they fell back in this pit-black drift to the best spot they could find for standing off an attack. Using loose ore and rock which had crumbled down between the shore timbers, they threw up a barrier behind which they could crouch. There they fell to watching for whatever was to come first.

They had not long to wait. It was Grumpy who jerked out suddenly, "By gravy, they're comin' with a light!"

He spoke truly. Down the drift appeared the wavering flicker of some sort of illumination. Soon they were able to see it clearly. It was a candle, and there was something mysterious about its unsteady advance; for it threw no light on anyone near at hand and seemed to be moving along close to the ground.

Rainbow was the one who hit on the answer. "They've stuck that candle on the end of a plank," he murmured, "and they're shovin' it along ahead of them!"

"Purty clever stunt," his companion returned grudgingly. "All the same, I'll jest see if I can't break that little game up!" He raised his gun. Rainbow stopped him before he could fire.

"Hold on! Maybe this is the chance we've been lookin' for."

"What yuh mean?"

"That 'll be Slack and Cully, and maybe a couple others behind that candle. They'll be watchin' sharp ahead—waitin' for the lead to start flyin'. If only we can find a hole to climb into and hide till they get past . . ."

"I get it!" Grumpy chuckled. "We'll jest let 'em waltz by without knowin' they're doin' it!"

That was Rainbow's idea.

Giving over all thought of smoking out the advancing men, they fell to examining the walls of the drift for some hiding place which would answer their purpose. The shadows were too deep to see much; nor had they a moment to spare. Suddenly, however, Grumpy gave vent to a muted sound in his throat and his eyes bugged out. Rainbow looked in the same direction. His surprise was as great. They had been so long in darkness in this ghostly place that they could not be sure they were not seeing things; and yet, it seemed that at a point about halfway between them and the advancing candle, a gigantic, twisted form was swinging down through the mine timbers from a hole in the roof of the drift. That grotesque figure could be only one man.

"Tim Bucktoe!" Rainbow breathed. "He's got his eyes on Slack and the others!"

Freezing, they watched. Bucktoe moved with

the stealth of a specter. Crouching behind a mine timber, he waited with Indian patience while the candle on the plank approached. The dull scrape of boots over the tunnel floor could be faintly heard; the low whisper of voices. Bucktoe drew back as the circle of light neared his hiding place. Rainbow and Grumpy waited breathless to see what he would do.

Suddenly the malformed giant galvanized into action. For a second it was impossible to divine his intent, for he seemed to have gone mad; then Rainbow understood. With his tremendous strength, Bucktoe was pushing out the rotten upright which supported the roof of this drift. Slack, Slicer and the others spotted him and let out a yell of surprise. Slack was the first to recover from it, unerring recognition sending a knife thrust of fear through him.

"Drill him!" he yelled to his men. "Blast him down! He'll kill us all if we don't get him first!"

Springing up, they didn't wait for explanations. Their danger was plain enough. Guns thundered hollowly, just as a great section of the rock roof came rumbling down. Turning, they tried to race back to safety. Rainbow got a flash of Slack himself, his face distorted with terror. A man beside him was struck down, flung on his face. He scrambled up, only to be caught a second time by a rocky mass that crushed the life out of him.

Still Bucktoe labored on, tore at the mine timbers with maddened ferocity.

"I told yuh I'd be yore finish, Slack, yuh double-crossin' hound!" he screamed. "By God, this is the last time you'll buck my game!"

Desperate, Slack whirled to throw a slug at him. If the shot took effect, it was not apparent. Before he could fire again the walls and roof of the drift caved in with a tremendous roar, closing the tunnel.

It was an avalanche in which the cripple suddenly found himself caught. When he sought to swing up and away, the trap closed over his legs. His grip was wrenched free and he went down, pinned.

No part of the significance of what had passed escaped Rainbow. With a lightning-swift flash of illumination the truth hit him, Bucktoe's embittered words explaining everything that had puzzled him so long. This warped and twisted giant was the real mastermind behind all the rustling and lawlessness which for two years had gone on unchecked. Slack was no more than his tool—a tool which, it was plain, at last had turned in his hand. But that was as nothing compared to the fact that the man they had sought for so long, revealed suddenly before their eyes, was in danger of being buried here forever along with his secret.

Breaking from the vise of his surprise, Rainbow

sprang forward and, grasping Bucktoe about the shoulders, attempted to drag him free.

"Help me, Grumpy!" he exclaimed. "This is the gent we came on this range to get! He'll never be any good to us if we don't get him out of here in a hurry!"

Grumpy had gathered the truth as quickly; he lost no time in doing as he was bid. Together they managed to extricate Bucktoe and pull him back as another section of the roof fell that would have crushed them all had it caught them.

Bucktoe had been struck on the neck by a jagged piece of quartz. It was an ugly gash. Although partially stunned, he had his wits about him as he struggled up to glower at them malignantly.

"I know yuh!" he rasped. "Yo're Ripley an' Gibbs!"

"That's us," Rainbow told him, the repelling ugliness of the man sending a cold chill through him. The dull rumble of a fresh cave-in in another drift warned him that all these old workings might collapse. "Bucktoe, what do you know about Jim Goodnight?" he jerked out hurriedly. "Is he somewhere here in the mine?"

Bucktoe only glared, his beady eyes glinting in his flat face. "Come on, open up!" Grumpy advised roughly. But still Bucktoe stood there as if this was a situation he didn't know what to do about, as indeed it was; for his discovery by this pair threatened to overthrow all his calculations.

His only chance lay in getting them out of the way and doing it in a hurry. Something of his thoughts must have shown in his eyes, for Rainbow exclaimed,

"Grab him, Grumpy! Don't let him get away!"

Grumpy started to lay his grasp on Bucktoe's arm. With a sudden movement the cripple flung him off, and whirling, headed the other way. Rainbow tried to stop him, crying, "Hold on, Bucktoe! You ain't goin' nowheres! Not if we have to stop you for keeps!"

Tossing both of the partners aside as easily as though he was dealing with children, Bucktoe leaped toward the mass of débris on the floor of the drift. Rainbow and Grumpy closed in again. With them hanging to his great body but unable to stop him, the giant hauled himself up to the gallery overhead. Once there he brushed them off like flies. Then with lurching fleetness he started away.

Only the knowledge that this vicious human gorilla was a menace as long as he remained at large persuaded Rainbow to do what he did then. Whipping his gun out, he sent a shot lancing after Bucktoe through the gloom of the drift. Grumpy followed suit. The next moment Bucktoe answered with a wicked fire.

It could not deter them. "After him!" Rainbow exclaimed as they sprang in pursuit.

It was soon evident that with his knowledge of

the mine Bucktoe was able to avoid them easily. Racing from one drift into another, blundering into the walls and other unseen obstructions, it was all they could do to keep from being shot down themselves. Bucktoe's gun spat again and again in their direction, the slugs droning close, until the hopelessness of pursuit drove home.

"It 'll take some doin' to git out of here with a whole hide, let alone catchin' him!" Grumpy jerked out tensely.

For the moment, Bucktoe seemed indeed to have given them the slip, but Rainbow continued to probe their surroundings with wary alertness. "What's that?" he queried suddenly, pointing. "It looks like daylight."

"It *is* daylight!" Grumpy broke in. "An' that's the out Bucktoe's headin' for! He must be!"

They started hurriedly toward the light. It was a long way up a steeply slanting drift, and they knew that at any point that snarling fiend might be lying in wait for them. Nor were they mistaken. They were still half-a-dozen yards from the tunnel mouth when something hurtled through the air and fell rolling at their feet, something that sputtered and fizzed with fiery life. It sent a shock coursing through the marrow of them both.

"Good God!" Rainbow ejaculated. "Get out of this! Get out, before that dynamite tears loose!" Grabbing Grumpy by the shoulder, he whirled him violently toward the open.

Scarcely had they burst through the mouth of the tunnel high on the flank of Superstition before the blast went off with a hollow, snarling roar. The jar and crunch of loosened rock was like an earth tremor; the tunnel closed with a collapsing crash. Grumpy whirled.

"Hell's hinges!" he whipped out. "Bucktoe's shucked us an' slammed the door in our face! We've lost him, Rainbow!"

The other assented curtly. "We're wise to the setup at any rate," he added. "The thing now is to get down the mountain and go for help!"

"Small chance of gettin' our broncs back."

"No, Slack's crowd 've picked up our horses by now. We'll have to follow the railroad tracks on foot till we can cut over to the Wishbone."

They looked down the slope, where the smoke of the Nevada Midland locomotive could be seen. Rainbow studied it in puzzlement. He knew that a train was being loaded down there. "Darn queer that Slack should be shippin' tailin's on top of what's happened," he said thoughtfully. They could make nothing of it, but the circumstance gave Rainbow an idea. "If we can get a mile or so down the tracks in time," he said, "we can climb on and ride the rods instead of havin' to hoof it."

It was half an hour after dark before they struck the right of way, footsore and weary. The train had not passed them, and they were satisfied. At the head of a grade where the locomotive would slow down, they waited.

Rainbow sized up the situation concretely when he said, "We've been after small fry up to now. It wasn't Slack who knocked the hotel out from under us or tried to kill us with the ore car. The wreck—everything was Bucktoe's doin'! Slack is just a dangerous crook. Bucktoe is a madman."

"Right," Grumpy agreed. "If he's playin' a lone hand now, he may not stick around the mine a minute longer than he has to."

"Slack's gang may hold him there," Rainbow argued. "Our move is to grab the whole bunch of 'em the minute we can get a posse here."

Their nerves were worn thin with waiting before the faint echoing scream of a whistle advertised the fact that the train had started. They crawled behind a rock till the engine rumbled past, then sprang out and made for the cars. Swinging under the last one, they pulled themselves up on the rods. They had not been seen. A moment later the train was picking up speed.

It was no easy task to hang on against the jar and jolt of the car over the uneven roadbed. Grit blew up in their faces. They lay stretched out, their hands gripping the rods tightly.

Suddenly Rainbow felt a drop of something wet fall on the back of his hand. Queer! It hadn't rained for days; there could be no moisture in those tailings. He looked up at the car floor, and another drop splashed on his upturned face. It felt warm, sticky. He tested a drop with his tongue and knew what he had found. It wasn't water that had splashed him. It was blood!

"Grumpy," he said slowly, "I know where Jim Goodnight is."

"Huh?" Grumpy was startled. "Where?"

"He's buried under these tailin's over our head; his blood is leakin' through the car floor!"

"You mean he was in the mine—that Bucktoe's killed him?"

"That's what I mean!"

It didn't take long to convince Grumpy.

"By God, we got evidence now! But don't you be too shore we'll ever git Bucktoe an' Slack to trial. More apt to be a short rope an' a quick one for 'em when folks learn the facts!"

Rainbow agreed thoroughly. "We're stayin' on this train," he announced, "till we get to Crazy Horse. The sooner we get the sheriff lined up the better!"

The thought flashed on him then that there was someone else in Crazy Horse to whom this news would come as a shock, and that was Sharon Longstreet. He knew what Goodnight's death would mean for her. He would have done anything in his power to spare her the blow.

The train rumbled through Indian Wells not long after. It seemed an endless time while it whirled down through the winding canyons to Crazy

Horse. As the train pulled in, Rainbow and Grumpy tumbled out from under their car and darted for the shadows beside piled ties. Rainbow led the way toward the main street. It was nearly midnight, but he was confident that Lint Granger would be somewhere in evidence.

The lawman was. The street proved empty, but no sooner had they stepped in the door of the Golden Palace than they saw Granger at the bar. Rainbow's glance fell on the man he was talking with and he stopped dead, his jaw dropping. An exclamation of amazement burst from his lips.

"Good Lord!"

Grumpy was no less startled. The man standing at the bar with Granger, a glass at his elbow, was Jim Goodnight!

19

The fact that Goodnight was still alive was a jolt to Rainbow, but it was not his chief concern now. His gaze flicked to Lint Granger's face.

"What's on yore mind, Ripley?" the sheriff asked, noting his excitement.

"Plenty!" Rainbow assured him. "With your help, we're ready to put an end to the hell that's run this country ragged for two years." To Goodnight he said, "This will interest you. We've found your rustler; and we can explain a good many things besides that have been puzzlin' you."

Granger's jaw bulged. "I'd guess yo're talkin' about just one man, Ripley," he exclaimed gruffly. "Yuh mean Slack?"

"I mean Tim Bucktoe!"

If he had expected to surprise them, he was not disappointed. "Bucktoe!" Goodnight ejaculated incredulously. "Why, that's nonsense! Bucktoe isn't even in the country!"

"Don't be so sure of that," Rainbow retorted. "He's been livin' in the Buckskin Mine for months, and he's had plenty of help."

"Help?" Granger snorted. "Now yuh *are* meanin' Slack!"

"Right!"

"Bucktoe and Slack!" Granger exploded. "A madman and a rattler!"

"You've had Grumpy and me wrong from the start, Goodnight," Rainbow ran on. He quickly explained why he had accepted Slack's offer. Before he finished, Goodnight and the sheriff had the complete story of all that had happened at Lost Angel and the Buckskin Mine.

"I've certainly made a mistake about you and your partner, Ripley," Goodnight admitted. "You've been doin' a fine job."

"The last I'd heard of you, you'd disappeared," Rainbow continued to Goodnight. "None of your friends knew where you were. That was three days ago. I had you dead."

"What yuh mean, yuh had him dead?" Granger demanded.

Rainbow told him of his discovery on the train.

"I've been in Salt Lake," Goodnight explained. "Maybe I can set you right about the blood in the car. I got the idea that Slack might be gettin' away with butchered beef. So I went to Salt Lake to check up on his shipments. I didn't find out anything. But this blood drippin' through the car floor sounds mighty interestin'!"

Granger nodded grimly. "We're investigatin' them cars," he declared.

Leaving the saloon, they headed for the Nevada Midland station, where Slack's train stood on the tracks. There was a light in the office. They found Sharon still there, going over the books and figuring anxiously. As they stepped in, her glance fell on Goodnight.

"Jim!" she exclaimed. "You are safe! You've come back!"

There was a world of meaning in her tone, but Goodnight chose to ignore it. Sharon hesitated, attempting vainly to cover her agitation at the coolness of his greeting. Grumpy threw Rainbow a significant glance. But Granger drove straight to the business in hand.

"Miss Longstreet, I'm havin' a look at Slack's cars. Will you have Rucker push 'em on to the sidin'?"

Sharon quickly mastered her surprise. "I will," she said, "if Clem is still in the yard."

Not bothering to slip on hat or jacket, she led the way out into the night. They found Rucker in the smoke-blackened shed which housed the locomotive.

Once the cars were on the side track, Rainbow, Grumpy and Goodnight climbed aboard, armed with shovels. The others watched with interest in the flickering light of a lantern while they attacked the tailings. At first it seemed the quest would prove fruitless as the load got lower and lower and nothing came to light. At last Grumpy exclaimed:

"Wal now, take a look at that!"

On the floor of the car the carcass of a freshly killed steer could be seen. Soon others were unearthed. The discovery made incontrovertible the means by which the rustled cattle were being got out of the country.

"It makes Bucktoe's game clear from the beginning," Rainbow declared. "He got Slack in his hands when he saved him at that trial; he's been workin' through him ever since. Organized this gang to do the rustlin', beefed the steers in the mine and shipped them under the tailin's, which probably paid the freight and made the rustlin' all gravy. Not that the money was all that mattered to Bucktoe."

"That's gospel!" Goodnight exclaimed. "It was his way of gettin' even!"

"Believe me, he's cunnin'," Rainbow continued.

"He's been givin' all the orders, plannin' all the moves—likely it was his idea to keep Grumpy and me on the outs with you cowmen. He may even be figurin' to get the Nevada Midland in his own hands: Slack has made the first moves in that direction. But somethin' went wrong, and they quarreled. They'll kill each other if they get the chance—the same way Bucktoe tried to kill us! Whatever happens, the rustlin' will go on till we've cleaned up that crowd."

"We'll put an end to it!" Granger thrust in grimly. "Bucktoe's a mad dog—rabid! He's got to be stopped. I'll swear in a posse—"

"Hold on!" Goodnight halted him as he started to turn away. "We ain't wastin' a minute, Granger! Bucktoe's got to be stopped all right; but he's dangerous—a hundred times worse 'n Slack and his rustlers. He's got a grudge against every man that walks, the kind of a crazy grudge that 'll balk at nothin'! You'll need some real men with you to round up that outfit."

"You're right," Granger agreed. He whirled to Clem Rucker. "Get steam up on that locomotive! We're pilin' aboard and ridin' to Indian Wells. I'll swear in a posse of rangemen and push right on through the hills. We'll have Superstition Mountain surrounded before daylight!"

It meant a night's hard riding, but half an hour before dawn the posse—twenty strong—rode out on a ridge that faced the mine.

"There she is," Granger rumbled. "We're here in good time."

"I hope so," Grumpy muttered to Rainbow.

Soon after midnight, Slack, Slicer Cully and several others had gathered in the main tunnel of the Buckskin to confer. All looked worried. "We've been through them drifts with a fine-tooth comb!" protested a man whom Slack had been grilling. "There ain't a thing there, Slack! Ripley an' Gibbs seem to 've crawled in their hole an' pulled the hole in after 'em!"

"They ain't been seen since Bucktoe pulled down them drift timbers," another seconded. "Mebby they got buried in the fallin' rock," he added hopefully.

"Like hell they did!" Slicer retorted flatly. He had a blood-stained rag tied around his head. "They got away clean, I tell yuh! Right now they're probably miles away an' stirrin' up plenty of trouble for us!"

Slack was afraid he was right. That Ripley and Gibbs should disappear so completely passed belief. He had little doubt that Tim Bucktoe was in some manner responsible. It rendered him incapable of determining just what should be done about it. He floundered in a morass of indecision.

"Damn yuh, yuh knew Bucktoe was in there all the time, didn't yuh!" Slicer charged in sudden fury. "It was him saved yore skin at that murder

274

trial. An' yuh been hidin' him ever since. I always suspected yuh of a double-cross, Slack, an' now, by God, I'm sure of it! Bucktoe will knock us off if we go back in there now! He's already tried his hand at it. It was him rolled that dump car down the drift the other day an' like to smashed half-a-dozen of us!"

Only yesterday Slicer would not have dared use that tone to Slack. But things had changed, and Slack chose to ignore the other's open insolence.

"I didn't know a thing about Bucktoe bein' in there!" he protested. "I'm as willin' to get shut of him as you are—that ought to be proof of what I'm sayin'. We'll blow up the mine," he suggested suddenly. "That 'll fix Bucktoe—and Ripley and Gibbs too, if they're still in there!"

"We'll do no such a damned thing!" Slicer cut him off bluntly. There was iron in this man. It came out now. "We worked too hard gettin' them steers to bury 'em that way! What yuh say, boys?"

There was a restless mutter of agreement. All too plainly the men sided with Slicer in this argument. They stared at Slack with growing contempt. "Bucktoe may have some dynamite himself," one of them pointed out thinly. "Reckon yuh know what that means fer us if we go back in there!"

Slack was at his wit's end, and they read it in his face. It was Slicer who took command decisively in this emergency. "We'll all go to hell in a hand basket, the way yo're handlin' things," he hurled at Slack. "From now on I'll be the boss, an' you'll like it!" He turned to the others. "We'll guard the mine at this end, boys," he told them, "an' keep a watch fer a while to see what's goin' to happen. Meanwhile we'll try to figure some way of smokin' out Bucktoe an' squarin' our account with that pair of sneakin' skunks!"

There was a chorus of assent. Slicer placed his men where he wanted them. Desperate, dazed, Slack saw the reins slipping out of his hands. He flung away to the mouth of the mine in a black mood, prowling up and down.

But it was not he who saw the first sign of the sheriff's posse. One of Slicer's guards, posted in an upper drift, came hurrying down the slope, wildly excited. "Cully," he burst out, "there's over a dozen men closin' in on us! I seen 'em jest as they started to spread out! We better clear outa here in a hurry—"

"Hold that!" Slicer was curt. Though he guessed what it meant, he went on hardily, "We ain't stirrin' a step till we know jest where we stand. Pass the word to the boys, an' don't let nobody get close to the mine!"

Five minutes later a rifle cracked suddenly, then a second. The fire was answered by shadowy horsemen in the brush. There was this brisk exchange while the light slowly strengthened, and then a hail rang out. "Yuh might's well give yoreself up, Slack! We got yuh dead to rights!" It was Lint Granger's voice.

"Go to hell, Granger!" Slicer hurled back. That was all. He didn't ask why the sheriff was here with a score of armed men at his back. Matters had gone beyond parleying, and all knew it. Slicer's crowd was gathering at the mouth of the Buckskin, tense and ugly. They looked to him for orders, ignoring Slack.

Out in front, Lint Granger turned to glance grimly over his posse. They were dismounted and spread out. Granger made a forward-sweeping gesture with his arm and they began to crawl toward the mine, firing as they went. The rustlers responded hotly.

"They're droppin' back in the tunnel," Grumpy muttered to Rainbow.

It was true. The move enabled the posse to close in, but they were not deceived; they knew they had a bitter fight on their hands. Just as they were pushing into the mine, a man rode up on a lathered bronc and flung out of the saddle. It was Bart Galey.

"Lemme git into this!" he jerked out. "I want my whack at them curly wolves!" He had his gun out. Rainbow stared at him.

"Where 've you been keepin' yourself, Galey?"

"I've been ridin' my own trail," Bart evaded. "I only jest heard what was goin' on. Wal, are we talkin' all day or doin' somethin'?" he rasped, as

Slicer's men sent a blast of lead droning through the gallery.

Though the posse took advantage of any cover that offered, they were at a disadvantage from the start. Bide Jennis was the first man to be hit. A slug tore half of his ear off and scraped his scalp. Rainbow tied up the wound for him. Before long nearly all of them had scratches to show for the flying chips and fragments of rock knocked down by ricocheting bullets. Undeterred, they closed in, hoping to pin the enemy in a blind drift. Every foot they gained was a fight, for the rustlers were determined not to be driven back into the mine, where Bucktoe awaited them.

Neither side dared advertise its position with lights; there were only the lurid muzzle bursts of the guns to go by. "Danged if yuh can tell what yo're shootin' at!" Grumpy grumbled to Rainbow.

Lint Granger heard him. "Shoot at anythin' yuh kin see," he jerked out harshly, "an' worry about yore mistakes afterwards; we're cleanin' up on this bunch an' no mistake about it!"

It seemed that someone else was bent on taking his advice, for only a moment later a slug which he would have sworn had come from the rear, tore through Rainbow's shirt at the collar. Whirling, he ran a few steps and made a sweeping grab—and found himself grappling with Bart Galey.

"Lay off, Ripley!" he grated. "What are yuh makin' a pass at me for?"

"If I could be certain it was you who fired that slug, I'd make more than a pass at you!" Rainbow bit off. "Get up in front there, Galey, where you won't be shootin' all of us in the back. And see to it that you stay there!"

Bart muttered angrily under his breath, but he didn't take the matter up.

For ten minutes they inched forward, lead whistling about their heads. The stench of burnt powder here was strong. Suddenly Goodnight jerked out, "I can hear the steers bellerin'! They must have a bunch of 'em in here!"

"They won't be here much longer!" Granger grunted, trying to ignore the fact that things were at an obvious stalemate. But to Rainbow he muttered, "Dang hard drivin' them birds back! Seems like they jest ain't budgin' a foot—"

"It's not so strange," Rainbow told him. "They know what's layin' in wait for them if they get shoved far enough back in this mine! Bucktoe is probably only waitin' his chance to bring these workin's crashin' down on all of us. He's in here, and he's got dynamite; you know he tried that game on Grumpy and me last night."

Grumpy turned from this talk to lift his nose and sniff suspiciously. A moment later he burst out tensely, "Smoke! Somethin' burnin'!"

Rainbow was sure of it the next instant. "You're right!" he exclaimed. "The workin's are afire!"

They would have understood the cause could

they have seen Dan Slack crouched in a recess midway between Granger's posse and the gang he once had bossed.

Slack had found himself caught between the opposing forces. Wildly he racked his wits to find a way out of his difficulties until his desperate need spurred him to inspiration. If he fired the mine timbers, the tunnel would soon fill with blinding, choking smoke. It would drive out the posse and Slicer's cohorts, suffocate the steers of which Cully sought cunningly to rob him and even spell the end for Bucktoe. It might spell his own finish, but he was willing to risk even that if he could square accounts with that grinning devil.

Feverishly he pawed through his clothes for letters, a notebook—anything that would burn. A moment later his match flared, caught. The dry timbers began to smolder with a thick volume of smoke.

In less than ten minutes a lurid, flickering light glowed in the tunnel. Slack watched, a feverish madness in his eyes. At last he had found a means of breaking the grip Tim Bucktoe held on his tortured spirit.

Bucktoe at that moment was not far away. Following events closely, he knew how matters stood. He cursed himself for making use of such a fool as Slack. Never had his warped brain been keener and more vindictive. He knew the game was up as far as the mine was concerned. The knowledge stung like a burning brand.

Here he was with success almost in his grasp, only to have it snatched away. The rustling had been discovered and his part in it exposed; even his hiding place was lost to him now. And it was Slack's doing—Slack's incompetence. All the venom of which his mad brain was capable welled in him, poured through his veins like the fire that was slowly but surely eating through the mine timbers.

The smoke was denser now. It got into his lungs and set him to coughing. Tears sprang to his beady eyes. They were tears of rage. A few minutes more and that smoke would drag a man down. In this moment he could have torn Slack limb from limb like the jungle gorilla he so much resembled.

In the lurid glow of the flames licking the timbers overhead he glimpsed a crouching figure near the spot where the fire had started. A galvanizing shock ran through him.

"Slack!"

The name was wrenched out of him in a tortured shriek. Slack was the fool who had brought this last disaster down on his head! Bucktoe went blind with hatred of the other.

"By God, I'll tear his heart out!" he screamed.

Only the mad bellowing of the steers, keyed to a wild crescendo by the crash of shots and the terror which lay in the thickening pall of smoke, prevented men from hearing that wild cry. Bucktoe had not forgotten them, however. All his enemies were here in this mine—Slack and the men who had turned against him, the lawman who had long threatened him, Ripley and his partner, even the cowmen he had long sought to ruin. A kind of frenzy gripped Bucktoe at the thought. He wanted to crush them all, stamp the life out of them. In his twisted mind it was no more than justice. They would never let him get out of the mine alive, he knew. Even as the desperate desire ate into him, he had the answer.

Both Slack's men and the posse were in the main tunnel. The cattle were penned in a drift running off from it. He could hear them crashing vainly into the gate that held them imprisoned. Released, they would stampede through the tunnel, sweeping everything before them. He waited no longer, willing to snuff out his own life to wreak his vengeance.

Rainbow and Grumpy got a flash of his bent and twisted bulk in the flickering light of the flames as he hurled himself toward the penned steers. Although the gagging smoke had them nearly helpless, they were holding their ground.

"It's Bucktoe!" Rainbow cried. "There he goes!"

Granger had his gun up at the moment. Drawing a bead on the giant, he blazed away. But even as he fired a gust of coughing shook him. The next moment Bucktoe had merged with the writhing smoke shadows.

The mouth of the lateral drift was closed by a stout wooden gate behind which the steers were milling. It was locked, but a blow with a sledge opened it. The steers bolted forward, horns tossing; their bellowing grew to a swelling roar. Bucktoe flung the gate wide and leaped back. With a rush, the terror-stricken herd sprang through the opening into the tunnel and thundered toward its mouth, heads down, death for anything in their path.

No one could miss that mad bawling and rumble of hoofs. Rainbow caught it and was the first to read its meaning. He sprang to his feet. "The steers! They've busted loose!" came from his lips hoarsely.

Regardless of danger from the rustlers' guns, the posse scrambled up. What they saw froze them in their tracks.

In the wild light of the flames the horde of stampeding steers could be plainly seen. They were racing at them, filling the tunnel from side to side and surging forward with the resistless flow of floodwater, a mad wave of slashing hoofs and goring horns. Rainbow wheeled. "Get back!" he yelled. "It's our finish if we're caught here!"

The words broke the spell. Already Slack's men were on the move. They were even nearer to that tossing sea of horns than the posse. Rainbow saw them frenziedly hauling themselves on the unburned mine timbers, searching desperately along the walls for a cranny to crawl into. Then he looked beyond—saw something which held him momentarily rooted to the spot.

Flinging open the gate and springing aside as the steers spilled out, Bucktoe had caught sight of Slack, retreating toward him. A wild blaze of vengeance, sweeping through his big frame, carried all reason before it. The next instant Bucktoe sprang forward, caught Slack by the shoulders, whirled him around.

"I warned yuh!" he snarled. Smoke choked him, but he drove on gratingly, "Yuh thought yuh could make a mock of me; but yuh'll pay now, Slack! Yuh'll pay in full!"

Slack let out a scream of terror as those great, ruthless hands closed on him. Bucktoe began dragging him toward a shaft near at hand. A second later Slack read his design as his enemy flung him toward the pit. Strength born of his naked fear made him cling to the other like a leech. Bucktoe tore him loose, thrust him over the crumbling brink. Again Slack grappled desperately.

Bucktoe's giant strength was too much for Slack. But it took him a second too long to shake the man off, for even as he stood there, his great muscles knotted, a maddened steer barged into him. Bucktoe clutched at the wall for support. It crumbled in his hands. Reading his danger, he screamed. Then his grasp slipped off; and with Slack's arms wrapped around him, they plunged downward to destruction with a yell of terror, the frantic steer hurtling after them.

"God!" Grumpy cried hoarsely. And then, "Come out of this, Rainbow! We're goners if we don't reach that side drift in a hurry!"

Rainbow swung out and they fought through the smoke. Some of the posse had almost reached the mouth of the side drift, the cattle pounding close upon them. Rainbow saw Lint Granger stumble and go headlong. Grumpy was at the sheriff's side in a flash. Lint was heavy, raw boned, but Grumpy picked him up in a single movement, hurled him forward toward safety.

Thrusting his partner ahead of him, Rainbow was the last to gain the safety of the drift. The thunder of the onward-sweeping steers was deafening. Flashing a look back, Rainbow saw that mad wall of beef rush by. The steers were jammed so close together that a number were forced into the drift in which the posse had taken refuge. One charged forward, head down, with a menacing flirt of horns.

Rainbow's gun cracked. The steer went down with a sliding thud. It did not wholly check the others. Soon they were crowding into the drift, bellowing their maddened bewilderment. The smoke here was nearly as thick as in the main tunnel. "Get farther back!" Granger cried. Like Rainbow, he was firing over the heads of the steers in the effort to hold them.

Still the herd thundered by through the main tunnel. Rainbow scarcely dared ask himself what had become of the rustlers. If they had escaped annihilation it could only have been by a miracle. A moment later he caught a change in the sound of those stampeding hoofs. It was slacking off, drawing away toward the mine entrance. The next instant he heard a new sound, one that jerked him taut.

In some far-off level the flames had reached Bucktoe's store of dynamite. The dull thunder of that explosion was followed by the muffled concussion of countless tons of settling rock as those workings collapsed.

A cry reached him as he stood there. It was answered at once. Rainbow read the meaning of it in a flash: the rustlers were running down the main tunnel, fleeing the mine!

"It's Slack's bunch!" he jerked out. "They're makin' for the open!"

The posse galvanized into action with a rush. At risk of their lives, they jammed past the steers which had penned them in this side drift; dashing out into the main tunnel, coughing and choking, they were in time to see the fleeing rustlers just as they broke from the mine entrance. The few hasty shots flung after them had no effect.

"Right after 'em!" Lint Granger roared.

As they burst out into the daylight a gasp of dismay rose from them. Slicer and his men had not only succeeded in escaping unscathed from the mine but had seized the horses belonging to the posse and were even now striking out toward the Calico Hills at a gallop. Already they were beyond range of the posse's guns.

20

Grumpy came running back a moment later, breathless with haste. "They didn't wait to turn their own broncs loose!" he burst out. "They're down here in a corral!"

He led the way to it. Rainbow, Goodnight and the others were not far behind. Bart Galey did his best to hamper their efforts to get up ponies in a hurry. "We'll never snag that bunch now!" he rasped. "The hell with them! They'll leave the country—let 'em go!"

Goodnight whirled on him. "Stow that talk, Galey! Stand back and keep out of the way! We'll get them, with your help or without it!"

Galey started to curse him. Lint Granger stepped between them before anything could come of it. "Save it till later!" he snapped. "We're losin' time!" Galey breathed a threat, his face ugly.

They flung into the saddle hastily. Raking the

287

spurs home, they started after the fugitives. Superstition Mountain loomed higher as they left it behind. Soon they were in the Calicoes. And now the forced exchange of horses proved an unexpected advantage, for the mounts abandoned by the rustlers were both sound and fleet, and they were fresh. Although the escaping men had disappeared from sight, the posse soon began to draw up.

With his first glimpse of the quarry, Rainbow, in the lead, struck straight across the hills at them. The way led through the wild land fringing the Wishbone range. Here Lint Granger and the others were entirely at home. So, it appeared, were the rustlers.

Tas Johnson was first to open up with his gun. The rest immediately followed suit. Slicer's men answered hotly. Knowing they would be cut down unless they changed their tactics speedily, they struck into a wild, tangled maze of malpais and broken gulches.

"Circle around!" Goodnight cried. "We can pen 'em up in there!"

The possemen spread out and began to strike into the rocks. Knowing they were trapped and without sufficient opportunity to hole up, the rustlers scattered. Rainbow saw Goodnight shoot the bronc out from under Slicer Cully. The gunman leaped clear, started to clamber up the rocks.

"I'll git him!" Bart Galey jerked out. He sought to force Goodnight roughly aside. The latter pitched into him with a wrathy exclamation. Galey slashed at him wildly with his gun. The barrel of Galey's gun caught him in the head, and he slid out of the hull.

Galey flashed a furtive look around. He didn't see Rainbow. The next instant Bart deliberately threw down on Goodnight, firing at point-blank range as the other writhed on the ground.

Rainbow choked down his surprise. From the first he had vaguely suspected Bart Galey of more than hotheadedness. Now his suspicion was confirmed; for Galey was feverishly signaling Slicer Cully, waving him into the rocks. It made plain the understanding between them. Rainbow's wrath boiled up sharply.

"Galey!" he called.

Bart fired even as he wheeled. He knew he had been found out. His slug tore past Rainbow's throat with a snarl. And then as Rainbow's bullet took him in the chest, he stiffened with a jerk, tried to level his gun again, and even while swift amazement raced across his features, pitched forward out of the saddle.

Slicer Cully's shot droned so close that Rainbow felt its flutter. But Grumpy had appeared on the spot in the nick of time. Before Slicer could shoot again, he fired once. Slicer dropped his guns to clutch his stomach. Slowly he sat down and slid to the foot of the slanting rock, his face graying as death caught up with him.

Lint Granger rode up as Rainbow started for Goodnight's side.

"So yuh got Cully!" he rumbled deeply. "I got one of 'em myself over there in the rocks a piece. We'll soon have the rest of 'em rounded up!" He saw Goodnight then. "Jim! Are yuh hit bad?"

Goodnight had a bleeding head and a creased side. He struggled up with Rainbow's help. "Never mind about me," he gritted. "I'll be all right."

"The hell yuh will!" Grumpy exclaimed bluntly, leaping to Rainbow's aid. "You'll keel plumb over in 'nother two shakes!"

The prediction was scarcely out of his mouth before Goodnight fulfilled it. They lowered him while Granger stared in real concern. "Yuh better git him to Lost Angel right off," he advised gruffly. "Our job's most done hyar, anyways."

Rainbow assented. He tied up Goodnight's wounds; he and Grumpy got him into the saddle, and holding him there, they started back to the camp. Before they drew beyond earshot of the scene of the fight, the firing ceased. Rainbow was satisfied the cleanup would prove complete.

It was no light task getting Goodnight all the way to Lost Angel in his present condition. He had regained consciousness, but remained dazed. When they reached the camp, riding in with

Goodnight held upright between them, they went directly to the store.

They were hauling up before the place when somebody burst through the door and down the steps on the run. It was Sharon.

"Jim!" she cried as Rainbow and Grumpy lifted Goodnight down. "You are wounded!" Her voice broke when she saw that he seemed scarcely to recognize her. She got control of herself then, turning to Rainbow. "What happened, Rainbow? Is it serious?"

Despite his real interest in this girl, looking into her face now Rainbow could no longer delude himself in the slightest about her feeling for Goodnight. For better or worse, she loved him. Her tortured eyes cried the truth without any effort at concealment on her part. Rainbow's lips stiffened.

"Men get hit harder and live," he assured her. "He'll pull through."

"Bring him inside!" she said breathlessly. "We must do something for him!"

They got Goodnight in the store. Sukey Withers said there was a cot in the back room. They placed Jim on it. A few sips of whisky brightened him up.

"Jim, speak to me!" Sharon cried, bending over him, her anxiety tearing at her. "If only you'll say something."

Goodnight met her gaze as if suddenly

awakened; and despite himself his eyes flicked to Rainbow as if he read an unescapable connection between the two. "What shall I say?" he countered so coolly that the blood rushed to Sharon's face. Even Grumpy sensed the rebuff; and as for Rainbow, he was deeply sorry for this courageous girl.

Had there been any use, he would have spoken his mind freely to Goodnight. But there was not. Caught in the vise of his stiff, unbending pride, the latter had no intention of melting toward Sharon. But men were like that. Often they broke the hearts of women who loved them before they comprehended what it was they were doing.

Sharon hid her hurt by busying herself with Goodnight's wounds. They had to be cleaned and rebandaged. Goodnight pretended to ignore her, even when she took up a basin and turned away hastily. Rainbow gazed after her thoughtfully as she went out the door. He knew it wasn't to change the water in the basin that she had left; she was fighting pluckily to regain control of herself. Turning things over musingly, Rainbow determined to take a hand.

Grumpy noted the direction of his glance and stirred restlessly. "Wal, Rainbow," he got out anxiously, "our work is done here. Even Goodnight 'll agree to that after what happened today. It looks like we're due to collect our wages and be ridin' on."

To his surprise, Rainbow shook his head slowly. "Not this time, Grumpy," he made answer. "I reckon this is the end of the trail for me. I've been lookin' a long time for the right girl."

Grumpy said "Huh?" incredulously. Goodnight's head had come up with a jerk. He frowned, and his cheeks began to show a flush under the bronze. Plainly Rainbow's intentions got to him despite his determination to hold aloof from anything that concerned Sharon Longstreet. He opened his lips to speak, but before he could get a word out, the girl returned. Rainbow saw his eyes dart to her face with a new light hovering behind them.

"You don't need us here any longer," Rainbow told Sharon. "We'll just step outside and wait."

"I'll call you if you're needed," she nodded.

In the front of the store, Sukey and Cyclone Bradley were waiting to hear what had taken place. Rainbow and Grumpy accommodated them. Grumpy was right in his element here, talking thirteen to the dozen once he got started, and it was Rainbow who remembered, after some time, that Sharon hadn't called them. While Grumpy held the floor, he took a peep into the other room. What he saw was more than enough to assure him that his stratagem had worked.

Sharon and Goodnight were close in each other's arms, and the tender look on the girl's face was proof that all was well with her. For a moment Rainbow gazed, held by that sight. He could not pretend that there was no regret for him in this moment. Sharon was everything a man could ask for in a woman; more than once he had wished that he might be that man. But it was not to be.

He was just swinging away, wooden faced, when Grumpy finished his story and turned. He didn't notice anything wrong.

"She ain't called us yet," he said to Rainbow. "We better go in an' see what's what—" He started for the door.

Rainbow stopped him with a shake of the head. "No," he murmured, "we're goin' the other way, Grumpy." Turning his partner, he headed him for the door. "You were right. We're done here. We'll be driftin' on."

Bliss Lomax was a pseudonym for **Harry Sinclair Drago**, born in 1888 in Toledo, Ohio. Drago quit Toledo University to become a reporter for the Toledo *Bee*. He later turned to writing fiction with *Suzanna: A Romance Of Early California*, published by Macauley in 1922. In 1927 he was in Hollywood, writing screenplays for Tom Mix and Buck Jones. In 1932 he went East, settling in White Plains, New York, where he concentrated on writing Western fiction for the magazine market, above all for Street & Smith's *Western Story Magazine*, to which he had contributed fiction as early as 1922. Many of his novels, written under the pseudonyms Bliss Lomax and Will Ermine, were serialised prior to book publication in magazines. Some of the best of these were also made into films. The Bliss Lomax titles *Colt Comrades* (Doubleday, Doran, 1939) and *The Leather Burners* (Doubleday, Doran, 1940) were filmed as superior entries in the Hopalong Cassidy series with William Boyd, *Colt Comrades* (United Artists, 1943) and *Leather Burners* (United Artists, 1943). At his best Drago wrote Western stories that are tightly plotted with engaging characters, and often it is suspense that comprises their pulse and dramatic pacing.

Center Point Large Print
600 Brooks Road / PO Box 1
Thorndike, ME 04986-0001 USA

(207) 568-3717

US & Canada:
1 800 929-9108
www.centerpointlargeprint.com